X-MEN

THE LEGACY QUEST TRILOGY
Book 3

STEVE LYONS was born and lives in Salford, near Manchester, in the north-west of England. He has contributed articles, short stories and comic strips to many British magazines, from *Starburst* to *Batman* to *Doctor Who*. He has also co-written a number of books about TV science-fiction shows, including the official *Red Dwarf Programme Guide*. He is the author of a dozen original *Doctor Who* novels and two full-cast *Doctor Who* audio adventures, and the author of *X-Men: The Legacy Quest* Book 1 as well as writer of short stories for the Marvel-related anthologies *The Ultimate Super-Villains, Untold Tales of Spider-Man, The Ultimate Hulk,* and *X-Men Legends.*

MARVEL SUPER HEROES

Published by ibooks, inc.:

Spider-Man: Revenge of the Sinister Six
Spider-Man: The Secret of the Sinister Six
by Adam-Troy Castro

<u>X-MEN: THE CHAOS ENGINE TRILOGY</u>
by Steven A. Roman
Book 1: X-Men/Dr. Doom
Book 2: X-Men/Magneto
Book 3: X-Men/Red Skull

X-Men: The Legacy Quest Trilogy
by Steve Lyons

X-Men: Shadows of the Past
by Michael Jan Friedman

Five Decades of the X-Men
Stan Lee, Editor

X-MEN

THE LEGACY QUEST TRILOGY
Book 3

By Steve Lyons

Interior Illustrations by
Nick Choles

MARVEL®

ibooks
new york
www.ibooks.net

DISTRIBUTED BY SIMON & SCHUSTER, INC

bp books inc
New York

Author's Note:
This trilogy takes place shortly after
the events recounted in X-Men #87.

A Publication of BP Books, Inc.

Distributed by Simon & Schuster, Inc.
1230 Avenue of the Americas, New York, NY 10020

BP Books, Inc.
24 West 25th Street
New York, NY 10010

The BP Books World Wide Web Site Address is:
http://www.ibooks.net

ISBN 0-7434-7519-4

PRINTING HISTORY
First BP Books, Inc. trade paperback edition, October 2002
First BP Books, Inc. mass-market edition, October 2003
10 9 8 7 6 5 4 3 2 1

Edited by Dwight Jon Zimmerman

Special thanks to C.B. Cebulski

Cover art by David Rabbitte
Cover design by Mike Rivilis

Printed in the U.S.A.

CHAPTER 1

THE Black King of Hong Kong stood in his rooftop garden and surveyed his domain.

The landscape of this small island had changed a great deal in the four and a half decades of the King's lifetime. Its trees now jostled for position with towering constructs of glass and concrete, some of the tallest skyscrapers outside of New York City. But at night, in Sebastian Shaw's eyes, it remained one of the most beautiful places in the world.

He had spent a lot of time up here recently, in the pagoda atop the wide, single-story Hellfire Club building, just gazing out over the lights of Hong Kong Island and thinking.

He fancied he had much in common with Hong Kong. On the outside, he too was a mixture of the old and the new. His company, Shaw Industries, had made him rich by remaining on the cutting edge of technology. As a Lord Cardinal of the Hellfire Club's Inner Circle, however, he clad himself in old-fashioned finery. Currently, he was wearing a maroon smoking jacket and cummerbund, gray breeches and a white silk shirt and cravat. His black hair was tied back into a ponytail, secured by a red bow. This "uniform" may have appeared idiosyncratic, but it symbolized his organization's allegiance to the morals of a bygone era. The Hellfire Club had been birthed in England in the latter half of the eighteenth century, at a time when—in Shaw's view—a man's ambition had been limited only by his strength and determination to succeed. Today, great men had to contend with a multitude of strictures placed upon them by the less able and jealous.

Despite this, Shaw—like Hong Kong—had built himself from humble beginnings into a significant political and economic force. Through the Hellfire Club, he pulled the strings of businessmen and government officials alike. But, like Hong Kong, he had seen a lot of changes recently—and not all of them had been for the better.

Something alerted him to the presence of an intruder in his garden. He wasn't sure what it was; it hadn't been a sight or a sound. But Shaw hadn't lived this long without developing an instinct for such things. He turned slowly, a composed expression fixed upon his face, one eyebrow raised in mild query. He would not give a potential foe the satisfaction of seeing him disconcerted. He did not bother to disguise his distaste, however, when he laid eyes upon the mutant sorceress known as Selene.

She hadn't deigned to visit him in person, of course. "Sebastian, my dear," she purred, her thin red lips twisting into a mocking grin on her pale face, "I am beginning to get the impression that you are trying to avoid me. You won't return my calls; I have been forced to send my astral form over eight thousand miles to get your attention."

"I have nothing to say to you, Selene," he snarled.

"Oh, come now. I know you are making plans to celebrate the forthcoming solstice. You have been in contact with Kings and Queens of the Hellfire Club worldwide, and yet you have overlooked our most powerful branch. Why is that, I wonder?"

Shaw bristled at the well-chosen words. Selene had been his Black Queen once; he had ruled the New York Hellfire Club with her at his side. Even after she had betrayed him, he had given her another chance. But now, the treacherous witch ruled in New York alone—and as much as he loved Hong Kong, it felt like a poor consolation prize.

Shaw had spent most of his life moving forward; a few temporary setbacks had not worried him much at first. But increasingly, it seemed that he was having to fight harder and harder to keep what he had, let alone reclaim what had once been his. He had tried to rebuild his diminished power base, but his most audacious schemes had been thwarted by his many opponents, and his reborn Inner Circle had fallen apart around him.

He had thought about giving it all up. He had almost resigned from the Club itself more than once, but that would have been a backward step. It would have meant throwing away a lifelong dream, and he hadn't yet found a new dream, a new plan, with which to replace it.

Three weeks ago, Shaw had taken a trip to the future. He had seen what he was destined to become, and he had been appalled. He had sworn to avoid that fate somehow.

Selene moved closer to him, the lights from below shining through her black cloak and her faintly translucent body. "You can't still bear a grudge against me for our last encounter?"

"You stole something from me," Shaw reminded her. "Something of great value."

Selene laughed. "The X-Men had backed you into a corner, Shaw. All the resources you put into finding a cure for the Legacy Virus, all the sacrifices you made, and they were about to take it from under your nose."

"I had agreed to share my discovery with them."

"You and I both know, Shaw, that that cure was only useful to our organization if we could exercise sole control over it."

"I see," sneered Shaw. "You expect me to believe that you were trying to help me; that your theft of the cure was in some way staged to fool the X-Men?"

"What use is the Hellfire Club if its branches cannot support each other?"

It was an obvious lie—and all the more so because Shaw had seen the future, or at least a possible version of it. He had seen what Selene had intended to do with the Legacy cure, and he had seen himself humiliated by her. The memory of it sent a shiver down his spine. "It was thanks to your interference," he said tartly, "that the cure was lost."

"We played the game," said Selene as if it didn't matter. "It ended in stalemate. At least the prize was not claimed by those whelps."

"You are a mutant, Selene, as am I. The Legacy Virus was designed to attack our kind. We are dying out because of it—and you snatched away our only hope of salvation."

She waved a dismissive hand. "The strong will survive, as we always have."

"We may have been allies in the past," said Shaw coldly, "but no longer."

She frowned. "You're up to something, Shaw. I know it—and I will find out what it is."

"I am merely organizing a party," he said with a false smile.

He turned his back to her, and looked out across the island again. It was a calculated insult, about which Selene, in her insubstantial form, could only seethe. She couldn't even read his mind. She couldn't know that he had deceived her as she had tried to deceive him.

She didn't know that the cure to the Legacy Virus still existed after all.

Eventually, sensing that the witch had gone, Shaw let out a controlled sigh. Selene had been right about one thing. He *had* been reluctant to deal with the X-Men—and her attack had presented him with a welcome opportunity. Now they, like she, believed the precious cure destroyed, and he was rid of their interference.

To his continuing frustration, however, the prize was not yet his alone.

In the course of his quest to cure the Legacy Virus, he had acted as he always did. He had made alliances where they seemed prudent, using and discarding people like pieces on a chessboard. But some pieces were more powerful than others, and more difficult to discard at the game's end.

Shaw had not intended to share his prize with anybody, but he had been outmaneuvered. And his current partner's plans for the cure scared even him.

He stayed in the pagoda for a few minutes longer, hands clasped behind his back, his expression stoic although nobody was around to see it. He listened to the calming orchestral music that drifted up from the Hellfire Club's ballroom, and he breathed in the warm evening air and basked in a gentle breeze.

Hong Kong, arguably, enjoyed its most pleasant weather in the final weeks of the year, when the burning heat of Summer had subsided. But Sebastian Shaw still yearned for the biting winds and the snow of New York.

Shaw had kept his visitors waiting for over an hour. It was his way of showing his contempt for them, and his power over them.

He greeted them, at last, in his office, seated behind his desk with his fingers forming a steeple in front of his nose and mouth. A ceiling fan beat the air and caused the bamboo blinds behind him to clatter against the window. The wall hummed with the continuing strains of the music behind it.

The woman was well known to him: Emma Frost was another remnant of an Inner Circle that had once been unbeatable. She was wearing the white bodice, the thigh-length boots and fur-trimmed cloak of the White Queen. Her blonde hair hung straight down to her shoulders, framing a face that was young but already hard and cold.

The man was less familiar, although Shaw recognized him. He too was dressed in white, but he seemed uncomfortable in the high collar and starched shirt of his formal Hellfire Club attire. He appeared to be a normal, middle-aged man with deep frown lines etched into a grim face and dark brown hair swept back from his forehead. But appearances were deceptive. Daimon Hellstrom was the mortal son of a powerful demon—and despite his calm demeanor, Shaw fancied that he could detect a hint of brimstone about him.

His personal assistant, Tessa, announced the pair in her usual prim manner. She took up a position at her master's shoulder, lips pursed, hands tucked into the sleeves of her kimono. Her innocent eyes betrayed none of the furious activity of her enhanced brain. Shaw thought of her as his living computer, possessed as she was of a phenomenal memory and analytical skills. She also had rudimentary telepathic abilities, and he could feel her presence in his mind. She had built a wall of static around it, boosting his psychic defenses. Frost was a more powerful telepath than Tessa—but if she wanted to read Shaw's thoughts now, she would have to fight for them.

Hellstrom extended a hand toward Shaw. He ignored it. With a curt, unsmiling nod, he indicated that his visitors should sit. He waited for them to break the awkward silence.

"We want to talk to you about your plans for the solstice," said Frost.

"Oh?" Shaw raised an eyebrow. "And of what concern are they to you?"

"I never formally resigned my post as White Queen," she reminded him.

"But you have shown little interest in Hellfire Club affairs of late."

"Perhaps it is time that changed."

"Do I detect a hint of jealousy in your actions, Miss Frost?" Shaw twisted his lips into a smile, but he didn't allow it to reach his eyes. "I spoke to your sister, Adrienne, only a few days ago. She is doing a fine job of rebuilding our London branch. Unlike you, my dear, she will make an excellent White Queen."

Her smoldering expression confirmed that he had hit a raw nerve. Was she regaining some of her old fire? He hoped so. Unlike many of his former allies, Emma Frost had never actually betrayed Shaw. She had simply disappointed him by proving to be weaker than he had thought. When her team of young mutants in training had been slaughtered, she had run into the waiting arms of Professor Charles Xavier, the X-Men's altruistic founder. Now, she trained another team of youngsters, inculcating in them not the proud beliefs and the will to succeed of the Hellfire Club but rather Xavier's own naïve principles. It gave her a sense of purpose, a way to redeem the mistakes of her past. She needed that for now. But Shaw wondered how much longer it could last, how long before she returned to the fold.

"As for you, Mr. Hellstrom," he continued, "you appointed yourself to the rank of White King of the Inner Circle in New York. Selene does not recognize your position, and nor do I."

Hellstrom spoke in a low, threatening rumble like a building storm. "I would have expected you of all people to appreciate the need for a balancing force to Selene's Black house."

"And where were you, Mr. Hellstrom, when your Black Queen launched a brazen attack upon me and stole the cure to the Legacy Virus?"

His eyes flickered downward. "I was . . . otherwise engaged."

"The point is," said Frost firmly, "that we still have contacts in the Hellfire Club, and we are both concerned about the rumors we are hearing."

Shaw got to his feet abruptly. "As these 'contacts' of yours have no doubt told you," he said with an air of scorn, "the Hellfire Club is indeed planning to mark the solstice in two days' time. At the hour of midnight in each of their respective time zones, our major branches will launch specially designed fireworks that will erupt at the upper edge of the atmosphere. Each firework will create a pyrotechnic display in the shape of a giant Hellfire Club trident. As one trident fades, another will be created as midnight strikes in another locale. From Sydney in the east to Hawaii in the west, our symbol will light the night as it moves across the sky. It will be visible to all."

"And this . . . this cheap publicity stunt is so important to you that you have traveled the world to supervise the preparations in person?" Hellstrom's disbelief was plain.

Shaw clasped his hands behind his back and walked around his desk. "Our organization has been sorely tested in recent years. I felt it was time to make a statement, to boost the morale of our remaining loyal members." He reached the door and opened it, giving his visitors a meaningful look. The pair rose from their chairs, but they made no move to leave.

Frost shook her head. "I know you, Shaw. You are power-hungry but never this vain. You would not go to this much trouble simply to massage your ego. You are hiding something."

Shaw gave an indifferent shrug. "To our pagan ancestors, the winter solstice—the shortest day of the year—was a time to celebrate the rebirth of the sun. Here in the southern hemisphere, of course, it is the height of summer; nevertheless, what better time to reaffirm our allegiance to a proud tradition and to announce our own symbolic rebirth?"

Frost fixed him with an icy glare, and he had no doubt that she was worming her psychic tendrils into his mind, looking for the information that he was keeping from her. By now, she would have found Tessa's shields. She could choose to withdraw quietly or she could show her hand by bludgeoning her way through them and taking what she wanted by force. Once, she would have done the latter without hesitation. Shaw was faintly saddened, then, when she dropped her gaze to the floor, defeated. She had spent too long with Xavier and his ilk.

"On the night of the twenty-first of December," said Shaw, "the wealthy elite of every civilized country in the world will enjoy the biggest and best party that even the Hellfire Club has ever thrown. Neither of you, I regret to say, are invited."

Hellstrom's eyes flashed as he clenched and unclenched his fists. "We will find out the truth, Shaw, one way or another."

"You are welcome to try." Shaw was well aware that Hellstrom had the physical power to destroy him. Like Frost, however, he did not have the will to use it. He held the inner rage that was part of his demonic heritage at bay. He was not ruthless enough. That was why the Black King would always better his rivals in the long run.

"Your arrogance will be your undoing one day," snarled Hellstrom.

"So I am often assured. Now, if there is nothing more, I am extremely busy. . . ."

With a tight smile, Shaw motioned his visitors out through the door—and this time, they took the hint and left.

The White King and Queen swept out of the Hellfire Club building, framed by the light from its veranda behind them. They marched down a short flight of wide steps and passed the fire-breathing stone dragons that stood sentry at the entranceway. Their anachronistic costumes drew hardly a glance: this area of Hong Kong was relatively secluded, and most of the people on the street were Club members joining or leaving its night-long revels. The balmy air deadened the harsh sounds of slamming car doors and drunken giggling.

Hellstrom let out a sigh of exasperation. "That man tries my resolve. I have half a mind to go back in there and coax his secrets from his lips with hellfire."

"Patience, Daimon," said Frost. "The way to deal with Shaw is not with physical force. He will already have set his scheme in motion. Unless you are prepared to kill him—and perhaps not even then—you won't stop it." She allowed the hint of a smile to tug at her lips. "In any case, we never expected him to confess to everything, did we?"

"I presume you weren't able to read his mind?"

"As we anticipated, his lapdog shielded it from me." Hellstrom looked despondent, until Frost continued: "However, young Tessa is not as adept a telepath as she would like to think. I did glean one important fact."

Hellstrom raised an eyebrow in her direction. "You don't sound entirely happy about it."

"I am not," said Frost shortly. "I don't know what Shaw's plans are, but he has not formulated them alone. His partner's name was close to the surface of his thoughts." She shook her head and muttered to herself: "I can hardly believe he would trust him again. I was there the first time, I remember what happened. But then

Shaw has always been one to make a bargain of necessity. Always playing his games. . . ."

Hellstrom cleared his throat, and Frost's eyes focused upon him as if her mind were returning from a faraway place. He didn't have to put his question into words.

The White Queen took a deep breath and said: "Shaw has allied himself with Magneto."

When Raul Jarrett had closed his eyes, he had expected it to be for the last time.

He had settled into a deep, dreamless sleep, his fear of the unknown tinged by relief as the pain had ebbed from his body at last. He had known little but pain all his adult life, and in some ways he had felt that death would be a blessing.

As a carefree child growing up in the prosperous city of Hammer Bay, he had never given much thought to the people who tended his garden, swept the streets and drove the trains and buses. He had known that his country, the East African island nation of Genosha, was blessed to have such individuals, such willing slaves whose paranormal abilities made them ideally suited to their menial tasks. But he had never spoken to one of these so-called mutates. He had never wondered where they came from, nor where they went to after sundown.

He had never imagined that he, Raul Jarrett, the youngest son of a well-heeled, well-connected family, could have become one of them.

The darkness lightened, and he was aware of himself again, lying on his back. His eyes were still closed, and he could hear nothing over the sound of his own breathing. This in itself was a puzzle: when consciousness had slipped away from him, he had been sprawled across a gurney in a filthy, narrow corridor in an overcrowded hospital, his ears full of the coughs and groans of the dying. Doctors and nurses had hurried by, but there had been too few of them and too many patients for them to spare time for a lost cause. His lungs had burnt as he had sucked in air, but now his chest felt as if a weight had been lifted from it. His muscles no longer ached. He began to wonder if he still had a body at all, or if he had passed into an afterlife. The thought unnerved him, and he didn't dare look to prove or disprove his theory. He remembered his mother bursting into tears as the magistrates arrived at his home, brandishing his test results. Gene-positive. He had been numb, disbelieving. There had been no history of the mutant gene in his family; surely there had to have been a mistake?

He hadn't really understood what was happening at first—but he remembered the moment of sheer terror as they wheeled him into the operating room, the anaesthetic fighting to take hold. He had glimpsed the blurred face of the feared Genegineer above him and he had realized that, mistake or not, this was happening. It was happening to him. Just one moment. And after that he had felt nothing else, no strong emotions of any kind, for over a decade.

They had altered Raul Jarrett. They had activated his latent mutant gene and sculpted it, controlling its effects upon his body. They had needed somebody to speed up mining operations beneath the Ridgeback Mountains—somebody who could chase seams of iron ore into areas that even the air could hardly penetrate—so they had given him the power to stretch himself into a narrow thread and to store oxygen reserves in his stomach. They had bonded a skinsuit to his flesh, to afford him protection from the harsh conditions underground and to mark him out inexorably as a creature without rights. They had shaved his head and tampered with his brain so that he had accepted his new station unquestioningly. He had followed the magistrates' orders and devoted himself to his country even though his bones had protested with each use of his newfound abilities. He had ignored the shooting pains and the knowledge that the work was killing him. And only in his feverish dreams had he recalled the life that he had once lived.

To all intents and purposes, Raul Jarrett had been dead then. He had become Mutate #6014.

It was an unbearable irony to him that he had clawed his way back to life only to be singled out by a cruel Fate—or a vengeful deity—again.

In truth, he had seen little of the mutate rebellion. He had spent most of that bewildering, turbulent time cowering in his squalid little cell in the settlement zone in the Genoshan Highlands. He had not joined in the fight against the magistrates, he had not risked his life—but at least he had won the inner struggle against their conditioning, and he had been proud of his small triumph. And if his country had no longer been the Utopian land of his youth, if its slave-based economy had collapsed and its streets had been claimed by fear and looting and arbitrary death, then at least he had been Raul Jarrett again. He had been free.

But that was before the Legacy Virus. That was before the mutate population of Genosha had been targeted again, and this time they had had nobody to rebel against.

"How are you feeling?"

Jarrett felt a cool hand on his forehead, and his eyes flickered open. He blinked uncomprehendingly. He was in a clean, well-lit room. It wasn't large—but at the public hospital, an area of this size would have held at least five beds, not just one. Standing beside him was a slender young woman with short blonde hair. Genosha's former slaves no longer wore their numbers, but her purple skinsuit betrayed her nature nonetheless. Some mutates had been quick to shed the symbols of their servitude, despite the long and difficult operation involved. Others, like Jarrett himself, had decided to wait until an easier way to reverse the bonding process had been found. Once the Legacy epidemic had begun to soak up their country's resources, of course, they had had no choice in the matter.

There had been a movement toward reclaiming the skinsuits as a symbol of racial pride. Many people still wore them openly, and kept their heads bald, proclaiming their identities to the world. They were mutates: no longer something lower than the common herd of humanity, but something better.

"I'm Jenny Ransome," said the woman, and Jarrett felt his eyes widening. He recognized her name. She was the chancellor of the new government; the government formed by the man who had been heralded as his country's savior. She must have known what he was thinking, because she smiled and said: "I was a nurse before the war. You're in safe hands."

"I can't . . . feel anything. . . ." he murmured.

The woman frowned. "Nothing at all?"

"I mean . . . no pain . . . it doesn't hurt any more. . . ." Jarrett's tone was full of wonder. He felt strange. Empty, somehow, and numb. He flexed his fingers and toes, and was pleased to find that his body was the right shape. In recent weeks, as the virus had progressed and stolen his control over his powers, his limbs had lengthened and become weaker, and he had been unable to pull them back together. By the time he had been taken into the hospital, even standing had been beyond him. He had lain across the gurney like a tangle of over-tensed elastic.

Jenny Ransome smiled again. "We tried a new treatment. We injected a special type of cell into your bloodstream. It fought off the Legacy Virus and reversed the damage it had done within a matter of hours."

"You mean I'm . . . cured?" He hardly dared voice the hope. "The virus won't come back?"

"It's too early to be sure," said Jenny, "but the indications are positive. Very positive indeed. Raul—your name is Raul, isn't it? —there's somebody here who wants to see you."

Jarrett couldn't imagine who she might be talking about. He had no close friends. During his years of enslavement, he had been forbidden to speak with other human beings unless spoken to, and he had known his fellow mutates only by their numbers. Since his liberation, he had enjoyed a certain kinship with those who shared his situation—but, like many of them, he had needed time to build up his confidence. The virus had denied him that time.

He thought about his family. He didn't know if they had survived the war or not. They had been forced to disown him, but perhaps they had not forgotten him after all. He wondered if he would still recognize them.

A tall, cloaked figure strode confidently into the room, and Jarrett's heart leapt into his throat. This was the last person he had expected to see, especially here, especially taking an interest in him. For a second, he thought he was dreaming. Perhaps the virus had claimed him after all, and this was some form of fever-induced hallucination?

"Mr. Raul Jarrett, I presume?" said Magneto.

Raul nodded nervously. His jaw was working, but his throat had seized up and he was unable to talk. Magneto looked every inch a king, clad in royal colors of red and purple. His hair was gray, and his face lined by age and bitter experience—but as he towered over the room's single bed, Jarrett saw that his eyes were steely with resolve. Beneath one arm, he held the metal helmet that had become such a potent symbol to the people of Genosha. Resembling a gladiator's headgear of old, it indicated that Magneto was not afraid to fight for his beliefs—indeed, that he would make a formidable opponent.

Raul Jarrett had never seen this man in person before, but he had heard much about him. Magneto was a mutant himself, the master of magnetism. He was Genosha's new ruler, and reputedly the hope of the mutate race. In recent days, however, Jarrett had come to doubt this. Believing himself on the verge of death, he had cursed this so-called Savior, this man who had offered only false hope. Now, he felt as if his troubles had been but a test of faith, and he feared that Magneto could look into his soul or read his mind and see that he had failed.

"M-my liege . . ." he managed to croak.

"You look as if your condition has improved. I trust you are feeling well?"

The nurse, Jenny, came to his aid. "Mr. Jarrett is feeling much better, Your Eminence. I still have a few tests to run, but he appears to be in perfect health."

"Thank you, Jennifer." The ghost of a smile softened Magneto's features. Belatedly, Jarrett wondered if he should get out of his bed and kneel, but the Savior did not seem to require it. "You, Mr. Jarrett," he said, "are privileged. You are the first of our people to receive the Legacy cure. Now that I am assured of its effectiveness, we will begin mass production. Genosha will be rid of this pestilence at last."

The Savior turned abruptly, his purple cloak billowing out behind him. As he marched back to the door, he said: "Let Mr. Jarrett rest now, Jennifer. Bring him to me tomorrow."

Jarrett's breath caught in his throat. He realized now where he had to be: in Hammer Bay, inside the former magistrate base that Magneto had converted into his command center. But what was he doing here? Why had he, of all the dying mutates, been singled out?

What could the Savior want with somebody like him?

"Los Angeles and Madrid both report that preparations are complete."

Shaw had asked Tessa to update him on the day's events; she stood before his desk and recited the details from memory, but he was hardly listening to her. He was thinking about Magneto, the man who had taken over his life. He was thinking about a future in which he had seen himself crushed beneath the heel of a despotic ruler, and he was trying to convince himself that it would not happen again. "Scribe has been in touch from the London branch," continued Tessa, "asking questions. I dealt with her. And apparently, Selene has paid a visit to the White Bishop of Boston, but he could tell her nothing. Sebastian?"

Realizing that his assistant was staring at him, Shaw refocused his attention upon her.

"There are no urgent matters to attend to," she said. "Would you prefer to do this tomorrow?"

He nodded wearily, his chin still cradled in his hands. "Thank you, Tessa."

She turned to leave, but he stopped her by speaking her name again. "Would I be right to assume," he said in a low, silken voice, settling back into his seat, "that you allowed Miss Frost to take some information from my mind earlier?"

It was rarely possible to read Tessa's feelings; she knew how to retain her composure in the most trying of circumstances. She had learned that from him. But Shaw's question caught her unawares, and there was no mistaking the fear that flickered across her features.

"Sir?" She frowned as if she hadn't understood him.

"You don't have to play games with me, Tessa," said Shaw. "I am not angry with you. I merely need to know exactly what it is that our enemies have learned."

"I . . . I apologize if I overstepped the mark," said Tessa, "but it was clear to me that you are not happy with your partner's plans for the Legacy cure. I thought that, if somebody else could deal with him. . . ."

"So, Frost and Hellstrom are aware of Magneto's involvement in my plans."

"But no more than that, sir, I swear."

Shaw nodded. "Very well, Tessa. You may leave me now."

She stared at him uncertainly for a moment, before she did as she was bidden.

Alone now, Shaw closed his tired eyes and sighed heavily. When he had accused his assistant of betraying him, he had only half-expected to be proved right. He had long thought of Tessa as his most loyal servant. He had trusted her, and Sebastian Shaw's trust was not lightly given. But his trip to the future had taught him something about her too.

He could not trust anybody now.

Frost would undoubtedly contact Xavier and his followers. After all Shaw's efforts to remove the X-Men from the board, they would rejoin the game. He ought to have been irritated about that—but a part of him suspected that, whatever Tessa's motives, she had made the right move.

Thanks to the X-Men's renewed involvement, Shaw might yet claim a victory after all.

CHAPTER 2

THE X-Man known only as Rogue was standing in the under-ground throne room of Selene, the Black Queen of the New York branch of the Hellfire Club.

When last she had been here, she hadn't had much time to take in her surroundings. She had been too busy fighting for her life against Selene's demonic cohort, Blackheart. He was looming over her now, a granite hand poised to kill her. His gigantic body almost filled the room, and his eyes burnt in the darkness of his face. He wanted the prize that Rogue was clutching to her chest: the glass container in which was stored the blood of a friend.

Last time, she had been rooted to the spot as Blackheart had manipulated her emotions, increasing her fear of him. This time, it was different.

This time, Rogue could leave her body and move—and the demon, trapped in her past, could do nothing to stop her. She could safely ignore him, and explore her memory of these events, taking in features of the room that had not fully registered with her before. She peered into shadowy alcoves and inspected the frozen flames of black candles. Some areas were blurry—she had not seen everything—but she was amazed at the level of detail that her subconscious mind had stored.

She found what—or rather, who—she was looking for behind the ornate golden throne. Sebastian Shaw, a longtime foe of the X-Men but their ally against Selene, had taken cover here. He wore a green combat suit, and squatted on his haunches. He was keeping out of sight, but there was no fear in his expression. His eyes were alert and calculating.

"We were right," said Rogue aloud, in her broad Southern drawl. "Shaw's here. I mean, he *was* here. He must have stayed behind when the others took the fight with the Black Queen upstairs. I must have caught a glimpse of him. I can't believe I didn't remember it before."

You had a lot on your mind, Rogue, said the reassuring voice of her mentor inside her head. It was through the telepathic powers of Professor Charles Xavier that she was able to revisit her recent experiences like this.

"Ain't that the truth!" she said ruefully, glancing back at her own body as it cowered before its attacker. It felt weird to see it from this perspective, to look into its terrified eyes and at the distinctive white stripe in its long brown hair as if they belonged to somebody else. She remembered how she had felt in that time-stopped moment of three weeks ago, and she shivered.

The Rogue of the past was dressed, like the insubstantial Rogue of the present, the costume covered her entire body but for her head—and its hood could always be pulled up too, should she have need of the additional protection.

Rogue was a mutant, part of a tiny vanguard of the next generation of humanity, born with special abilities—but she had come to see her particular power as a curse. Whenever she touched another person, skin to skin, she absorbed his or her memories and physical characteristics. It was a process over which her control had lessened with time. The bodysuit protected her from accidental contact. It also marked her out as a member of the X-Men: a team of mutants who had banded together for the common good of their kind, and of the world, and yet were perceived as outlaws by a frightened, distrustful public.

The X-Men existed to pursue the dream of Xavier, their founder: a dream of a future in which humans and mutants lived together in peace. Not everybody shared their goal, however. Some mutants believed that *homo sapiens superior* were the dominant species of Earth, destined to replace the lesser *homo sapiens*, and that they should be treated as such. Others used their powers for personal gain, caring nothing about the wider implications.

Sebastian Shaw fell into the latter camp. His greed had set into motion the chain of events that had ended here. He had bent the considerable resources of the Hellfire Club—and of his own company, Shaw Industries—into an effort to find a cure for the deadly Legacy Virus; not for the benefit of its mostly mutant victims but for the political and financial power that would accrue to the sole possessor of such a cure. Selene's ambitions, on the other hand, had been more extreme. She had intended to use the cure to black-mail mutants into serving her. The X-Men had spent some time in a possible future in which she had already made Manhattan Island her own, and they had been determined to avert it.

Everything had come to a head in this room. The cure had existed, for a short time, in the bloodstream of one of Rogue's teammates, the mutant known as the Beast. Selene had kidnapped him and brought him here to exsanguinate him; the X-Men had halted the process just in time to save his life. As Phoenix had rushed the Beast to a hospital, and the rest of the team had engaged Selene in combat, Rogue had gone back for his blood and the precious super-cell that it contained. Blackheart had cut off her escape. She had managed to get past him, barely, but she had lost the cure in the process.

She looked at the glass container now with a wistful sigh, wishing that she could pluck it from her past self's arms, prevent it from shattering against her chest as it was destined to do. But all this was just a memory, after all: she could not change what had already happened.

"I don't understand, though," she said. "I've got the container now. There's no way Shaw could have got his hands on it before . . . you know. . . ."

Clearly, mused Xavier, *his plan was to take the cure for himself.* Rogue was startled to find the Professor standing beside her, wearing the same light gray suit that he had been wearing in the conference room, his brow furrowed into a frown. Xavier's physical body was confined to a hi-tech hoverchair, and Rogue still wasn't used to the fact that its limitations didn't extend to his psychic form. *But perhaps you foiled his plans when you retrieved it. It could be that he was forced to flee empty-handed, after all.*

"You think we're barking up the wrong tree here?"

Unless we are missing something.

"We must be!" said Rogue, setting her lips into a determined pout. "Let's try moving forward again, just a little at a time. There has to be something. . . ."

The image of herself came to life in a series of slow, jerky movements, like the picture on a videotape played in slow motion. It tensed itself, preparing to spring past Blackheart, to make its ill-fated bid for freedom. She had to tear her eyes away from it. She glared at Shaw, and muttered to herself, "What are you thinking? What are you planning?"

She turned, and the answer struck her between the eyes, almost literally.

A dark red globule was hanging in the air in front of her. No, not hanging; as more time inched by, Rogue realized that the globule was moving, describing a ponderous arc. She flinched from it, expecting it to hit her until she remembered that she was not really here. She followed its sluggish progress until it splattered against the Black Queen's throne in a silent explosion, which took several seconds to play itself out. And then she retraced its trajectory, and saw where it must have come from.

The Beast had been held in an alcove, hanging upright, attached to the wall by a mass of organic tendrils that had burrowed into his veins and begun to drain the blood from his body.

Rogue had torn him free, with Phoenix's help. But now, as more seconds passed like minutes, she saw that the tendrils were still alive, still twitching and writhing. Another droplet of blood appeared at the ragged end of a flapping tentacle, and as she watched, fascinated, it grew larger and more bulbous until it was finally shaken free.

"That's it!" she cried in triumph. "I know how he did it."

Professor Xavier nodded sagely, and the throne room faded around them, leaving only a black void. But this too soon dispersed, and Rogue found herself back home.

It took her a moment to readjust to her surroundings, familiar though they were. In contrast to the candlelit gloom of Selene's inner sanctum, the morning sun streamed through the windows of the venerable old mansion that was known to the outside world as the Xavier Institute for Higher Learning. Set back into its own grounds at the top end of a rarely traveled lane in the quiet Westchester town of Salem Center, the building attracted a minimum of attention. Few people suspected its true purpose.

"Our hunch was correct, then? Shaw *could* have taken the cure?" The words were spoken by the X-Men's field leader, Cyclops. His tone was grim, his expression equally so. A golden visor with a single red lens concealed his eyes, and made him seem even less approachable. Rogue knew, however, that he didn't wear it by choice. Like her, Scott Summers had little control over his mutant ability; the visor's lens was made from ruby quartz, the only material capable of keeping his devastating optic blasts in check.

At the head of the long conference table, Xavier opened his eyes and lifted his head as if waking from a light doze. "Rogue's memories do appear to confirm our suspicions," he said.

Rogue explained what she had seen. "Friend Shaw only had to wait until he was alone in that room. He could have squeezed the last drop of Hank's blood out of one of those tentacle things and made a run for it."

"Always assuming," said Doctor Henry McCoy, "that he could have improvised a refrigeration system. The super-cell could not have thrived long in an environment of room temperature." To an outsider, the cultured voice might have sounded incongruous, coming as it did from the lips of a blue-furred creature with a heavy brow, pointed ears and fangs, who wore only a pair of stretchable blue trunks. However, Hank's monstrous form was belied by his calm, analytical nature; he had been a respected scientist longer than he had been a Beast.

"There was ice on the floor," recalled Xavier. "I saw it in Rogue's memories." Rogue suppressed a shiver at this reminder that she had allowed a visitor into her mind. She had known Professor X for a long time, and she trusted him, but the very notion of sharing her most private thoughts still freaked her out a little.

She wondered if he knew that she had been thinking of Joseph.

"Mea culpa," said Bobby Drake, holding up a hand. "Selene sent two fire demons against us, remember? I hurled a lot of ice at them." Bobby was a young man with mousy brown hair, clad in a formfitting, two-tone blue costume with red "X" logos on the shoulder and belt buckle. In combat, that costume disappeared beneath the hard, translucent shell of the incomparable Iceman. Even now, Bobby was keeping his hands occupied by condensing ice cubes out of the air and juggling absent-mindedly with them.

"It makes sense," said Cyclops. "Too much sense for my liking." He counted off points on his yellow-gloved fingers. "Shaw tried to find a cure for the Legacy Virus using Kree technology. We know he had a partner in that endeavor; somebody who raised a Kree island from the seabed for him. And thanks to the White Queen, we also know that, three weeks after we thought the cure lost, Shaw is working on another secret project with none other than Magneto. I think all those facts could be connected."

"And now," said Wolverine, "we got a pretty good idea how." He clenched his fist, and three claws popped out of the back of his hand with a soft *snikt* sound. The claws, like his skeleton, were sheathed in adamantium, the hardest known metal. Wolverine's yellow and dark blue costume, with extensions jutting out of his mask like long ears, combined with his restless nature to lend him the semblance of a rare breed of wild animal. He also had an animal's enhanced senses and awareness, and an accelerated healing factor, which allowed him to enter any combat hard and fast without undue concern for the consequences.

"Precisely," said Xavier. "That is why I gathered you all here. The eight of you were present when the cure was supposedly destroyed. By searching your memories, I was hoping to prove that Shaw couldn't have taken it after all. Unfortunately, there appears to be a very real possibility that he did."

"And if he did take it," said Rogue, "then Magneto has it now too."

Her statement was greeted by a reflective silence. A month ago, some of the X-Men might not have been able to imagine how even their most dangerous mutant foe could do much harm with a serum designed to save lives. Since then, however, they had seen New York City enslaved. And Magneto was a far more ruthless opponent than Selene. His goal was nothing less than the total subjugation of the human race by its evolutionary successors.

Once, not such a long time ago, Rogue had met a young man called Joseph. They had come to care for each other; given more time, they could have fallen in love. The irony of it was that Joseph had been cloned from Magneto's DNA. He had had Magneto's personality, but he had not shared his memories of a lifetime of persecution. He did not remember the death camps and gas chambers of World War II, nor the mutant-hunting Sentinels of more recent years. He had been a good man. But unfortunately, good men sometimes die.

Wolverine finally spoke up. "Then we've got us a second chance," he growled. "People are crying out for that cure, and now we know where we can find it."

"It may not be that simple," said Storm. Before Xavier had

found her, Ororo Munroe had been worshipped as a goddess in the rainforests of her native Kenya. It was easy to see why. Apart from her mastery over the elements, she retained a regal poise and a confident grace, and her flowing white hair—held back from her forehead by a black headband—still marked her out as something different, something exotic. Sometimes, Rogue fancied that she could see the lightning itself in Storm's eyes.

"Ororo's right," said Phoenix, brushing her long red hair off the shoulders of her combat suit. Like Xavier, Jean Grey was a telepath. But more important—and much more powerful—were her telekinetic (or TK) abilities. On occasion, Phoenix's telekinetic powers had seemed limitless, uncontrollable, and had worried even her teammates. What kept them in check was Jean's infinite compassion. "Magneto's rule of Genosha is recognized by the United Nations," she said. "We can't just storm in there and take the cure from him by force, much as we'd like to." Cyclops, her husband, flashed her a tiny smile.

"So you say," muttered Wolverine under his breath.

"We'd be in violation of international law, Logan!" said Cyclops tersely.

"Maybe," said Nightcrawler quietly, "but how many lives might we save as a consequence?" Like Hank McCoy, Kurt Wagner's personality and appearance presented a sharp contrast. His particular mutant gene had played a cruel trick on this gentle, religious soul by making him resemble a shadowy demon out of folklore. His skin was indigo blue with a texture like velvet, his eyes a luminous yellow, and his long, prehensile tail came to a wicked barb. As if in compensation for being thus marked out, he had the power to teleport from place to place. For a time, he had found a promising niche as a circus performer—part freak, part acrobat—in his native Germany. Having ultimately been hounded out of his home, however, he had found a new one here.

"It's worth remembering," said Phoenix, "that Genosha has a Legacy epidemic. Its people are dying by the hundreds."

"Which is half the reason the UN handed the place over to Maggie," added Iceman. "They thought it'd keep him busy and out of their hair for a while."

"Yeah," said Rogue, "that and the fact that he was threatening to destroy the whole world if he didn't get his way."

"And I said at the time it was a mistake," grumbled Wolverine. "Magneto wants power. You give him some, he'll come back for more every time."

"Give him some credit, though," persisted Phoenix. "He has the mutates' best interests at heart, unlike the old government. I know it seems unlikely, but perhaps he only wants the Legacy cure for humanitarian reasons?"

"So, what do you think will happen when he has an army of healthy mutates under his command?" asked Wolverine. "They already look to him as some kind of savior."

"Would you rather see those mutates die, *mein freund*?" asked Nightcrawler.

"Nevertheless," said Cyclops, "Wolverine has a point. At the very least, I would feel much happier if we could know what Magneto's plans are."

"Law or no law," said Rogue, "don't we have a right to that cure? Shaw couldn't have developed it without the Beast's help. The deal was that we'd share it."

"And Shaw welched," said Iceman. "Big surprise!"

"Then perhaps we should take our grievance to Shaw himself," suggested Storm, "confront him with what we have deduced." Rogue recalled that Ororo had seemed to reach an understanding of sorts with the Black King when last they had met. She wondered if that newly forged relationship could work to the X-Men's advantage.

"And you think he'll just put his hands up to everything?" sneered Wolverine.

"Whatever his reaction," said the Beast, "we have good reason to believe that Shaw is engaged in nefarious activities of some description. Our evidence of Magneto's involvement is circumstantial at best. Our most logical course is to question Shaw in the first instance."

"In case you hadn't noticed," said Wolverine, "Frost and Hellstrom already tried that."

"Magneto is the greater threat here," said Nightcrawler. "We can't just ignore him."

"I'm inclined to agree," said Xavier, his considered words bringing the discussion to a halt. He held his fingers together in front of his lips, and his eyes were hooded. He always seemed like this when Magneto was mentioned: subdued, as if he had resigned himself to fighting this battle over and over again for the rest of his days.

"According to our information," the Professor continued, "Shaw is planning a worldwide Hellfire Club party on the night of the solstice—tomorrow night. I think it's reasonable to assume that his plans, whatever they are, will reach fruition then."

"Which doesn't leave us much time," said Phoenix.

"Quite. I think we need two teams: one to confront Shaw in the hope that this can be ended quickly, and the other to investigate the situation in Genosha—in case it can't."

"Rogue has been to Genosha more recently than any of us," offered Cyclops.

Rogue nodded, thinking about Joseph again. He had sacrificed his life to save the world that Magneto had imperiled—but when she had flown to Genosha alone in search of its new ruler, it had not been for revenge. She had hoped to find Joseph again, buried somewhere in the heart of his corrupted template. She had hoped to redeem a tortured soul. Perhaps she had been naïve, but she had wanted to believe that such a thing was possible. After all, she had found redemption with the X-Men herself: Xavier had accepted her into his team, his family, despite her past misdemeanors.

"The place is a mess," she reported. "Everything the Genoshans built with mutate slave labor has been torn apart—and thanks to the Legacy epidemic, they've hardly started to put the pieces back together. As Wolvie said, the mutates have welcomed the new order with open arms, but the baseline humans can't get away from the island fast enough—those who haven't decided to stay and slug it out, that is. The war might be over according to Magneto, but some of his 'loyal subjects' haven't realized it yet."

"Could you lead a team of four into the country undetected?" asked Xavier.

"Shouldn't be a problem. I flew right in there a month or so back without anyone noticing."

"Magneto might have beefed up his security since then," Wolverine pointed out.

"There's no way of knowing," said Cyclops, "not with news from inside the country as scarce as it is."

"Be careful," advised Xavier sternly. "I would rather not spark an international incident if we can help it. Your task for the present is simply to reconnoiter."

"Understood," said Rogue.

"Take Wolverine, Nightcrawler and Iceman with you," said Cyclops. "Storm and the Beast have had the most contact with Shaw recently, so they'll accompany Phoenix and me to the Hellfire Club in Hong Kong."

"Sounds like a plan to me," said Rogue with forced levity, trying to ignore the fact that her heart was heavy at the thought of this mission.

She had to forget the past, she knew that. She had to deal with Magneto as he was now, as she had always known him: as an implacable foe. She had to accept what she had discovered when she had confronted him at last, when she had stolen his soul and looked into his innermost being.

She had to forget the man that he could have been—because that man was long since dead.

CHAPTER 3

ONCE, Hammer Bay had been lauded for its dynamic, forward-thinking architecture. The Genoshan government had had the old buildings torn down and replaced by the latest designs, their angles rounded and their lines softened. The skyline had been a wondrous sight, majestic, almost natural. The insides of its buildings, like the streets, had been clean and welcoming, fitted with every modern convenience. Everything had been built to a plan, each structure complementing those around it perfectly. No compromises had been made, no corners cut for the sake of expediency or cost. Government officials had received award after award, taking the podium at a string of international events with modest smiles and enterprising words that everybody wanted to hear.

A few people had wondered how Genosha had become so prosperous, how it had achieved so much in so short a time. Some had even suspected that the country had hidden resources. But nobody had asked too many questions. Not until it was too late.

Now, Hammer Bay's award-winning buildings were broken. Some had been gutted or felled, and there were noticeable gaps in the meticulously sculpted skyline. From Wolverine's vantage point, a few miles off-shore, the city resembled a ruined castle.

Lights still shone from its windows, but they were relatively few now. Smoke billowed from more than one street, and the night sky was washed in angry shades of red.

He sniffed the air, scowling at the acrid smell of burning. It was faint—so faint that he wondered if the others, without the benefit of his enhanced senses, could detect it. They certainly couldn't have caught the scent of the man who was flying out of the city toward them under his own power—although they might have seen him by now, a black shape growing and detaching itself from the darkness.

"Incoming," he muttered.

Iceman's knuckles tightened on the side of the small powered boat as the figure reached them. He was wearing a green uniform festooned with holsters and ammunition belts, but the top of a yellow skinsuit was still visible around his neck. His face was concealed by a dark blue gas mask into which was set a filtered speaking grille and a reflective eyepiece. A green cap was pulled down over this.

"Never thought I'd see a mutate in magistrates' clothing," grumbled Wolverine.

The mutate's size and demeanor betrayed the fact that he was a boy, no more than fourteen or fifteen years old—but Wolverine knew better than to underestimate him. Not only did he carry a rifle, but there was no telling what other powers he might possess.

The boy hovered about ten feet above the boat, glaring at each of its occupants in turn. "You have invaded Genoshan territorial waters." He was trying to sound menacing, but his voice hadn't broken yet. "Turn back now or suffer the consequences!"

Nightcrawler responded with a stream of his native German, of which Wolverine only understood the occasional word. A natural actor, Kurt played the part of the bewildered tourist well. Of course, his appearance would have given the game away had it not been for his image inducer. The device cast a holographic field around him, which made him look like a tall, wiry man with a pencil-thin moustache. The rest of the X-Men didn't need such aids to hide their mutant natures, although they had eschewed their usual colorful costumes for less conspicuous attire. Wolverine wore a light khaki shirt and shorts to keep him cool in the heat of the near-equatorial day. He had also donned a sombrero hat, which he tipped back to regard the mutate with a quizzically raised eyebrow.

Rogue joined in the protestations of innocence. "Come on sugar, can't you give us a break? We're just trying to take in some of the sights here." Even in this climate, she had wrapped herself in a red, hooded jogger top for safety.

"A five-mile exclusion zone is in force around our island."

"Well, we didn't know that," complained Iceman.

"I do not believe your story," said the mutate boy. "We have turned away many journalists from our shores. We will not be spied upon."

Rogue glanced at Wolverine, then looked back at the mutate with a wry grin. "OK, sugar, you caught us. We just wanted to get a bit of footage for the evening news, you know? But if you feel so strongly about it, we'll just mosey on back to where we came from."

The mutate gave her a curt nod, then folded his arms and remained in his hovering position. Evidently, he was waiting for her to carry out her promise.

Reluctantly, Rogue gunned the outboard engine and steered the boat around until it was pointing in the direction of Madagascar, from which it had been hired. As it cut a white trail across the calm surface of the Indian Ocean, the mutate watched it go, a silent sentry. It wasn't until Hammer Bay was little more than a dot on the horizon that Wolverine, with his sharp eyes, saw the boy turn and fly back to his concealed guard post at last.

Rogue killed the motor again, and let the boat drift. "Looks like you were right," she sighed. "Magneto's closed his borders. This is going to be trickier than I'd hoped."

"He can't have mutates watching the entire coastline, surely?" said Iceman.

"Probably not," said Wolverine, "and from what I've heard, he's as keen to keep Genosha's non-mutant population in as he is to keep the rest of the world out. His troops have got to be over-stretched!"

"Nevertheless," said Nightcrawler, "that leaves us with a problem. How do we find the weak points in his surveillance from five miles away?"

"I have an idea," said Rogue, "but I'm not sure any of us are going to like it."

They took the boat in a wide arc around the distant lights of the city before silencing the engine again and breaking out the oars. They approached the island as quietly as they could; Nightcrawler scanned it through binoculars and guided them toward what looked like a secluded nook. He was alert for any sign of move-ment, any indication that they had been sighted again.

The X-Men's plane—a Lockheed Blackbird souped up with alien technology—had brought them to East Africa in record-shattering time, but Kurt felt as if it had already been a long day. The time difference was probably to blame. Genosha was nine hours ahead of New York: his body thought it was mid-afternoon, but his senses insisted that it was midnight.

In this part of the world, he thought with a chill, it was the twenty-first of December already. Further east, the sun was on the verge of dawning. The Hellfire Club's solstice celebrations would be underway in as little as fourteen hours.

Wolverine stopped rowing. "I think this is as close as we can safely get," he said.

"See anywhere we can use?" asked Rogue.

Nightcrawler squinted through the binoculars, trying to make out shapes in the darkness. Fortunately, his night vision was excel-lent. "I'm looking at a cliff face with a small copse on top," he reported. "It's just a few miles from Hammer Bay—and I can't see any guards."

"Sounds perfect," said Rogue.

"So long as you don't go 'porting into a tree," cautioned Wolverine.

Nightcrawler nodded grimly. For him, this was the most dangerous part of Rogue's plan. Such a long-distance teleport would be a strain, but it was perfectly feasible; what worried him was that, without a precise idea of the layout of his destination, he could easily materialize inside something else. In that case, he would suffer a quick but agonizing death.

He fixed his sights upon a particular spot at the top of the distant cliff edge. He tried to visualize it from all angles, to reconstruct the site inside his head. It would have been better to appear further into the trees, but it would also have been much riskier. This way, he would be visible to any onlookers for a second before he could take cover. Reaching through his illusory light-colored suit and into a pouch in his red fighting tunic, Nightcrawler thumbed off the image inducer and revealed his true form. Another side-effect of his mutant gene was that he became almost invisible when cast into shadow; it was just the advantage he needed.

"Good luck," said Iceman, crossing the fingers of both hands.

Nightcrawler took a deep breath, concentrated on the place in his mind and envisaged himself there. His ears were momentarily deadened by a pop of imploding air, and his nostrils assailed by the stench of brimstone that always accompanied his teleports: another cruel irony. He sprinted through a cloud of dark smoke and into the trees; he didn't even give himself time to feel relieved that he had reached Genosha in one piece.

Picking out a tree with particularly dense foliage, Nightcrawler took a prodigious leap onto its trunk and scuttled into its uppermost branches, narrowing his headlamp eyes lest they betray his presence. He prayed that such precautions would prove unnecessary—but to his dismay, he soon heard footsteps approaching.

A mutate passed beneath him, the top of his head just a few feet below Nightcrawler's perch. He looked scrawny and malnourished, his green uniform hanging off him like rags from a scarecrow: he was probably ill with Legacy. His lips were pinched and his expression haunted. He moved slowly, uncertainly. Perhaps he only *suspected* that he had heard or seen something. . . .

But as he passed Nightcrawler's hiding place, the mutate faltered and sniffed the air. He cocked his head to one side suspiciously, and Kurt realized that, like Wolverine, he had the ability to detect another person's scent.

Inwardly cursing his luck, he sprang from his hiding place and somersaulted to land feet-first on his would-be hunter's neck. Fortunately, as his appearance had suggested, the mutate had not been blessed with great physical defenses. He emitted a tiny, high-pitched groan and collapsed into the undergrowth. Nightcrawler stooped beside him and checked his pulse. He was alive, but he would be out for a while at least.

Time was of the essence now. The mutate had a belt-mounted radio handset, and it couldn't be too long before he was expected to report in. Nightcrawler listened for a moment, but heard nothing to suggest that there were more sentries about. Moving quickly but lightly on his feet, darting from tree to tree, he made his way back to the cliff edge.

With the moon behind him and the lights of Hammer Bay some way down the coast to his left, he couldn't see the X-Men's boat on the sea—but he knew it was out there. He teleported again, more confidently this time, aiming for a point some four feet above the one from which he had started out. As he had expected, he materialized above cold, dark water: the boat had been anchored, but it had still drifted a short way on its chain since he had left it. Before gravity could take hold of him, he got a fix on its new position and vanished again to reappear neatly beside his teammates.

"One guard," he reported. "I was forced to deal with him."

"Did he get a look at you?" asked Wolverine. Nightcrawler shook his head.

"Either way," said Rogue, "the sooner we get back over there, the better." She removed a long black glove, and gave Nightcrawler an apologetic look. "You ready for this, sugar?"

"When you are," he replied, trying to sound cheerful.

As bad as this would be for him, he knew it would be far, far worse for her.

Rogue reached out and brushed her fingers across Nightcrawler's cheek; just a brief, gentle caress, but the result of it hit her like a sledgehammer between the eyes. Everything that Kurt Wagner was, everything he thought and felt, was rushing into her, trying to displace her own identity. She gritted her teeth and concentrated on her sense of self. She tried not to focus upon the stray thoughts, the odd recollections, that were sluicing through her brain to light up the insides of her eyelids. She remembered how unsettling it had been to let the Professor into her mind, and she wondered if Kurt was feeling the same about her now.

The onslaught subsided, and she was aware of her own lungs heaving. She looked down at her uncovered hand and saw that the skin was dark blue.

Nightcrawler was holding his head in his hands—but after a moment, he looked up and grinned at her bravely. He was resilient. He had been through this—and, like all of them, much worse—before. He would recover, faster than most of Rogue's victims did.

There was an image in her mind: a small patch of land surrounded by trees, in which a uniformed mutate lay face down. Instinctively, she knew how to get to that place. She replaced her glove, put her arm around Wolverine's shoulders and drew him to her side.

Alone, Nightcrawler wouldn't have been able to take all three of his colleagues to Genosha. He found it a strain to teleport with even one passenger, especially over such a distance. To do so three times in succession would have killed him. This way, Rogue could take some of that burden from him. She could teleport herself and Wolverine to the island now, before her stolen powers began to fade. In a few minutes' time, Nightcrawler would be healthy again, and he could follow with Iceman.

But Kurt had warned her, in no uncertain terms, that it would hurt.

Rogue closed her eyes and teleported. The world exploded around her, and she was enveloped in dark smoke, feeling as if a giant hand had seized her internal organs and twisted them forty-five degrees clockwise. She let out a scream, feeling shamed by Wolverine's stoic refusal to do likewise: he must have been feeling almost as bad as she did.

Thankfully, it was over in a second. The sweet smell of pollen hit Rogue's nostrils, overwhelmed an instant later by that of brimstone, and she saw the felled mutate at her feet. She hadn't even had time, she realized giddily, to wonder what might have happened if he had woken up and begun to wander about. She was only vaguely aware of Wolverine beside her; she didn't know what condition he was in. Her legs felt like jelly, and she collapsed against a tree, breathing heavily, her stomach heaving.

"Remind me," she panted, "to never, ever do that again."

Iceman felt sick.

He sat hunched up with his back against a tree-trunk and his arms around his knees, putting all his efforts into regulating his own body temperature and waiting for the nausea to pass.

It was all right for the others, he thought: Nightcrawler was used to this, Wolverine had his healing factor and Rogue was darn near invulnerable. They had all coped better than he had with the stresses that the teleport had placed on their bodies. They were standing around the unconscious mutate now, discussing what was to be done with him.

"Whatever you say, Logan," insisted Nightcrawler, "I will not agree that it's acceptable to take a human life."

"This guy knew what he was getting into when he took the job!" growled Wolverine.

"And who's to say he had a choice in the matter, *mein freund*?"

"We have to do something," said Rogue. "We can't afford to have our presence here discovered." Her skin hadn't quite returned to its normal color yet; it still had a blue tint.

"Nothing else we *can* do," said Wolverine. "As soon as our mutate friend wakes up, he'll put a call in to his boss. Best we toss him into the sea now and nip the problem in the bud."

Nightcrawler shook his head vehemently. "All he can report is that somebody attacked him from behind. He didn't see me."

"But," said Rogue, rubbing at her chin thoughtfully, "when Magneto hears the report of that other sentry, he might just put two and two together and make X."

"Who's to say he won't do that anyway, if one of his guards goes missing?"

"At least we'll have bought ourselves some time," said Wolverine.

"You know what Cyclops would say if he was here," said Rogue.

"But he ain't here, is he!"

It was a familiar argument, and one that Wolverine must have known he would lose. But he had his say nonetheless. He believed that, as the X-Men's foes grew deadlier and more ruthless, so too did they have to change their methods. He believed that a war could not be won without sacrifices. Iceman tended to steer clear of such disputes; in theory, he agreed with Nightcrawler's principled stance, but he could see Wolverine's point as well. Leaving the mutate alive was asking for trouble. It meant that, somewhere down the line, the X-Men's lives could be endangered, their vital mission jeopardized. Disposing of their foe—a man who would surely have done the same to them without hesitation—was the easier option. And life was difficult enough as it was for a mutant; for an X-Man, even more so.

Iceman would have shed few tears if Wolverine had killed the mutate. But he could never have delivered the fatal blow himself.

"It's your call, darling!" said Wolverine, looking at Rogue.

"We'll tie him up," she said decisively, "and hide him some-where."

Wolverine shook his head. "No point. If we're not gonna do the job properly, best leave him as he is. We don't to make this look too professional." The mutate groaned as he began to stir, and Wolverine dropped to his haunches beside him. He slipped his hands around the man's throat and applied pressure to his sensi-tive nerve clusters until he passed out again. "There—should keep him under for another couple of hours. Pile a few leaves on top of him. With luck, we'll be long gone before the alarm's raised."

Rogue nodded her approval to this course of action, and turned to Iceman. He sighed and climbed to his feet, nodding to signal that he was well enough to proceed. In fact, he was still feeling queasy, but he would just have to put up with that.

"So, which way to Hammer Bay?" he asked.

The question had been directed at Nightcrawler, but it was Wolverine who answered by setting off sure-footedly through the trees. The others followed him without question: they knew that his sense of direction was unparalleled.

Emerging from the copse, they hurried down a gentle slope into a moonlit field. As Wolverine led the way across it quickly, eager to reach the cover of more trees on the far side, Iceman looked at the dead earth beneath his feet. He could sense that it had not felt water in a long time; whatever seeds had been planted in it had been neglected, left to wither in the hot, dry climate. Genosha had once advertised itself as "a green and pleasant land," and the claim had not been an exaggeration. The field, he supposed, was sym-bolic of the state to which the human-mutate war had reduced a once proud country.

He couldn't help but wonder if America might one day suffer a similar fate. His instinct was to deny that such a horror was even possible—but what if an all-out war began there too? Who could predict how that might end?

The others had almost crossed the field, and Iceman made to

catch up with them—but he frowned as he caught sight of something. Something odd about one of the trees in front of them—but what was it? Had it moved? If he concentrated and looked at a certain spot in a certain way, then part of the landscape seemed off-kilter somehow, distorted. He ought to have warned the others, but none of them appeared to have noticed anything amiss, and that made Bobby doubt the evidence of his own eyes.

The air rippled like a heat haze, just a few feet in front of Nightcrawler and to his left, and suddenly he was sure. "Guys," he said, "I think there's something up there!"

A shape formed out of nowhere. It was a woman, her hands clasped to her cheeks, her eyes and mouth stretched into wide saucer shapes. She was insubstantial like a ghost, and Iceman could see the trees through her. She must have blended herself into her background, masking her presence somehow even from Wolverine's senses.

She was screaming, and her voice was a shrill alarm signal. Wolverine leapt at her, his claws springing from their housings, but she dissipated on the air and left him to slice through green mist. The scream sounded as if it were coming from all around the X-Men now, boring into their skulls and filling their brains with its intensity. Iceman put his hands over his ears, but it didn't keep the scream out. Rogue threw an experimental punch, looking aggrieved but not at all surprised when she connected with nothing. She tried again anyway, and Iceman saw a faint green shimmer as something recoiled from her fist.

Quickly, he brought up his hands and condensed the moisture in the air around it. A large, jagged lump of ice thudded into the ground between the four X-Men, and Iceman was gratified to see that he had trapped a green blur in its depths. The screaming had stopped.

"Good work, Bobby," said Rogue. Iceman's ears were still numb, and the words sounded distant to him. "Now let's get out of here before someone comes to investigate that racket!"

"Too late," said Wolverine grimly.

* * *

Wolverine's keen ears had detected a familiar whining sound. Aircars, four or more of them, running on their quiet antigravity-powered engines. They had once been used by Genosha's so-called peace-keepers, its human magistrates, but he had no doubt that they would have fallen into the hands of Magneto's followers.

The others could hear them too now, and they followed him into the woods at a run. Bright searchlights stabbed through the trees and lit up the undergrowth, and Wolverine caught flashes of rounded silver panels through the leaves above him. A finger of light caught Rogue momentarily, followed by a barrage of blaster fire that ripped up the ground beneath the X-Men's feet. Nightcrawler was buffeted by an explosion, but he teleported instinctively before he could take shrapnel damage.

"So much for sneaking into the country undetected," he said ruefully.

"Looks like it's Plan B, people," said Rogue.

They all knew what she meant. They had discussed this on the boat ride from Madagascar. Now that their presence in Genosha had been discovered, they would be hunted down—and Magneto's forces outnumbered them by hundreds to one. If they stayed together, they could only fall together. Individually, however, each of them stood a chance of being able to keep out of sight—and they only needed one of them to complete the mission, to find evidence of their enemy's plans and to get that information out to the rest of their team.

The X-Men scattered, and even Wolverine had soon lost sight of his three teammates through the foliage. He could hear a commotion above him, though: Rogue had flown straight up into the sky and made herself a target for the aircars, distracting their pilots. Plucky lady.

And there was something else: a whooshing of air behind him. A flying mutate, and a fast one. He varied his path, putting cover between himself and his pursuer, but it was no use. The mutate kept gaining on him until Wolverine knew that he had to stand and fight.

A muscular figure flew at him like a cannonball. Wolverine stood his ground until the last possible moment, then leapt beneath his incoming attacker. But the mutate's speed was incredible, and he was still able to clip the X-Man's chin with a fist that felt like an anvil. It was only a glancing blow, but it was enough to rattle even Wolverine's reinforced bones.

He was still reeling when the mutate came in for a second pass. This time, he threw himself backwards and brought up his hands and feet, taking hold of the mutate's shoulders and simultaneously delivering a punishing double-kick to his stomach. His foe spun around in midair and hit the ground hard. He was already back on his feet by the time the X-Man could press his advantage—but Logan was fast too. The pair closed in hand-to-hand combat, and the mutate, for all his speed and strength, couldn't land a solid blow on his twisting, slippery opponent. Wolverine, on the other hand, made himself an opening and raked his claws across the mutate's arm. He felt them tearing through skin, felt a warm trickle against his knuckles, and grinned to himself through clenched teeth. "First blood," he snarled in triumph.

And then he caught another two scents. Three. Four. More mutates, alerted by the sounds of combat or perhaps by an inaudible distress signal. They were approaching from all sides, homing unerringly upon the X-Man's position. Fuelled now by urgency, he laid into his opponent, giving no quarter, and felled him with two swift adamantium-laced punches to the jaw. But his senses told him that it was already too late.

He was surrounded.

Nightcrawler was making slow but sure progress, leaping from treetop to treetop, a shifting shadow, melting into the darkness whenever he thought there might be eyes upon him. He was leaving the sounds of the aircars behind him, their engines protesting as they tried to keep up with their target. He feared for Rogue's life—but at least, he thought, while the aircars were still spitting fire, it meant that she was giving them something to aim at.

And then, he heard a new sound: the sound of a pitched battle from somewhere ahead of him and over to the right. The clanging of metal against metal, the shrieking of unfamiliar energy discharges. It had to mean that Wolverine or Iceman was in trouble.

Kurt hesitated. He longed to help with every fiber of his being, but the X-Men's plan forbade it. He was supposed to keep away from the others. It sounded very much like his teammate was outnumbered: if he went blundering in, then he was likely to get himself captured or killed too. But how could he abandon a friend in need?

Even before he had formed an answer to that question, he found himself heading toward the source of the disturbance. What harm could it do to take a quick look at least, to see precisely what the situation was? He could always teleport away if he had to.

And so it was that Nightcrawler found Wolverine, fighting savagely to keep himself from being overwhelmed by five green-clad mutates. The X-Man's khaki shirt was torn and his cheek bloodied. His claws lashed out this way and that, faster than Nightcrawler could follow, his eyes were wild and the only sounds to emerge from his throat were a series of guttural growls and grunts. Nightcrawler mumbled a quick prayer. Logan was his best friend—but when he surrendered all reason, when he gave in to his animal side like this, he scared even Kurt.

Ironically, though, it was when Wolverine lost control—when he allowed his finely-honed instincts to take over and guide him—that he was at his most effective in battle. Even the disapproving Nightcrawler had to admit that he was putting on an impressive display: the mutates couldn't lay a hand on him, and every time they tried, they received new cuts for their troubles. Even as Kurt hesitated, as he tried to decide if he should intervene or not, one of the mutates let out a gargling scream, clutched his hands to his stomach and keeled over. An instant later, a woman with fire for her hair was felled by a roundhouse punch. A younger man leapt upon his foe with an angry roar—he was wearing no mask, and Kurt could see that his skin was a deep jet in color, glistening like crystal—but his own momentum was turned against him. Thrown clear of the melee, he hurtled into a tree-trunk, and Nightcrawler thought he heard a sound like glass breaking.

Wolverine was left with only two opponents now, but even his luck couldn't hold out forever. He was tagged from behind by a young female mutate with long talons in place of fingers. Nightcrawler winced in sympathy as her nails slashed into his side, between his ribs, and Logan arched his back in pain. A broad-shouldered man whose steel body had burst out of his combat suit seized his opportunity; he stepped forward and took hold of Wolverine's head in his metal hands. When he failed to crush his enemy's skull, he looked confused and irritated, and he increased the pressure. The adamantium in Wolverine's bones was keeping him alive, but for how much longer? His expression was strained, his knees beginning to buckle. And the girl with the talons was moving in to strike again.

By the time she got close, Nightcrawler was sitting on the shoulders of the steel man, jamming his cap down over his eyes. He didn't have the strength to break the mutate's grip on Wolverine, but the distraction of his sudden, noisy appearance—and his cheerful cry of "Peek-a-boo!"—was enough to do the job. The mutate threw his hands up to his head, but Nightcrawler had already teleported away again.

In the meantime, Wolverine and the girl were fighting claw to talon—and Nightcrawler was alarmed to see that his teammate was losing. It wasn't that the girl was good—far from it, she seemed undisciplined and inexperienced, her fighting style amounting to little more than flailing at her foe and hoping for the best—but Wolverine was uncharacteristically slow, even clumsy. He favored his injured side, and Kurt realized that the wound was deeper than he had thought. It was bleeding. Logan needed a breather; time for his healing factor to kick in.

The steel man bore down upon Nightcrawler like a runaway train, his roar like a warning siren. It was easy enough to avoid him with a standing somersault and a handspring off the mutate's shoulder. But bringing him down would be another matter—and the flame-headed woman was already beginning to stir again.

"In this case," he muttered to himself, "I think discretion is very definitely the better part of valor." A space opened up between Wolverine and his opponent, and Nightcrawler teleported into it. He took advantage of the girl's bemusement to land a punch to her head, followed up by a kick to the stomach that sent her sprawling away from him. "Pardon my feet, madam," he said apologetically. Then he took hold of Wolverine and added, in a graver tone: "And pardon me for doing this to you a second time in one day, *mein freund.*"

Wolverine didn't say anything. He fell into Nightcrawler's arms like a dead weight. Fortunately, this tandem 'port was much shorter than the last—nor did it have to be undertaken blindly. Nevertheless, Kurt gritted his teeth and steeled himself as he visualized the open field through which he had recently passed.

Even as three mutates rushed them from opposite sides, Nightcrawler and Wolverine vanished in a puff of smoke.

Rogue had kept the aircars occupied for as long as she could—she had certainly given her teammates a valuable head start—but a few near misses had convinced her that it was time to think about herself now. She dropped back below the treetops and flew a random pattern around the trunks, hoping to shake off her pursuers. It was no use, though. She couldn't reach her top speed, not without sacrificing maneuverability—even now, her gloved hands were raised to keep branches from whipping across her face—and no matter where she flew, the probing searchlights from above still found her. She suspected that the aircars' onboard computers had locked on to her genetic pattern, that there was no escape for her now.

Suddenly, she ran out of cover. She shot past the last of the trees, out into the open, and the aircars swooped in behind her again, preventing her from turning back. Of the original four, only two had remained doggedly with her—but each held two uni-formed mutates. And now that they could see her, they were using their vehicles' blaster weapons again.

Rogue twisted and turned, making herself as difficult to hit as possible—but the very air around her was erupting in flames, and she was buffeted fiercely. Through a haze of smoke, she saw the lights of Hammer Bay ahead of her, and she wondered if she might find shelter among its buildings. But the capital was still too far away, and she was too exposed.

She changed tactics, flipping herself over and rocketing toward the foremost aircar, her fists outstretched in front of her. She wished she could see the expressions of its masked occupants, but their body language at least suggested that she was unnerving them. She had also given them the opportunity to take one point-blank shot.

She closed her eyes and grimaced as the fiery pain washed over her. It was almost unbearable, even to her. Her heavy clothing burst into flame, but she was determined to keep going. She heard a mutate cry out in alarm as she smacked into a warm body. She was in the aircar now, fighting blindly, lashing out at anything that touched her, feeling the crack of bones beneath her knuckles.

By the time her teary eyes had cleared, she was the only person left standing. She felt dizzy, and her jogger top was charred and half-melted. An unconscious mutate lay at her feet; she must have knocked the other one overboard. The aircar was out of control, losing height as it screamed toward Hammer Bay. Fortunately, she had flown one of these things before.

Pulling back heavily on the joystick, Rogue wrestled the vehi-cle's nose up; its undercarriage almost scraped the ground, but it began to climb again. She ducked as blaster fire sizzled past her ears. The second aircar was on her tail. Smiling maliciously to her-self, she turned her vehicle around and set it on a head-to-head collision course with its pursuer.

The mutates in the second car tried to swerve around and below her, but Rogue threw her car into a steep right bank and effectively dive-bombed them. They leapt out of their cockpit an instant before the unavoidable impact, as did she. She flew as hard and as fast as she could, but she didn't get very far before she was rocked by the explosion of two engines.

Winded by the blast, disoriented and hurting, it was all Rogue could do to keep moving, to put as much distance between herself and her hunters—whether they were alive or dead—as she could before she passed out. She didn't even know which direction she had taken, how high she was, how far she flown already. All she was aware of was the pain in her body, and the blackness that was encroaching ever further upon her vision and then, after what seemed like a lamentably short time, the realization that she couldn't control her muscles any more and the sensation of falling . . . falling. . . .

Rogue hit the ground in an untended field about a mile outside Hammer Bay. The earth itself shook with the impact. And there she lay, unmoving, in a crater of her own making.

Until somebody found her.

CHAPTER 4

T HE Hellfire Club's New South Wales branch stood on the southern shore of Sydney Harbor. The building, of necessity, was conspicuously more modern than the organization usually favored. However, it was well situated in one of Australia's most wealthy areas, and the famous Harbor Bridge bisected the view from the front windows of its main ballroom.

Behind those windows now, a fight was nearing its conclusion. The Hellfire Club had thrown almost thirty of its best mercenary agents, dressed in blue and red uniforms with dehumanizing blank flesh-toned masks, at just four intruders. They were losing.

Skilled and highly trained as they were—not to mention armed with lightweight machine-guns—the agents were no match for their genetically gifted foes. The Beast had the strength of several men, and his agility kept him three steps ahead of them; Phoenix snatched their weapons from them with telekinesis while Storm's control over the winds kept them off-balance; and Cyclops's optic blasts could fell two or three agents at a time.

This wasn't going at all how the X-Men had planned it.

Cyclops had hoped, in the first instance at least, to be able to talk to the man who had no doubt approved the order to attack. After dropping off their teammates in Madagascar, he, Phoenix,

Storm and the Beast had taken the Blackbird on to Hong Kong, only to find that Sebastian Shaw was not in residence at the Hell-fire Club's headquarters there. An interminable wait had followed before some desk clerk, grumpy from being roused in the early hours of the morning, had finally informed them that they would have to travel even further east. It made sense, Scott supposed; Shaw had told Emma Frost that the solstice celebrations would begin in Sydney. It was just like him to want to be there.

They had reached their destination shortly after eight, local time. The morning sun had already been hot, and Cyclops had been glad of the cool air currents along the waterfront. His body had insisted that it was still five o'clock the previous evening.

They had been greeted by Shaw's assistant, Tessa, which in itself had all but confirmed that the Black King was indeed here. She had informed them, in a brusque tone, that her employer had had a late night, that he was sleeping and that they should come back later. Mindful of his encroaching deadline, Cyclops had been just as insistent in return. Tessa had refused to discuss the matter further, slamming the door in his face—but he had shot out its lock with an optic blast and followed her into the building.

That was when the fight had begun.

It ended now with three sharp retorts. The figure of Sebastian Shaw was framed by one of the ballroom's arched doorways. He was dressed in a black silk dressing gown, a golden dragon pattern running down one side. His black hair was ruffled, not yet tied into its usual ponytail, and his expression was an approaching thunderstorm. Tessa had adopted her customary position at his shoulder. The clapping of Shaw's hands had been a signal to his costumed pawns. They ceased their attack and withdrew quickly, carrying their fallen with them. Their heads were bowed as if they had been shamed in the sight of their leader.

"Did my assistant not make it clear," he said in a voice that dripped ice, "that I do not wish to receive visitors this morning?"

The X-Men lined up to face him, Cyclops bristling at Shaw's easy air of superiority. He was about to issue a rejoinder when

Storm spoke quietly: "We apologize for the intrusion, Sebastian, but our business here will not wait."

Shaw sneered at her. "Do not presume upon the understanding that we once shared, woman. We could have been allies. We are not. That makes us enemies, now and forever."

Storm withdrew as if stung. Even Cyclops hadn't expected Shaw to be quite this irritable. Normally, he was inscrutable, his thoughts and feelings hidden beneath a cultured veneer. *Perhaps he just doesn't do mornings*, Phoenix's telepathic voice quipped inside his mind.

"If friendship does not influence you," said the Beast, "then how about the plain, old-fashioned concept of a gentleman's honor? You and I had a deal, Shaw. You could not have developed the Legacy cure without my experience in the field, just as I was reliant on your resources. We agreed to share it."

"An agreement made under duress, and one that you are powerless to enforce."

"We know you have the cure, Shaw," said Cyclops, "and we're prepared to take this building apart brick by brick until we find it."

"It would do you no good. It is not here."

"You admit, then, that you took it," said Storm pointedly.

Shaw shrugged. "I see no need to play word games with you. Yes, I have the cure. I took it from Selene's throne room while you were otherwise engaged. And as you no doubt know, I have great plans for it: plans that involve a certain business acquaintance of mine."

"Magneto," said Cyclops, tight-lipped.

"Indeed. Beyond that, I am not prepared to discuss the matter."

"What about this fireworks display of yours?" asked Phoenix.

"I have already been quizzed about this evening's festivities by your associates, Frost and Hellstrom. I have no more to say. Now, if you will excuse me, ladies and gentlemen, I have another busy day ahead of me." Shaw smiled and bowed courteously to his visitors, but his contempt for them showed in his eyes.

Cyclops clenched his fists. "You don't expect us to let you walk out of here, do you?"

Shaw straightened. "And how do you intend to stop me, Mr. Summers?" His tone had softened; now, he sounded genuinely amused. He crooked the fingers of one hand, challenging the X-Men's leader to approach him. "Feel free to attack me if you must. Pit your mutant powers against mine. Beat me to within an inch of my life if you can. You will learn no more than I have already told you."

"There are other ways of gaining information, Shaw," said Phoenix.

The Black King raised an eyebrow. "Ah, the X-Men's resident telepath. Yes, Miss Grey, I have no doubt that you could tear my secrets from me if you so wished. I also expect that you would cause me much pain in the process, should I choose to resist—which, of course, I would." He spread his arms wide in a gesture of helplessness. "So, the decision is yours. Will you do what your White Queen would not? Will you violate me?"

Cyclops and Phoenix exchanged a glance. They could have communed in secret through the permanent telepathic link that, as husband and wife, they shared—but there was no need. They knew each other well enough for each to know what the other was thinking.

Phoenix had always known how easy it would be to abuse her powers. When Shaw had talked of violation, he had chosen his words carefully, reminding her that she had pledged never to invade another person's privacy, never to force her way into somebody else's thoughts without good reason. Cyclops admired her restraint. He was a firm believer in the philosophy that a hero was only as pure as his or her methods. But he was also a pragmatist. He knew that, sometimes, when the stakes were high enough, compromises had to be made.

"Do it," he said.

* * *

Closing her eyes, Phoenix tuned out the distractions of the physical world. She trusted in her husband and her teammates implicitly. She knew that if it came to it, if Shaw or more of his lackeys attacked her physical body, then she had the best possible protection.

The psychic plane was incomprehensible to human senses, but Jean Grey's mind could translate it into images that she understood. She was standing in a white void, the only feature of which was a long, tall wall built from red bricks. She could not see its top, nor its end in either direction. The wall represented Sebastian Shaw's mental defenses. For a non-telepath, it was impressive—but Phoenix could see the cracks in the brickwork, the crumbling mortar, that would allow her to force her way through it.

"I will not allow you to do this."

The voice did not surprise her. She did not even have to turn to see who had spoken. "Unfortunately," she sighed, "I must—and you cannot stop me. It would be better for all concerned if you talked to your employer, persuaded him to give his information freely."

"Sebastian will not pander to such as you, X-Man."

"Your Black King is a ruthless man, his partner even more so. We cannot ignore the fact that they have gained this advantage. If they intend to misuse the Legacy cure, then we have no option but to oppose them—and we will defeat them, Tessa."

"Then you will have to go through me first."

Phoenix faced her opponent at last. In the ballroom, Tessa had been dressed demurely in a neat black jacket, short skirt and high heels. Here, she wore the leather teddy, knee-length boots and cloak of a Black Queen, and she appeared to have increased in stature twofold. Phoenix wasn't impressed. Here, both she and Tessa could look like anything they wanted to; it was no real test of their abilities. Jean chose to present her true form: it was not worth the waste of energy to cloak herself in a lie.

She let Tessa make the first strike. Black tendrils burst out of the white ground at her feet: dead and rotting plant matter, reanimated by hatred. They wound themselves around Jean's ankles and held her fast. She made no move to escape from them. Her attacker's features showed no sign of triumph, no emotion at all. Tessa didn't even meet her gaze. Her concentration was reserved for the matter at hand.

The tendrils had bound her legs beneath the knees now, and they were pulling at her, trying to drag her down. Still, Phoenix didn't move. She reached out with her mind and felt the cold, dead creepers, as surely as if she had run her fingers across them. She tore at them, feeling resistance but overcoming it almost too easily. She watched as Tessa's lips twisted into a sullen pout—then, the black-clad young woman gestured sharply with one hand, and the tendrils burst into flame.

That was when Phoenix fought back, putting the full force of her mind into a single, decisive strike. She gathered up the flames, sculpted them into a roiling, blazing fireball and hurled it. Tessa threw up her hands and screamed as she was suddenly engulfed. The fire was not real, but it could have killed her nevertheless. She blinked out of sight, having withdrawn from the psychic plane before her mind could be destroyed. Phoenix took little pleasure from her victory. Tessa's telepathic abilities were slight: she could not have hoped to match the X-Man, especially not after choosing psychic flames as her weapon. Jean's most difficult task had been to shield her, to ensure that she was not harmed before she could retreat.

"Now, Shaw," she muttered, turning back to the brick wall, "let's see what you've got!"

From the Beast's point of view, it all happened in seconds.

Phoenix closed her eyes, and suddenly Tessa cried out and almost fainted. She leaned against the wall, gasping for breath. And then, Shaw let out a pained grunt through gritted teeth. He shifted his balance awkwardly, and Hank could see that he was making a Herculean effort to remain standing. Phoenix's eyes flicked open, and they were an infernal red. For an instant, she and Shaw locked glares, each as intractable as the other, although

Shaw was trembling and his forehead was drenched with sweat. Then Jean's expression softened, and her eyes faded to their natural green color. Shaw's eyes almost rolled back into his head, and he let out a shudder that was part dismay and part relief. He sagged like a puppet with its strings cut, but he recovered himself and rose shakily to his feet. He adjusted his black dressing gown and made an effort to regain his habitual composure—but when he spoke, his voice was a little hoarse and it sounded smaller than usual.

"You have what you came for, then," he said. Dryly, he added: "Congratulations!"

Phoenix was staring at him with a mixture of disbelief and contempt. "I can't believe that even you would countenance something so . . . so monstrous!"

Shaw turned his back to her. "You are trespassing in this building. Leave now, or I will be forced to summon the police."

"What is it, Jean?" asked Cyclops. "What did you see?"

Phoenix was already heading for one of the exits from the ballroom. "Come on," she said urgently. "We don't have any time to lose. I'll explain on the way."

Cyclops followed her without question, Storm a footstep behind. The Beast hesitated for an instant in the doorway, and glanced back at Shaw and Tessa. The Black King returned his gaze with a dark stare, and Hank was certain that a smile was pulling at his lips. Almost as if he knew something that the X-Men didn't.

He followed his teammates out of the room, and was alarmed to find that they were already out of sight. A corridor stretched ahead of him, its walls studded with doors and openings at irregular intervals. He could hear footsteps receding along the nearest side passageway, but how could the others have reached it so quickly? He had only been a second behind them.

Pushing that question to the back of his mind, the Beast loped after them—but by the time he had rounded the corner, the footsteps had stopped and he was alone again. He hurried along the corridor, becoming more and more worried as he passed each junction and saw nobody. He called out to his friends, but their names were swallowed by silence. He came to a halt, realizing that he was getting nowhere. "It's high time I took a moment to apply some logical deduction to my predicament," he muttered to himself. He paced the corridor in which he had found himself, pulling at his lower lip. The disappearance of his teammates was a physical impossibility—and the telepathic Tessa had been present when it had happened. It wasn't hard to guess, then, that she had messed with his mind somehow, probably in that moment when he had looked back. But what exactly had she done to him?

He tried the nearest door, applying his strength when it proved to be locked. With a splintering of wood, the Beast gained access to a small but expensively furnished office, smiling grimly to himself as he found what he was searching for. A wall clock told him that the time was twenty past nine. Almost an hour had passed since the X-Men had faced Shaw, and he had been completely unaware of it.

The question was, what had happened to the others during that lost time?

The X-Men had run into more Hellfire Club agents on the stairs. They had seemed fresh and alert, their uniforms immaculate. Cyclops couldn't imagine that they were the same people who had just been so comprehensively defeated in the ballroom. He had wondered just how many more mercenaries Shaw had stationed here.

Storm and the Beast had delayed their attackers, while Cyclops and Phoenix had cleared a path through them and headed deeper into the basement levels of the building. *We can't let the Hellfire Club set off that trident firework tonight,* Phoenix explained in response to Cyclops's telepathic questioning. *We have to destroy it!*

He was about to ask why, but then his wife threw open a door and they found themselves in a room which, to Jean's evident surprise, had been decorated like a nursery. The wallpaper was patterned with block capital letters of various colors, and building blocks littered the floor. Somewhere, a music box was playing a tinkling lullaby.

Sebastian Shaw stood beside a small crib in the center of the room. Cyclops didn't stop to question how he had beaten them here: a secret staircase or elevator, no doubt. He was more concerned with the fact that Shaw was holding a sleeping child in his arms. The boy was younger than when he had last seen him—no more than a year old—but Scott knew him all the same. "Nathan!" he gasped. The child stirred and gave a tiny gurgle at his father's voice.

Shaw was looking at Phoenix, a smirk on his face. "I'm sorry, my dear—is this not what you were expecting to find? It would seem that Tessa is a more accomplished telepath than you gave her credit for, no?"

Cyclops took two steps toward him, but held himself back. He couldn't risk harming the baby. "Get your filthy hands off my son!"

"I wondered if you would recognize him after all this time," said Shaw. "But you are mistaken, I'm afraid. Young Nathan is *my* son now."

Phoenix moved to Cyclops's side. "What are you talking about, Shaw?"

"Originally, it was to be a surprise for the boy's mother. She missed him so."

Scott's stomach tightened at the mention of his first wife. He had believed Jean Grey dead when he had married Madelyne Pryor. She had reminded him of his first and only love—not surprisingly, as she had proved to be an imperfect clone of Jean. But when Jean had returned, when Madelyne had lost her child and her husband, she had become bitter and, in time, twisted. She had joined the Hellfire Club and seduced its Black King.

"Nathan was taken to the future for a reason," insisted Scott. "He was suffering from a techno-organic virus. We had to accept that he was gone."

"Or perhaps you didn't love him enough to fight for him. Perhaps he was inconvenient. He got in the way of your aspirations, your dreams of saving the world."

"That's a lie!"

"You remember Fitzroy, of course: another former associate of mine. With his ability to create portals through time and space, it was a simple matter to locate young Nathan and pluck him out of his timeline, to give him a second chance of life here."

"You can't do that," said Phoenix quietly. "We spent time with Nathan in the future. We watched him grow up. He has a destiny to fulfill."

Shaw shrugged as if it didn't matter to him. "When Madelyne left me, of course, I had no further use for the boy. Nevertheless, after the considerable effort I put into obtaining fake documentation—birth certificate, vaccination records and the like, all of which confirm Madelyne and I as his natural parents—I think I'll keep him."

"Over my dead body, Shaw!" growled Scott, starting forward again.

"I don't think it needs to come to that."

Phoenix laid a comforting hand on Cyclops's shoulder. "You know you won't get away with this," she said, addressing Shaw. "We'll demand a DNA test!"

"And it will mitigate in my favor," said Shaw. "You are forgetting, my friends, that in this world of ours, money is the only universal language."

He's trying to provoke a response, telesent Phoenix. *Don't give him the satisfaction.* She was telling Cyclops nothing he didn't know—but her calming influence helped him to believe it. He took a deep, cleansing breath and tried to overrule his emotions. He had always possessed self-control in ample quantity: without it, his mutant power would have been a danger to everybody around him.

"Oh, I don't doubt your persistence," continued Shaw. "You may even take the boy from me in time. But how long? Five years? Ten? Certainly long enough for Nathan to learn the values of my organization, to become the worthy heir that Fate has denied me."

"Why are you showing us this?" snapped Cyclops.

"I am not a heartless man," said Shaw, turning away as he lowered the child into his bed. "I thought you might wish to spend a few minutes with him—to say goodbye."

Scott knew there was more to it than that. Shaw wouldn't have shown his hand like this without good reason. Or perhaps it was just that he couldn't enjoy his victory over his long-time foes unless he could tell them about it. Perhaps he enjoyed the anguish in Cyclops's expression, the ache that Shaw must have known was in his heart. Now that he was no longer holding Nathan, Scott wanted to punch him, blast him, return some of that hurt. But his son was awake now, and reaching through the bars of the crib to him.

"You have ten minutes," said Shaw as he passed Cyclops on his way to the door. "And be advised that this room is surrounded by armed mercenaries. Should you attempt to take my son, then their orders are to shoot him first!"

That was the final straw. Cyclops whirled around, swore at Shaw and opened his visor. A full-strength eye-beam struck its target in the back, but Shaw was unfazed by it. He would have absorbed the concussive force of the blast, Scott realized; its energy component would have caused him some pain, but not nearly enough.

Shaw paused in the doorway and looked back at Cyclops with one eyebrow raised in mild amusement. Ashamed that he had let himself be pushed over the edge, Scott made no further move until after the Black King had left and there was silence in the nursery.

Then, Jean linked her arm gently with his, and they approached the crib together.

The Beast had retraced his steps to the ballroom, planning to confront Shaw and Tessa. But as he approached the open doorway, he was greeted by a sight that filled him with horror.

The morning sun shone through the ballroom windows and fell upon three bodies. They lay in a heap, unmoving, and their blood was soaking into the deep pile carpet.

Hank ran to them with a despairing cry. Cyclops and Storm were already dead, their throats torn out by the claws of some wild animal. Phoenix's eyes fluttered open, but they widened in fear when she saw the Beast. She took a sharp intake of breath and tried to ward him off with a feeble hand, tried to cry out for help. "It's all right, Jeannie." Hank was so distraught that he hardly knew what he was saying. How could this have happened? It still seemed like only minutes ago that the X-Men had had the upper hand. "It's only me. It's Hank. It's all right now. I'm here. Everything will be all right." But Phoenix's fear didn't fade—and even as the Beast watched, the light fled from his dear friend's eyes.

It was too much to take in. It had all happened too quickly. He felt numb. There were claw marks on Phoenix's throat too. He thought about her reaction to him, and was hit by a dreadful realization. He didn't want to do it, didn't want to look down at his own hands, didn't want to face the proof of what he already knew. But he had no choice. He had to see.

An eternity seemed to pass as the Beast stared at his torn nails, at the blood that matted his blue fur, and everything else was blotted out by the awful truth of what he had done.

"Your worst fear, is it not?"

He looked up, shaken back to reality, only dimly recognizing the voice of Sebastian Shaw.

"Ever since your mutant gene manifested itself," said the Black King, "ever since you coined your own ironic code name—all these years, you have dreaded the next stage of your evolution. You immersed yourself in science and literature, exercising your intellect for fear of losing it. You always knew that your body chemistry could change, that your mind could snap at any moment—that you could become a Beast in deed as well as in appearance."

The Beast didn't stop to wonder how Shaw knew so much about his innermost feelings. He lunged at him, hoping to take him by surprise. "You made me do this!" he cried.

And then he was in hand-to-hand combat, but his foe was unmoved, simply absorbing the kinetic energy of his blows. The Beast tried to unbalance Shaw with leverage rather than force, but he only found himself staring into his eyes and seeing the harsh gleam of triumph therein. "Tessa tells me," said the Black King smugly, "that you were easy to manipulate. You were so close to becoming a savage already."

"I'll kill you, Shaw!" he roared. But his blows had added to Shaw's own strength, and he was outmatched. The Beast's hold on his foe was broken, and he was hurled across the ballroom by an almost casual sweep of an energized arm. He managed to turn his flight into a flip and land upright, but he was crouching beside the corpses of his colleagues now, and he could feel their blood, wet on his bare feet. His stomach performed a nauseating pitch and he could no longer think about fighting back. He could only think about what he had done, what terrible part of himself had been unleashed by Tessa, and he wanted to roll himself into a tight ball and shut out the rest of the world until the pain and the guilt had gone away.

"He's all yours, gentlemen," said Shaw—and the Beast became aware of the fact that four more people had entered the room. Police officers. They approached him warily, their guns trained upon him, but he made no move to resist them. One of the officers hauled him to his feet, wrenched his arms behind his back and cuffed his wrists together. Another read him his rights, but Hank wasn't listening. All he heard was the charge that had been laid against him: murder. That one word echoed through his mind, and chilled his blood.

But as he was led toward the exit, a defiant spirit rose within him. He was no good to the remaining X-Men, no good to any-body, if he was locked in a prison cell. And Shaw had to be stopped: Phoenix had said as much, even if she hadn't had time to fill in the details.

It was the work of seconds for the Beast to wriggle free of his handcuffs. But one of the policemen saw that he was free, and shouted a warning to his fellows.

As Hank made for the exit, gunfire exploded around him.

The Hellfire Club building was closing in around Storm.

Its walls and its ceilings were shifting, but never when she was looking directly at them. She just knew that the corridors were narrower and lower than when she had first entered them. She tried to tell herself that she was imagining things, that there was no need to panic. But each door she opened, every corner she rounded, only led her into another corridor, identical to the last but for the fact that it was almost imperceptibly smaller. Even when she tried to turn back, she found that the layout of the passageways had altered behind her. She was walking round in circles—and she was certain that the lights had dimmed.

"Cyclops?" she called, her voice more timid than she had intended. "Phoenix?"

No sound came back to her, but for that of her own heavy breathing.

She could place her hands flat against the ceiling now, or against both walls at once. The building was definitely shrinking, like a living thing, trying to smother her.

She offered a whispered appeal to her deity. "Bright Lady . . ."

Ever since childhood, Ororo Munroe had had a fear of enclosed spaces. She kept on moving, kept on hoping, because she couldn't afford to stop, couldn't let herself think too hard about what was happening. She couldn't think about being buried again.

A part of her railed against the unfairness of it. She had come to terms with her claustrophobia; at least, she had thought she had. She knew that it would never go away, but she had reached a point where she had felt able to cope with her problem. Until recently.

Recently, her resolve had been sorely tested. Three weeks ago, Storm had been trapped in a cave-in at an underground installation. A week before that, she had been buried alive. Or rather, she reminded herself, she had been forced to *believe* that she was buried alive by another of Shaw's telepathic associates. Not that it made any difference. The all-consuming darkness, the stale air and the cramped confines of the coffin still haunted her dreams.

It was typical of the Hellfire Club to zero in upon the weakness of a foe and to exploit it for all it was worth. Storm bitterly resented what Madelyne Pryor had done to her. She resented the anguish that she had been put through simply for having the courage to stand up for what was right. And her resentment manifested itself all around her as the temperature began to drop and a buildup of electricity made the air itself sizzle.

"I am not prepared to play your games, Shaw!" she shouted, sure that somehow her tormentor could hear her. She lashed out with a lightning bolt: it stabbed into the wall where the corridor turned, some way ahead of her, leaving a jagged hole in the plasterwork and in the bricks behind it. Storm soared toward it, carried by the wind, and climbed through.

She found herself in another corridor, identical to the one she had just left—but now she had to stoop to keep from hitting her head on the ceiling. She turned, and caught her breath as she saw that the hole she had made had sealed itself up, leaving no sign that it had existed.

She was panting now, on the verge of hyperventilation, and she could hear her heart beating. "Goddess," she muttered to herself, "this cannot be happening!"

And suddenly, unexpectedly, Ororo found a fragment of hope to cling on to: the hope that this really *wasn't* happening, that it was another of the Hellfire Club's mind tricks. And once that hope was born within her, it grew, and it comforted her with its perfect logic. Closing her eyes, she tried to forget the walls around her, to concentrate on the hope, which she repeated like a mantra. "This cannot be happening, this cannot be happening. . . ."

And slowly, she drew herself to her full height, and nothing stopped her.

Ororo Munroe smiled, experiencing in her relief a tiny moment of blissful serenity.

And then, she opened her eyes to find that she had never left the ballroom.

Shaw was still there, as was Tessa. And there was a third person present: an attractive young woman whom Ororo found vaguely familiar. Her brunette hair fell straight down to her shoulders, and she was clad from neck to toe in form-fitting black leather. Her lips were pursed into a smirk to match Shaw's own.

"Very impressive," purred Shaw. "Of all the X-Men, I expected Phoenix to see through your illusions first."

"She could dismiss them with ease," admitted the woman. "She has the power. But she has to choose to employ it—and she does not yet suspect anything."

"You can see now why I hold Miss Munroe in such high regard."

Storm was still trying to take in her new situation. Cyclops and Phoenix were on their knees, distraught, their arms wrapped around each other. The Beast was struggling as if with unseen assailants—but as Ororo watched, he seemed to break free of them. A shadow of concern flickered across Shaw's face as the X-Man bounded toward the door. "Miss Wyngarde . . .?" he said.

"I have it covered," said the young woman confidently—and suddenly, the Beast stiffened and fell as if he had been shot in the back.

That was when Storm remembered where she had seen the woman before. She had studied a photograph of her after Wolverine and another fellow X-Man, Gambit, had reported encountering her in London. She had been using the name Martinique Jason, but a little research had exposed her as Regan Wyngarde, the daughter of one of the X-Men's oldest enemies.

Jason Wyngarde had gone by the code name of Mastermind. He had died a few months ago, another victim of the Legacy Virus—but this new Lady Mastermind was carrying on the family tradition. Like her father, she had the mutant power to create sophisticated illusions—but hers were more effective than his had ever been, because she was also a low-grade telepath. She could rifle through the minds of her victims, finding inspiration for her creations in their nightmares.

Storm was sick of being manipulated by people like her.

The quickest way to free her teammates was to remove the source of their delusions. Storm tensed herself, and whipped up a wind on which to sail—but even as she started toward Lady Mastermind, she slammed into an unseen barrier. Groggily, she picked herself up to see that Shaw's smirk had widened, almost reaching his ears now. And there was somebody else in the room; somebody who had entered quietly behind her.

"I do beg your pardon," said Shaw. "I have not introduced you to the final member of our quartet. But then, I believe you two have met."

Storm already knew who had felled her. She had recognized his power signature: the application of pure magnetic force. She had felt it many times before. And she knew now that the battle was lost. Shaw and Tessa, she could have bested; Lady Mastermind too, at a pinch. But not him. Not the X-Men's first, deadliest and most bitter foe.

Not the mutant known as Magneto.

CHAPTER 5

ICEMAN was exhausted. He felt as if he had spent the whole night running, although in fact he had spent much of the past few hours in hiding, crouching in the shadows of the forest and waiting for the sounds of footsteps or voices or aircar engines to recede.

He had been forced to fight just once: he had been lying in the shade of a thorny bush, straining his ears to confirm that what he had heard ahead of him had been no more than a rustle of a bird's wings, when a mutate had stumbled across him. To his chagrin, the woman had been a heat-generator. Mindful of the need to take her down before she could raise the alarm, Iceman had pushed himself to his limit. He had dampened her down with a snow coating and rendered her unconscious with his fists. Then, sacrificing caution, he had run, getting as far away from her as he could before she was found.

Throughout his nerve-wracking flight, he had remained in his ice form, comforted by the limited protection that his frozen armor would afford him from unexpected attacks. Now, he was beginning to regret that decision. A familiar muzzy feeling told him that he had overextended himself, he was using his body's moisture faster than he could replenish it. Narrow rivulets of water were already beginning to run down his chest, but he didn't dare return to his human form. Not now.

He had reached the edge of the woods, and he could see man-made structures and a few lights ahead of him. He was disappointed, but not surprised, to see that the architecture was wrong for Hammer Bay. He had tried to head toward the Genoshan capital, but he had become disoriented in the darkness. Nevertheless, any reasonably-sized settlement offered him a chance to lose himself in its streets, to become anonymous among its people. The only problem was, he would have to cross a wide area of open scrub land to reach this one. He would be exposed.

He hesitated for long minutes, pondering the wisdom of his plan. But he concluded that he had no choice. He had detected no sign of pursuit for over half an hour now—and the sooner he got this over with, he told himself, the sooner he could rest.

He gathered up his courage and made a run for it. But in the scant moonlight, he had misjudged the distance to the buildings: no matter how many steps he took toward them, they never seemed to draw closer. And suddenly, he heard an aircar engine behind him.

He glanced back over his shoulder, his eyes wide with fear. The silver vehicle had appeared from nowhere, swooping toward him from above the trees, its two uniformed occupants shouting and pointing at him. Iceman gritted his teeth and tried to ignore them, tried to ignore the protesting of his leg muscles and the pounding of his heart against his chest as he drove himself on. He created an ice slide for himself, forming each section in front of his feet an instant before he skated onto it. It was his customary mode of transport, whenever he needed speed; he had not used it before as its residue would have pointed straight to him, but that hardly mattered now. However, the effort required to maintain the slide was almost too much, setting off a trip hammer inside his head.

The village loomed before him, tantalizingly close. He was almost upon it now.

But then, a well-placed shot from one of the aircar's blaster weapons shattered the slide behind him. Its anchor to the ground destroyed, it collapsed. Iceman hit the hard turf in a hail of fragments, and his armor dissipated. He was flesh and blood and vulnerable, and the aircar sounded as if it were directly above him. Panicking, he clenched his fists and tried to force his unwilling body to "ice up" again. To no avail. The pain in his head was extreme, and his vision misted over. He scrambled back to his feet and set off again with lurching, faltering steps, not sure how far he had to go, not knowing even if he was heading in the right direction. He expected to be engulfed in flames at any second.

There was an explosion of sound behind him, and Iceman cried out as he flung himself to the ground, in no doubt that he had just heard the killing shot. He would die with his nose and mouth full of Genosha's barren soil. But slowly, incredibly, his muddied brain began to register the fact that there was no pain, no dimming of the light. Just the sound of his own shallow breathing as it echoed inside his eardrums.

And then footsteps, thundering across the earth to each side of him.

Nightcrawler's progress through the forest had been painfully slow. He had expected his teammate to recover at any moment, but if anything his condition had worsened. Wolverine had staggered along at Kurt's side, their arms around each other's shoulders, but Logan had become heavier as he had leaned increasingly on his friend for support, his chin sagging further toward his chest. At one point, he had started to mutter nonsensical words as if he had become delirious, and his forehead had been hot to the touch.

Kurt had inspected the gash in Logan's side, dismayed to find that it was still bleeding. He had torn his friend's shirt into strips and used it to bandage the wound. Fortunately, it was a warm night. He would have used his own shirt, had he been wearing one—but his civilian clothing, like his human face, had been an insubstantial product of the image inducer. He wore only his fighting clothes: a one-piece red tunic with a plunging neckline.

Hoping to confuse his hunters, Nightcrawler had headed away from his true target, the capital. When the village had come into sight at the edge of the woods, he had decided to take a chance. With the aircars still loud above him, he hadn't wanted to risk dragging his cumbersome charge across open land, so he had teleported with him instead. They had materialized in the shadow of a burnt-out building, Nightcrawler feeling as if his insides had been put through a blender. Wolverine had been sick on the ground, and had responded to Kurt's expressions of concern with a series of grunts.

The village was much smaller than Hammer Bay, its buildings shorter and more angular. Still, it looked as if it had once been a pleasant enough place to live. But now, its office blocks had crumbled and its houses had been firebombed out. Walls were blackened with soot, the streets ankle-deep in litter. The sewers had backed up, and a rotting stench permeated the night air. The lawns and parks had been neglected, their flowers strangled by weeds, and small, unidentifiable creatures nested in the uncut grass.

Nightcrawler had found a place to rest, on a pile of refuse sacks behind an overflowing dumpster in a dark alleyway. He hadn't wanted to investigate any of the buildings, empty though they seemed, for fear of finding squatters. Neither of the X-Men was in any condition for another fight. One of the sacks had split open, oozing rusted tin cans and soft food waste. He didn't like to think about what was in the rest of them.

Wolverine shifted and groaned in his arms. He had passed out for a few minutes, but now his eyes fluttered open. He looked confused, lost, but he tried to drag himself to his feet. Kurt held him down, relieved all the same that he was moving again. "Take it easy," he said, "you took a nasty scratch back there. You need to give your healing factor a little more time to do its work." His gaze flicked involuntarily to the scraps that bound Wolverine's side. His blood had soaked them through.

"Feels . . . different," murmured Logan. "What did that . . . witch do to me?"

"Nothing your body can't handle," said Kurt, "if you give it a chance."

Wolverine shook his head insistently. "Didn't just . . . cut me. Feel dizzy, sick . . . poisoned my blood. . . ." He closed his eyes again and took a long, shuddering breath.

Nightcrawler hadn't realized before how pale he looked. "It will pass, *mein freund*," he assured him, but he was no longer sure of anything himself. Kurt had been counting on Logan's remarkable physiognomy to pull him through this, to restore him to health. Now, he was beginning to worry that, whatever had happened to him, it was far too serious for that.

Iceman didn't want to move. But he had to know what was happening.

With a supreme effort, ignoring a dozen aches and pains, he rolled over onto his back and tried to make some sense of what he could see from his worm's eye point of view.

There were scraps of metal in the scrub, and he realized that the aircar had crashed. That must have been the noise he had heard: the rending of metal, although he was sure there had been something else too, something more insistent and high-pitched, more dangerous. One of the car's former occupants was lying facedown, limbs splayed out, beside the main body of the wreckage. The other was on his feet, but he had come under attack. He appeared to possess great strength, and he was fighting hard, but he was outnumbered. The six newcomers varied in age and gender: a teenaged boy had leapt onto the mutate's back and was pummeling at his head, while an elderly woman was aiming swipes at him with a metal walking cane as she hurled choice insults. Nor did they identify themselves with costumes or uniforms. They wore normal, everyday clothes, a little untidy perhaps—and as far as Iceman could see, they had no supernormal powers.

Nevertheless, the mutate fell to his knees beneath the sustained onslaught. And that was when a middle-aged, heavyset man with a graying beard stepped forward, reached under his loose-fitting, khaki-colored shirt and produced a gun from his waistband.

The rest of the group deferred to the bearded man, stepping aside as he approached the defeated mutate and leveled the gun at his temple. Their expressions were calm, almost neutral, and this fooled Iceman into thinking that the man did not intend to pull the trigger, that the weapon had been drawn only as a threat. That was why he didn't say anything, why he didn't try to stop the cold-blooded execution until it was too late.

Not that he could have done much. As he pulled himself to his feet, he felt his head spinning and his stomach lurching, and not only because of the grisly sight he had just witnessed. He almost fell again, but he settled upon the compromise position of stooping to rest his hands on his calves as he tried to get his breath back.

He hadn't realized until now how close his mad flight had brought him to the outskirts of the village. Its nearest building was only a few yards away. His unlikely saviors must have come from there. They must have seen that he was in trouble. He didn't know whether to feel grateful to them or just sickened by what they had done to their helpless captive.

Then, the bearded man blew imaginary smoke from his gun barrel like a cowboy in an old Western movie and, in a gruff voice, he said: "Score two points for our side. That's another pair of stinking muties who won't be polluting our good, clean air any more!"

And even Iceman's powers could not allay the prickly chill that broke out all over his skin as his erstwhile rescuers moved to surround him.

"Mutates in magistrates' clothing," mumbled Wolverine for the fourth time, shaking his head in lethargic disbelief. His eyes were closed, but he seemed to want to keep talking, to keep his mind active. Nightcrawler, for his part, longed to sleep—but worrying about his friend's condition and the possibility of discovery kept him awake and alert, albeit with a dull ache spreading slowly behind his eyes.

"I know what you mean," he said. "These are our own kind, and yet they have been turned against us. It does not seem so long ago that they would have welcomed us into their land."

"X-Men . . . helped to free them . . . we told . . . we told the world. . . ."

Kurt nodded sadly. He had not been with Wolverine and the others when they had first visited Genosha, when they had exposed its darkest secret, but he had heard the story. He thought about everything that had happened here since, all the misery that civil war had brought to this once-fair island, and he wondered briefly if his colleagues should have left well enough alone. But that would have meant condemning many more people—an entire race—to generations of slavery, of being denied their very identities. Sometimes, it was important to make a stand, whatever the consequences.

"And now," he sighed, "they see Magneto as their one hope of salvation. They will do anything for him. How did it come to this, *mein freund*? Should we have done more?"

"Magneto," snarled Logan, his hatred for Genosha's ruler seeming to energize him temporarily. "He did this. He took their pain and their anger, and he used it. Did what the . . . the humans did to him . . . made them as bitter and twisted as . . . as he is. . . ."

"He made them paranoid, taught them to distrust anyone who is different."

"He . . . put them in . . . magistrates' clothing."

Kurt added quietly: "Magneto has turned the mutates into everything they once hated."

The pair lapsed into a reflective silence, then, and Kurt soon realized that his friend had drifted off to sleep. He hoped it would do him good—but Logan's breaths rattled in his chest, and his skin was now cold to the touch. Kurt didn't like to untie the blood-sodden bandages to see if his wound looked any better, if the tissue had begun to knit back together. All he could do was keep him warm with his own body heat, and say a silent prayer for him. He feared that it would not be enough, that Wolverine might not survive the night.

When he heard footsteps and low voices from the direction of the street, he was torn by indecision. Logan was making too much noise, snoring and rasping. If anyone stopped at the mouth of the alleyway to listen, they would hear him for sure. But it seemed cruel to wake him, at least until it was absolutely necessary.

He decided to reconnoiter. He untangled himself from his friend, laying Logan's head down gently on one of the refuse sacks, and padded softly toward the source of the disturbance. Hidden by the shadows, he peered out onto the sidewalk and saw a small group of people—two men and a woman—conducting an urgent, whispered conversation. They wore skinsuits, but no uniforms. They were probably civilians. Perhaps they weren't loyal to Magneto at all; even some of the mutates must have chosen to resist his rule.

Under normal circumstances, Nightcrawler would have assumed the strangers hostile. It was the safest way. But Wolverine, he had become convinced, was in need of proper medical treatment, and maybe they could provide it.

He strained to overhear what the mutates were saying, to get some idea of whose side they were on, but to no avail. He wanted to believe in human nature, in the essential goodness of the spirit, but he had seen its dark side too many times. Looking over his shoulder, he could just about make out his teammate's body, an unmoving lump. Then Wolverine stirred and let out a soft howl of pain like that of a dying animal, and Nightcrawler's decision was made.

In the X-Men's Blackbird, during the flight from America, he had programmed a few useful costume changes into his image inducer. He activated it now, leaving his features the same but clothing himself in an illusory skinsuit of blue and red. Then, he teleported past the mutates, thinking that if things went badly, at least he would have led them away from Logan. They reacted with predictable alarm to his sudden noisy appearance, and he threw up his hands and called to them, in his best Genoshan accent: "I mean you no harm!"

They didn't attack him, but he could see suspicion in their eyes. He took two steps toward them, and continued: "My name's Kurt. Kurt Wagner. I'm a mutate, like you. You can see that, can't you?" He just hoped that his fame as a member of the X-Men hadn't preceded him.

"What do you want?" asked the woman, regarding him through narrowed eyes.

"I don't recognize you," said the older of the two men. "Where are you from?"

Kurt tried to recall what little he knew of Genoshan geography, to find an area that was just far enough away. "Carrion Cove," he hazarded.

The mutates exchanged glances. "That's a human stronghold!" exclaimed the younger man.

Kurt nodded eagerly. "My friend and I were being held there. We were forced to keep serving the humans. We escaped two nights ago, and we've been on the run ever since. You don't know how relieved I am to see friendly faces again."

"Your friend?" repeated the older man.

Kurt took a deep breath before he told them about Logan—but he was winning these people over, and lying to them at this stage would only undo that. Still, he was deliberately vague about the nature and the cause of Wolverine's injury. The older man rubbed his stubbly chin in thought. Then, finally, he nodded. "We don't have much in the way of facilities, but we'll certainly do all we can to help a brother."

Kurt let out a sigh of relief. "Thank you," he beamed. "God bless you!"

He led the mutates to the alleyway, where they took in Wolverine's condition. A sad shake of the head passed between the older man and the woman when they thought Kurt wasn't looking. Nevertheless, they put Logan's arms around their shoulders and lifted him between them. He groaned again, but didn't open his eyes. "We'll do what we can for him," said the man. "We can make him more comfortable, at least. We'll take him to our main base."

Kurt nodded dispiritedly, and returned to the street at the rear of the unlikely procession. They trudged along in silence for a few minutes, before the younger man fell back to walk beside him. "If you've come from Carrion Cove," he confided, "you'll find things a lot better here. The humans don't come to this area much. Not if they know what's good for them."

"I had heard that, in the rest of the country, the war was over," said Kurt cautiously.

The man scowled. "It will never be over until the last flatscan has left Genosha."

Ahead of them, the woman started and looked around, as if afraid that somebody might have overheard him. "The Savior has decreed otherwise," she shot back.

"Of course," said the man hastily, "and I don't mean to question his judgement." Turning back to Kurt, he explained: "You probably know that our borders have been closed. Magneto doesn't want any more of the humans to leave."

"We need their skills," said the woman, "to rebuild."

"They kept us mindless, servile, for so long," said the young man bitterly. "We only know how to do menial jobs. But now, Magneto has set up training facilities for us. Within a few years, we will be self-sufficient. We won't need the flatscans any more." His tone made it quite clear how much he relished that prospect.

"In the meantime," the older man reminded him, beginning to struggle with Wolverine's weight, "we have to be careful. The humans are still out there."

"The Savior has instructed that our two races shouldn't mix," said the woman.

"But that doesn't matter to the flatscans," snorted the young man. "They're animals! All they know is hating and killing. Some of them will work for Magneto, because they're afraid, but secretly they still want us dead." He puffed out his chest with pride as he added: "Fortunately, they're weak and they're stupid. We've all but wiped them out in this area. This will be a pure mutate village soon, and we won't have to put up with their stink."

Kurt wanted to say something, to tell the young mutate that hatred couldn't be fought with more hatred. But, for Wolverine's sake, he couldn't afford to jeopardize his cover. He took Logan's arm from the older man, shouldering the burden of his teammate even though he was still tired himself, and walked on in glum silence.

Eventually, they turned into a narrow side street. There were streetlights here, but only one of them was still working, looking forlorn in the center of its orange circle. "No humans in the vicinity," reported the woman, who must have had some kind of scanning ability—and the group approached a battered, two-story house about halfway along a terraced row. The door hung open, its blue paint peeling, and the dingy, musty hallway showed no signs of recent habitation. However, the older man led the way confidently toward a smaller wooden door beneath the stairs, which he unlocked with a large brass key.

Nightcrawler was struck speechless again as he helped to haul Wolverine down a short flight of rickety steps. He was in what had once been a low-ceilinged cellar, but its side walls had been broken through to the cellars on each side, and he could see that the process had been repeated beyond them. The mutates had probably joined all the cellars on this side of the road together. Lighting was provided by bare bulbs strung on an electrical cord, which wended its way haphazardly through the base at head height. Most of them had been turned off for the night; either that or they weren't working. Most of the available floor area, at least as far as Kurt could see, was taken up by old mattresses and dirty, tattered sheets.

This room alone was home to at least twenty mutates, most of them still wearing the skinsuits that must have been permanent reminders of their days of slavery. Some of them stirred in their beds to look up at the new arrivals, but most slept on. A couple sat at a wooden table, devouring hunks of stale bread from cracked tin plates.

The older man glanced back at Kurt, and he must have seen his appalled expression because he smiled tightly and without humor. "Welcome to our home," he said. "We're free citizens these days, so they tell us."

"Th-there was no need to murder that man."

The lynch mob had closed in around Iceman now, and he was trying to stall them, trying to delay the moment when their gray-bearded leader would put the gun to his head too. He didn't have the energy to transform himself again, and his ice armor probably wouldn't have saved him anyway, not from a bullet at this range. Perhaps if he could buy a little more time, another minute or two, he might be able to gum up the gun barrel with slush. He might be able to take its wielder by surprise and run for it in the confusion. He might just stand a chance of escaping. A very small chance. But he couldn't think of any clever words to say, so he had just blurted out the first thing that had come to him.

The bearded man snorted with cruel laughter. "The only good mutant is a dead mutant!"

"He would have killed you," said a young, slim woman with dark hair, "without a qualm."

"Debs is right, love. It's the only language those genejokes understand." The elderly woman was waving her cane sternly, drawing Bobby's attention to her. His lips tightened at the insult but he said nothing. "It's kill or be killed these days, you mark my words!"

"What did you do?" The bearded man sounded surprisingly genial. Iceman turned to face him again, confused. "To get the GUMPs on your case? You tried to get out?"

"Um . . . yes," he stammered, guessing that the "GUMPs" were the border guards. "Yes, that's right, I was trying to get out." Bobby was beginning to realize that he had misread the situation.

These people mustn't have seen his ice slide, mustn't have seen him at all until after his powers had given out. They had no reason to suspect that he, because of an accident of his birth, represented everything they hated. As far as they were concerned, he was just a fresh-faced young man dressed in a simple T-shirt and slacks. He made a mental note to thank Rogue for insisting that he wear civilian clothing on this mission.

They were expecting him to say more, so, mentally crossing his fingers, he added: "I mean, I know Magneto doesn't want people ... humans, I mean ... to leave the country, but ... but, well, I didn't think he'd go this far."

"He's a mutant, isn't he?" said somebody behind Bobby. "They'll stop at nothing to make our lives miserable. They're animals!"

"What I mean is, I didn't expect his guards to shoot to kill. I ... I just wanted to get away from here." To his relief, the general reaction to his story was one of sympathy rather than disbelief. Hoping to change the subject while he was ahead, he added quickly: "I was lucky you came along when you did. How did you manage to bring the aircar down?"

"Sonic sphere," said the bearded man proudly. "Old magistrate technology. We set it up a few days ago. Those genejokes flew right into it; it shook their car to pieces. That'll show them who owns this town!"

"The thing is, dear," said the old woman, "even if we could leave Genosha, we'd never get away from them, not completely. They're everywhere these days, the muties, waiting to strike. You can't even tell who's human any more. Not these days."

"No," said Iceman, forcing himself to nod. He wasn't enjoying the irony of the situation at all. "I know what you mean."

"Even America's swarming with them," agreed the teenaged boy. "You see it on the news all the time—at least you used to, before it was censored."

"And they'll destroy the proud United States as surely as they've destroyed our country," said the bearded man as if making a casual statement of fact. "That's why you can't run, son. Oh, plenty have tried—many families made a run for it as soon as they heard we'd been sold out. They escaped before that mutant fascist arrived, and good luck to them. But what kind of a legacy are they leaving for their kids, huh? Somebody's got to make a stand. Somebody's got to draw the line somewhere, or human beings will end up as extinct as the caveman!"

"This used to be a green and pleasant land," said the old woman wistfully.

"And it will be again," the bearded man promised her, "if we can stand together!" He extended a hand toward Bobby. "The name's Hendrickson. Are you with us, son?"

Iceman stared at him, then realized that his uncertainty was drawing suspicion. "Bobby," he said quickly. "Bobby Drake." And he reached out and took the proffered hand, hating himself for doing it but knowing that he had no other option. "I'm with you."

The mutates had taken Wolverine into a former wine cellar, one part of which was sectioned off by high shelves and equipped with four real beds. He had been lain in one; the other three were unoccupied. His wound had been washed and redressed, and he had been given antibiotics and plenty of water. Nightcrawler hoped it would be enough. At least his friend appeared to be sleeping peacefully now.

He had insisted on staying with Logan. The chair beside his bed was uncomfortable, but Kurt had fallen into a light doze anyway. His dreams were populated by the mutates. Even when they had been slaves, they had at least been kept in comfortable conditions. But the civil war had bankrupted Genosha, and their current lives of poverty seemed a high price to pay for liberation. He only hoped that, one day, it would prove to be worth it.

Woken by a scuffling sound, he saw that several people had joined him at the bedside. The three mutates from outside were among them, but Kurt's eyes were drawn to a thin, bald-headed man with sunken eyes and bloodless, disapproving lips, who stood a head above the others. The man wore white robes—made out of a bed sheet, he fancied—over a yellow and black skinsuit. Looking at Kurt, he twisted his mouth into an approximation of a smile, exposing black-capped teeth, although his eyes had a steel glint. "I am sorry to disturb you," he said in a low voice that seemed to reverberate inside his chest, "but I believe your friend is in need of assistance."

"You're a doctor?" asked Kurt hopefully.

"In a manner of speaking. I tend to the immortal soul." The other mutates had gathered around the bed, and Kurt stood at its foot. This placed him directly opposite the bald man, who took Wolverine's head in his huge hands, rolled his own head back and closed his eyes. His thin lips fluttered as he recited incantations to himself. Then, he said: "The life force of our brother is weak. We must pray for him."

Nightcrawler's heart sank. Much as he believed in the power of prayer, he had hoped for—expected, for a moment—more practical assistance. He had hoped that this newcomer was a healer, if not by profession then by virtue of a mutant gene. Nevertheless, he bowed his head respectfully, as did the mutates, and clasped his hands in front of him. He concentrated on the words of the prayer and offered up his own plea to God.

"Lord, we beseech you to heed the words of your humble priest, and the hopes of your loyal supplicants. We, who have suffered so much and yet believe that you will lead us to a brighter tomorrow, ask that you show mercy upon our fallen brother. We ask that he be made well and strong again, that he might assist in the rebuilding of your green and pleasant land. We pray that you might grant him a small portion of your infinite power of magnetism."

Nightcrawler blinked, and his stomach performed a cartwheel.

"Amen," said the Priest and the mutates in unison.

The Priest reached out in front of him, his hands hovering above Wolverine's chest. And something crackled beneath his downturned palms: a bright blue discharge of energy, which grew to encircle his sleeping patient and then faded as if it had been absorbed into his body. The Priest's face softened into a beatific expression, and he whispered: "Thank you, Lord."

Then, his blue eyes snapped open, seeming to drill into Nightcrawler's head as if they could see the uncertainty, the discomfort, he was feeling.

"All praise to the Savior," intoned the Priest. "All praise Magneto."

"All praise Magneto," the mutates repeated. "All praise Magneto."

Nightcrawler tried to join in the chant, but his throat had stopped. He moved his lips instead, hoping that his inability to give voice to the words would not be noticed.

But he felt cold and sick inside.

CHAPTER 6

SUNLIGHT shone through Rogue's eyelids. The air was warm, and moist with morning dew. She didn't know where she was at first; she couldn't work out why there was hard soil beneath her cheek. But then, feeling an insistent toe between her ribs, she forced her eyes open, raised herself up onto her hands and found herself looking into a gun barrel. And behind it, the image still blurred, she could see magistrates' uniforms.

"On your feet, mutie," somebody snarled, "and don't try nothing. We got guns!"

"I can see that," said Rogue, picking herself up wearily. "Don't worry, I don't have the energy to make a break for it. So easy with those trigger fingers, you hear?"

"Well, this is a real find, isn't it? A real live mutie, lying in this field by herself. Where are your genejoke friends, mutie?"

Rogue blinked, and brought her captors into focus. There were six of them, their faces concealed by blue metal gas masks, each armed with rifles. Behind them, the sun was rising over Hammer Bay, washing its fractured buildings in a bloody shade of red that seemed unnervingly appropriate. "You aren't mutates?" she ventured.

The group's apparent leader spat through his speaking grille. Rogue saw stripes of rank on his shoulder. "We're human beings, you mutate bitch: pure, decent people. We've nothing in common with your kind." His comrades murmured agreement.

"What makes you think I'm a mutate?" asked Rogue. She tried to sound aggrieved at the accusation, but she was struggling to keep her temper.

"You came down with the aircars, didn't you?" said another man, nodding toward the wreckage that strewed the field behind her. "Only a freak could have survived that. Look at you—there's not a scratch on you!"

"I guess I must have been lucky," said Rogue evenly. "I must have been thrown clear. Anyway, you're the ones who are dressed like Magneto's militia!"

The magistrates' leader slapped her across the face. Fortunately, his hand was gloved. Rogue flinched as if the blow had hurt her— so long as they didn't know anything about her powers, she had an advantage—but she fixed him with a baleful glare.

"These uniforms used to be a symbol of authority," he snarled. "The magistrates used to keep order in these parts; we had respect. Now, we've got stinking gene freak terrorists and human traitors running around in our clothes."

"Magneto calls them the Genoshan Unified Military Patrol— what a joke!"

"Well, that's gonna change. We're gonna take back our uniforms and we're gonna take back our country!" A ragged cheer greeted the leader's words.

"Well, bully for you!" said Rogue dryly. "But in case you hadn't noticed, sugar, I'm not wearing anybody's uniform, and I don't want any part of this here squabble of yours."

She had intended to say more. She had concocted a story about how she, a normal human being going about her lawful business, had been kidnapped by fanatical mutates, how she had taken them by surprise and knocked their flier off-course. But she couldn't bring herself to tell the lie, to toady up to scum like this. Anyway, she was feeling better now: well enough, she was sure, to take them on if they came at her. The odds were only six to one, after all.

"I know you!" said one of the magistrates suddenly, stepping forward. The voice sounded female, although the heavy, padded costume made it hard to tell for sure. "You came here a few weeks ago. I saw you flying over Hammer Bay!" She turned to the others excitedly. "She *is* a genejoke, she is! She's one of those American mutants—X-Men, they're called."

"As if we don't have enough freaks of our own," somebody muttered.

"That skunk hair is a dead giveaway, honey!" said the woman.

Most of the magistrates took fearful steps away from Rogue, tightening their grips on their weapons. She shrugged as if she didn't care that they had seen through her deception. "So, you know who I am. Now, what do you think you're going to do about it?"

"Same as we'd do with any other freak," said the leader. Then, raising his voice, he barked out the command: "Fire at will!"

Ororo Munroe stirred in her sleep. She was distantly aware that she was being held fast by something cold and hard, which encircled her midriff and trapped her wrists and ankles. Part of her knew that she ought to wake up, but she was plunging back into warm darkness before she could even make the effort. She surfaced amid the bright colors and disconnected recollections of dreams, discomfited that her mind's eye had chosen to replay the details of her recent defeat to her.

Storm relived the moment when Magneto had entered the Hellfire Club's ballroom, when she had been surrounded by four formidable foes. Again, she summoned a lightning strike—and again, she aimed it not at Magneto or even at Shaw but at her teammate, Phoenix. She delivered as mild a shock as she dared: she didn't want to hurt her dear friend, but she had to get through to her, to penetrate Lady Mastermind's illusions. Shaken back to reality, Phoenix took in the situation and broadcast a telepathic wakeup call to Cyclops and the Beast.

By then, however, it was already too late for Storm.

If only she could have reacted more swiftly, if she had not let her weakness cloud her mind, if she had come to her senses a moment earlier. If she had had that extra moment to think, to develop a more effective stratagem. But then, what could she have done?

Again, Magneto manipulated the iron in Storm's blood, the pain no less intense for the knowledge that it was only an echo of what she had truly suffered. He could have torn her apart, he could have stopped her heart, but he contented himself with rendering her helpless. As she hit the floor, fighting unconsciousness, she saw her teammates rushing to the attack again, knowing—even more certainly than she had known the first time—that their efforts were in vain. Lady Mastermind fell first, doubtless the loser of a psychic struggle with Phoenix—but, while Jean was thus distracted, Shaw felled her with one punch. And then, the Beast's eyes rolled back into his head and his legs buckled beneath him, and Storm knew that Tessa had shut down his mind.

Cyclops took out the telepath with one shot from his eyes, and turned to Magneto—but his optic blasts were absorbed by his enemy's magnetic force field. Then, Magneto cut off the X-Man's connection to gravity itself, and he hurtled into the ceiling with an impact that sent spider-web cracks crazing across the white plaster.

That was when Storm's eyes had closed at last, and where the dream now thankfully ended too. All she remembered after that was the feeling of something covering her nose and mouth, and the sweet smell of chloroform. The part of her that knew she had to wake was screaming now as it struggled impotently in the depths of her psyche.

But it too faded as the blissful darkness enveloped her once more.

* * *

The magistrates' automatic rifles spat a hail of bullets, and Rogue leapt into action. The shells were armor-piercing: they still bounced off her near-invulnerable skin, but they hurt like hell. Gritting her teeth against the pain, she grabbed the leader's gun and bent the barrel back on itself so that it pointed at him. If she had expected him to be startled by this display of strength, however, then she was disappointed. He reacted instantaneously, discarding the weapon to aim an ineffectual punch at Rogue's chin. She tried to knock him away from her, but he ducked beneath her arm and took hold of her jogger top, using her weight and momentum against her and hurling her to the ground. She berated herself inwardly for not realizing that he would be combat trained and well used to fighting foes with special powers.

Determined not to make the same mistake again, she ploughed into the magistrates like a bowling ball, and scattered them. As two fell, two more jumped onto her back, but she twisted around and dislodged them, knocking one out with a punishing blow. The other jammed a gun barrel into her face and yelled out: "Chew on this, you freak!"

Recognizing the voice of the woman who had identified her, Rogue batted the rifle out of her hands and cracked her mask with a punch. "That's for the remark about my hair!" she quipped. She was actually beginning to enjoy herself. After a hard night, an easy fight like this was a good way to blow the cobwebs out of her brain. And she couldn't think of any more deserving targets for her fists than this bunch of xenophobes.

But then, a new noise reached her ears: a whine, increasing in pitch as it became louder. And she realized too late that one of her foes was holding a blaster weapon, almost the size of a small cannon. He was charging it for use, and the whining reached an ear-splitting climax before cutting out abruptly. Quickly, Rogue grabbed another of the magistrates and swung him around in front of her. His comrade fired anyway.

There was an explosion, but no sound and no pain, just a split-second of blackness and a sensation of disconnectedness from the world. Then, Rogue was surrounded by fire—but, for a moment, she thought she could fly through it, attack the magistrate before he could recharge his blaster again. Except that, when she tried to move her legs, she couldn't. And then she realized that she was falling, the ground rushing toward her in slow motion, and she tried to put out her hands to catch herself but she couldn't move her arms either.

And then she was down, her body twitching involuntarily but otherwise paralyzed, and she was screaming inside, desperately trying to work out what they had done to her.

Another toecap in her ribs. She was rolled over onto her back, staring up helplessly, oddly embarrassed as she felt a trickle of drool brimming over her bottom lip and could do nothing about it. Her human shield, she saw, had fallen too, and two of the other magistrates were dragging him away from her, making him comfortable. She was looking down the lead magistrate's rifle again, and she couldn't even engage her larynx to say a word.

He flipped up his mask to let Rogue see her executioner. He was surprisingly young, but his thin face was hard beyond its years. His brown hair was long and lank, and his chin sported a two-day growth of stubble. His eyes were wide and fanatical, his nostrils flaring as he grinned at his helpless victim in triumph. "What's up, genejoke?" he sneered. "Didn't think a few human beings were any match for you, huh? Well, surprise! We learned a few things in the service. We got ways of dealing with uppity freaks like you!" He dealt a vicious kick to Rogue's side, but it hurt a lot less than his inflammatory words. Burning with indignation, she tried to reach up to him, but she was still frustratingly helpless.

Another shape loomed over her: the female magistrate again. "Neural paralyzer, honey," she explained. "We just knocked out the connections between your nerve endings and your brain. The effect's only temporary, like—but for the next couple of minutes, you won't be able to move a muscle, so don't waste your breath trying."

"And that's plenty of time," said the leader, with a sadistic smirk as he worked the breach of his rifle and lowered its muzzle to hover an inch above Rogue's face, "to see if our bullets bounce off your eyes like they do the rest of you."

Rogue tried to say something, to stall him, but the only sound to emerge from her throat was an impotent mewl. She couldn't even close her eyes. They were beginning to water.

The leader let her sweat for a few more seconds, evidently enjoying his power over her. Then he withdrew the gun. "Unless," he said, "you tell us what we want to know."

"Think about it," said the woman. "You should recover your power of speech in a minute."

"Something else to think about," said the man. "They say that repeated shots from the neuralyzer can screw up your nervous system for good. I wouldn't try to escape if I was you."

"Thought . . . you were . . . gonna kill me . . . anyway," said Rogue. At least, that was what she tried to say—but her jaw wouldn't move, her tongue lolled in her mouth and the words came out without consonants.

"What do the X-Men want in Genosha?"

Rogue's curt answer was as indistinct as her last attempt at speech, but her forceful tone got the message across nonetheless.

The magistrates' leader scowled and hefted his rifle again. "We can make this quick," he spat, "or we can make it very, very painful for you."

With an effort, Rogue managed to lower her eyelids at last. She breathed in deeply, feeling control of her muscles slowly returning to her. She rolled her numb tongue around her mouth. Then, hearing the whine of the recharging neuralyzer, she opened her eyes again and saw that two more magistrates had gathered around her, their knuckles white on the grips of their respective weapons as they waited for her to make her move. She flexed a hand experimentally; it responded to her command, but sluggishly. If she made a break for it now, she would be gunned down before she could take two steps.

"OK," she sighed indistinctly, "I'll tell you why we're here."

"Did Magneto send for you?" asked the woman.

Rogue tried to shake her head, but the effort was too much for her. She managed a weak laugh instead. "The X-Men are no friends of Magneto."

"You're mutants, like he is!" snapped the leader in an accusing tone.

"So? You're a human; does that mean you support Adolf Hitler's policies?"

"You were one of the ones who freed the mutates," said the woman. "You started all this!"

"But it wasn't our idea to put Magneto in charge of your country, sugar. That was the good ladies and gentlemen of the United Nations—your own kind—and believe me, we're just as unhappy with that development as you are."

"Magneto has talked about the X-Men as enemies," offered one of the other magistrates in an uncertain tone.

"So, we're expected to believe that this gene freak is on our side?" sneered the leader.

"I'm sure you'll believe whatever suits you best," snarled Rogue. "That's how bigots operate, isn't it?" The leader's eyes flared, and he brandished his rifle as if he were about to strike her with its butt. Quickly, Rogue added: "But if you don't want the mutates getting the upper hand in Genosha, you'll at least listen to me before you make up your mind."

She was feeling better now, and she hauled herself into a sitting position. Nobody made a move to stop her. She took a moment to steel herself for what she had to do, for what she had been unable to do before. Then, in a low, throaty voice, she told them: "Magneto has found a cure to the Legacy Virus. We've come here to take it off him."

A murmur of disbelief and fear rippled through the magistrates.

"If this is a trick—" began the leader.

"It's no trick!" snapped Rogue, letting out some of her anger. "And the way I see it, the Legacy epidemic here is the one thing that stops the mutates from wiping out the likes of you for good and all. If I were you, I'd be getting very, very worried about now."

"So, why are you involved?" asked the leader. "What's in it for you?"

"Good question," said Rogue with feeling. "Moments like this, I'm tempted to just head for home and leave you to slug it out. But that's not how the X-Men operate—and believe it or not, we don't like the idea of Magneto heading up an army of perfectly healthy mutates any more than you do." She tried not to think about what Nightcrawler had said back at the mansion: *Would you rather see those mutates die?* She was loath to think that she could have any goal in common with her captors, but her survival depended upon convincing them of it.

"What do you think?" the magistrate leader muttered to the others out of the corner of his mouth, as if that would prevent her from overhearing him.

"It would make sense of the rumors we've been hearing out of Hammer Bay."

"There are always rumors. No one ever knows Magneto's plans for sure. He's a madman."

"As far as I'm concerned, the Legacy Virus is a punishment from God. I don't see how those genejokes *could* have found a cure for it."

"But what if they have? What about our own people?"

The leader nodded thoughtfully and turned back to Rogue. "We've had a few humans go down with Legacy too."

"Filthy mutant freaks," spat one of the other men, "spreading their infection to us."

"We'll come to the Citadel with you," decided the leader. "We'll help you find this cure on condition that you leave it in our hands." A cruel smile pulled at his mouth as he thought about the possibilities. "We'd soon have those genejokes dancing to our tune."

"Uh-uh." Rogue shook her head vehemently. "This is strictly a solo flight."

Scowling, the leader clicked his fingers in the direction of the magistrate with the neuralyzer. The weapon was brought up to cover the X-Man again. "I think you're forgetting who's got the upper hand here!"

"You're right," said Rogue, struggling to her feet. She was still weak, but at least her muscles were working now. "You're in control. So, it's time to decide. I'm leaving now. Shoot me in the back; I can't stop you. But if you kill me, Magneto wins. You'll wake up tomorrow or the day after to find your enemies ten times stronger than they were today. Leave me to get on with my business, on the other hand, and you can go back to fighting your petty little war as if none of this ever happened. You won't see me again. Your choice."

Her fierce tone had riveted the magistrates to the spot. Even so, as she pivoted on her heel and limped away from them, she didn't know how they would react. She fancied she could feel a prickling sensation in her back where the sights of the neuralyzer were trained on her.

She was relieved, then, when, having succumbed to the urge to look back over her shoulder, she saw that the magistrates were gone. But they had left her with a sick feeling in the pit of her stomach and a flush of shame in her cheeks. She had hated having to deal with them, to pander to their prejudice, and every word had left a bitter taste in her mouth.

She couldn't help but feel that, if the X-Men were successful in their mission, then it would be at the expense of every poor, persecuted mutate in this country.

Raul Jarrett pressed his face up against the ventilation grille, shocked by what he could see in the room beyond it. He was looking down at a lump of twisted metal: it looked like a modern art sculpture, but for the fact that it held four sleeping figures in a variety of poses in its inanimate grasp. Jarrett didn't recognize any of them, but their garish costumes reminded him of talk he had heard of the X-Men, staunch enemies of Genosha. The "sculpture," of course, must have been shaped around them by the Savior.

Sitting with her back to the prisoners, engrossed in a well-thumbed paperback novel, was Miranda. Jarrett had shared a cabin with her on the flight from Genosha to Sydney, but they had not talked. He had spent the journey in a state of nervous anticipation, aware of the brooding presence of the Savior and wishing that Nurse Jenny could have been with him. And the girl, he had come to understand, was deaf and mute. She was about sixteen years old, her blonde hair was beginning to grow out again, and she wore a pink skinsuit with a swirling black pattern on its front. He didn't know what her special abilities were. He resisted the urge to attract her attention with a wave—the Savior himself had instructed him to tell nobody, friend or foe, about his task—and crawled on.

The air-conditioning ducts of the Hellfire Club building were narrow; too narrow for most people. That was why Jarrett had been picked for this mission. By elongating his body, he could slither down the confining tunnels like a snake. With a little concentration, and some pain, he could even squeeze himself through the grilles that blocked his path at irregular intervals. He felt honored to have been chosen, that Magneto himself considered his humble skills useful. At the same time, however, he was scared. He thought about the four figures held in the metal sculpture. Might that be his future if he disappointed the Savior?

He followed his directions, and came to the grille that led to his target destination: the suite of rooms currently occupied by Sebastian Shaw. He poked a fingertip through the metal latticework and, taking a deep breath, compacted the rest of his finger, then his hand, then his arm, to follow it. His body oozed into Shaw's bedroom like silly putty rolled long and thin, pooling back into its humanoid form as it gathered on the floor. Jarrett was left feeling as if he had stretched his bones to breaking point. He lay on the carpet for a full minute, fighting back tears as he recovered from his ordeal, as his muscles settled gratefully back into their accustomed positions. Outside, the Australian morning was hot—but in here, the shades were drawn, and Raul Jarrett enjoyed the cool touch of the darkness.

It was dark in the outer room of the suite too, but by the time he had cautiously crossed the threshold, his eyes had adjusted. He glanced at the large wooden desk, the high-backed chair behind it turned away from him and toward the window. To his disappointment, the desktop was empty but for a penholder—but his eyes alighted upon a wooden two-drawer filing cabinet, which stood against the wall beside it. Quickly, Jarrett stole across the room and stooped in front of the cabinet, his eyes forever flicking toward the closed door of the office. The Savior had told him that, above all else, he must not be discovered in here.

The cabinet was locked, but Jarrett knew how to shape his forefinger around the tumblers and trip them. His trembling hands made the simple task more difficult—but still, the lock soon yielded to his manipulations. He pulled open the top drawer eagerly to find a small stack of papers therein, divided by manila folders. The bottom drawer was empty.

He was reaching for the topmost folder when something—some sixth sense that made the hairs on the back of his neck tingle—told him that he wasn't alone. Whirling around, he fell from his crouching position with a gasp as he met the burning gaze of the Black King.

Shaw was sitting in the high-backed chair, his face cast into shadow. He must have been there all along, not six feet away from where Jarrett now sprawled, his back against the incriminatingly open cabinet. He must have turned the chair around and watched in silence as the mutate violated his security. Jarrett tried to say something, but there was nothing he *could* say. He let out a defeated whine instead.

"Mr. Jarrett, is it not?" Somehow, the fact that Shaw knew his name made him even more uncomfortable. He and Miranda had been standing at their ruler's heels when Shaw had greeted Magneto at his private airfield, but they had not been introduced. Magneto had acted as if they weren't even present. Clearly, though, they had not escaped the Black King's attention. Jarrett shivered with the illogical feeling that Shaw knew everything about him. "And may I assume that this intrusion was instigated by your master, my so-called ally?"

Gathering his wits, Jarrett shook his head and stammered: "N-no, sir."

"Please do not lie to me," said Shaw evenly. "You will only force me to hurt you, and I do not think either of us wants that."

"I . . . I was just . . . the Savior instructed me to. . . ."

Shaw silenced the mutate with a raised hand. "You do not have to explain to me. Magneto does not trust me any more than I trust him. I would be surprised if it were not so. That is why I allowed him to believe that I was no longer in the building: to see what he would do. He has sent you to search for evidence of perfidy in my absence, yes?"

Jarrett swallowed and nodded. Shaw's features softened a little in approval of his belated honesty. "Fate has not been kind to you, has it, Mr. Jarrett? To have swapped the oppression of one regime for another. . . ."

"M-Magneto is the Savior of the mutates," he objected automatically.

"Then how is it that you are still a slave?" asked Shaw harshly.

"No! I . . . I mean, I . . ."

"No? So, you will happily go to your Savior now and inform him of your failure?"

Jarrett bowed his head, his cheeks coloring. "If I must," he mumbled.

"And you do not fear what he will do to you?" Jarrett didn't speak, but he didn't doubt that the Black King already knew the answer to his question. "Look at you," said Shaw with contempt. "How old are you, Mr. Jarrett? Twenty-five? Thirty? A grown man, and yet you act like a child. You call another man your master; you crave his approval, and you are terrified of his wrath. You have no control over your own life. You are pathetic!"

Jarrett didn't—couldn't—disagree with him. He cringed as Shaw stood suddenly, expecting a blow to come at last. But Shaw just clasped his hands behind his back and walked slowly toward his bedroom. "I am tired," he said languidly. "You are welcome to search my office while I rest, but you will find nothing. And Mr. Jarrett?" He had halted in the doorway, looking back over his shoulder with an unfathomable glint in his eye. "I think this unfortunate encounter should remain our secret, don't you?"

Jarrett nodded eagerly, his heart overflowing with relief and gratitude even as his brain tried to work out the Black King's motive for sparing him.

He conducted a thorough search of the office, awkward as it made him feel, always aware of the sound of Shaw's measured breathing from the next room. He looked through every one of the files in the cabinet, and even booted up the laptop that he found in a desk drawer and searched for text documents on its hard drive. Jarrett had never used a computer before, but Magneto himself had taken him to one side on the plane and taught him what he needed to know. He had absorbed the lesson, speaking only when he had had to and stumbling over his words when he did. For the rest of the flight—and for most of last night, in his simple quarters elsewhere in the Hellfire Club building—he had pored over the scrap of paper on which he had noted down his instructions, memorizing them, not knowing why the Savior wished him to acquire this new skill but determined not to let him down.

He hovered in the doorway to the bedroom for a long moment. Shaw was lying on his back on the bed, fully clothed in his velvet costume, a blackout mask over his eyes. His hands were clasped across his chest, which rose and fell rhythmically, but Jarrett couldn't quite bring himself to believe that he was asleep.

He had been told to search both rooms of the suite, but he was afraid. Anyway, he insisted to himself, he was unlikely to find anything in the bedroom, and even less so to leave it alive if he did. But what if Magneto—the Savior, his master—asked him outright if he had followed his orders? Could Jarrett lie to him? He had no choice, he realized. He already knew that he couldn't risk revealing the whole truth to him; what did one more detail matter?

He crept across the room as quietly as he could, and reached toward the ventilation duct. Then, he started at the unexpected sound of Shaw's voice behind him. "You may as well leave by the door, Mr. Jarrett," he rumbled, without moving. "I dismissed my sentries shortly after you entered the air-conditioning system."

Raul Jarrett left the Black King's suite as quickly as his legs would take him.

The sun had risen fully now, and Rogue was beginning to feel smothered by Genosha's oppressive morning heat. She sat on the gentle slope of a grassy hill on the outskirts of Hammer Bay as she considered her next move, grateful for every stray breeze that came her way. Up close like this, the capital looked more squalid than ever. Every crumbling wall, every letter of obscene graffiti, every pile of rubble or scorch mark was exposed by the uncaring daylight. But there was life among the wreckage too: she could make out distant figures, erecting scaffolding around the most precarious buildings and removing refuse from the streets. The rebuilding work had begun here, as Magneto had promised.

Rogue had hoped that the other X-Men would find her. She had seen and heard nothing of them since the mutate attack in the forest. Perhaps they hadn't escaped, or perhaps they had simply entered Hammer Bay from another direction. More than once, she had taken out her concealed communicator and looked at it. It was sturdy, and it still worked despite the punishment that had been meted out to it. But she herself had decreed that radio silence should be maintained if possible. She couldn't risk having her position triangulated—or giving away her presence in Genosha if a comm-set had fallen into the wrong hands.

Rogue knew what she had to do now, whether she liked it or not. The X-Men had agreed when they had formulated their plans. She had to assume that Wolverine, Nightcrawler and Iceman had been killed or captured. The effects of the neuralyzer had worn off long ago, and she was only wasting time by waiting here, nursing a forlorn hope. She had to go on.

She had to penetrate Magneto's command center alone.

d activate the latent mutant genes of the population, no
tes were being created. And one of the crueler functions
suits was to prevent the existing ones from reproducing.
re the Legacy epidemic, their race had been dying out.
an had obviously rid herself of her suit when she had had
. He allowed himself a grin at the thought that, even in
ranean gloom, life had found a way to flourish.

man saw his eyes upon her, and she smiled back at him.
beautiful baby," said Kurt. "What's he called?"
s," said the woman. "After our Savior."
faded from Kurt's lips.
feel His presence the day I knew that Magnus was
side me." The woman's eyes darkened. "His father was
see—ambushed on his way to his new job at the refin-
s helping to rebuild our country, but the humans
low him even that. But, by Magneto's grace, a part of
es on. Our Savior will let no harm come to this one."
er baby softly on his forehead.
t as we prove ourselves worthy," muttered a mutate
without looking up.
u—have any of you—ever seen Magneto?" Kurt real-
was starting along a dangerous path, but he couldn't

an shook her head. "Only on our television. But He
He speaks to us. He promises our people a better
realized, with a sudden pang, that the mutates
to being shown any consideration, to being acknowl-

e seen His works," added the man next to Kurt.
me when I tore my hide," offered a woman from
the table. Her mutation was more visible than most:
ray and wrinkled, and a horn grew out of the center
he looked like a baby rhinoceros given humanoid

second to process that information. "Through the

CHAPTER 7

T HE rising sun had brought no light to the mutates' underground home. However, at about eight o'clock, somebody had turned on the rest of the bulbs that were threaded through the cellars. Many of the mutates had stayed in bed anyway; others had risen and were reading old magazines or eating joylessly or sitting in corners with miserable expressions. A few—a pitiful few—had left to attend training schemes organized by the new government. A significant proportion of the remainder had gathered around the flickering screen of a battered television set, on which a black and white World War II movie was playing. The announcer had introduced it as "a reminder of what must never be allowed to happen again." There was some conversation, but it was muted. These people were going through the motions of life, taking no pleasure from it.

Kurt had hoped to leave here before now, but Wolverine was still asleep. When he had visited him, he had been tossing and turning and there had been beads of sweat on his forehead. Kurt had prayed that another few hours in bed might allow his teammate's body to do its work, or the fever to burn itself out, but this seemed increasingly unlikely.

He ought to have gone on alone, but how could he leave his

best friend here? He would give it a li
would talk to the mutates, find out n
expect to find when he reached Hamme

He followed the most persistent voi
the final cellar in the row. Peering th
wall that led to it, he saw that the roo
but by aromatic, multicolored candles
rows around a central aisle, which stre
table draped in white cloth. Atop tl
sculpture, hexagonal with angular, st
side of it. It took Kurt a few second
seen the design before: a two-dime
Magneto's helmet.

A short queue of people straggl
the table, a mutate knelt with his he
in front of him. Kurt suppressed a
sunken-eyed Priest, his bald head
light as he stepped forward and
mutate's head. The mutate mumbl
hear, and the Priest reached behin
slice of bread. He placed it on th
genuflected and hurried away. T
place.

Kurt stepped back from the
him. He had only just realized h
intention of joining the queue,
to an evil man—and a sworn en

He followed the mutate to
some chairs had been set out,
ing in silence. He was pleased
mugs on the table, and he too

He found himself sitting o
with a round, ruddy face and
turing a baby. It was a pleasa
sters in the cellars. He had

detect an
new muta
of the ski
Even befo
This wom
the chance
this subter

The wo
"He's a
"Magnu
The gri
"I could
growing in
killed, you
ery. He wa
wouldn't al
Michael live
She kissed h
"So long
beside Kurt,
"Have yo
ized that he
help himself
The wom
sees us, and
world." Kurt
weren't used
edged at all.
"And we'v
"He healec
further down
her skin was
of her face. S
form.
Kurt took

Priest, you mean?" The rhinoceros woman nodded, looking at him as if it should have been obvious. He began to wish that he hadn't drawn so much attention to himself. A few seconds ago, each of the diners had occupied his or her own private world; now, all eyes were focussed upon him, the stranger asking odd questions about their deity. He cleared his throat self-consciously, and said: "We didn't have religious leaders back in Carrion Cove. How do you know . . . I mean, how does somebody get to become a priest?"

"Our Priest was chosen," said the woman with the baby.

"He channels the blessed force of magnetism."

"The Savior uses him as a conduit for his great powers."

Kurt frowned. "Didn't he have those abilities before Magneto came to Genosha?"

The mutates looked at him blankly, and Kurt wondered if it was wise to press the point. As it transpired, however, the choice was taken out of his hands. He heard a commotion from somewhere behind him. Voices were raised in anger, but he couldn't hear what they were saying. Somebody cried out in pain, and the mutates at the table exchanged fearful glances.

It said something of the life that Kurt Wagner had lived that he hesitated before teleporting, asking himself what the reaction of those around him would be. He had to remind himself that everybody here had abilities like his own. Not one of them had commented on, or even looked twice at, his unusual features, although most of them could have passed for human themselves. Having rarely enjoyed such unquestioning acceptance, he felt a little ashamed that he had been so suspicious of the mutates' motives in return.

But then, he materialized in the central cellar, and everything changed again.

As he had guessed, the noises had come from here. Only this cellar, and the one at the far end of the row away from the chapel, afforded access to street level: the other exits had been barricaded from this side. Two skinsuited mutates—a man and a woman, neither of whom Nightcrawler recognized—were being manhandled up the rickety steps by a much larger group. They weren't being treated gently. The man screamed as one of his attackers poked a finger into his ribs and triggered a visible discharge of energy. The woman shrank to a fraction of her original size, and there was a dangerous scramble to recapture her.

More mutates were pushing up the staircase from below, jeering and shouting insults. From across the cellar, others hurled cups and plates, whatever they could get their hands on. Kurt was horrified at the change that had come over these once placid people. He picked out one phrase amid the babble: "We don't want your kind here!"

He intercepted a woman as she brandished a chair, placing restraining hands on her shoulders. "What's going on here?" he cried. "They're our kind—they're mutates!"

"They can't come in here!" she screamed in his face. "They're unclean! Unclean!"

The door was slammed and bolted behind the would-be refugees, to a tangible outpouring of relief. The mutates were still agitated, chattering in loud voices, drowning each other out, and suddenly Nightcrawler felt very lonely in the middle of the crowd.

He wanted to ask the woman what she had meant by "unclean"—but he was dreadfully afraid that he knew the answer already.

Iceman had woken to electrical lighting too—but in his case, it was stark, white and clinical, bleeding through the doorway of his dormitory. He had no way of telling the time, but he remembered staying awake until past dawn. The other beds were empty, and he suspected that most of the morning had passed.

He turned onto his back and stared at the ceiling, his brain picking up from where it had left off when exhaustion had claimed him at last, pondering his situation until it hurt.

His so-called rescuers had taken him to a tall building on the outskirts of their village. From the outside, it looked like just another abandoned warehouse. As Bobby had passed through its doors, however, he had felt the faint hum of machinery beneath his feet.

He had been taken through an airlock into an environment that was totally at odds with the world outside. A main atrium was packed from floor to high ceiling with consoles and computer banks at all levels, a system of ladders providing access to numerous raised workstations. Monitors relayed the output of hidden cameras positioned around the village, although Hendrickson had explained that many of these had been discovered and destroyed. Passages and staircases led off to personal quarters and who-knew-what else.

Of course, this had been a magistrates' base: one of many secreted around the country to help keep Genosha's precious peace. Its deceptive exterior had masked its function, and kept it hidden when riots had swept through the streets a few feet away.

"The magistrates took as much equipment as they could when they evacuated," Hendrickson had explained, "but we've salvaged guns and combat suits and a few other useful items. The mutates may have their freakish powers, but we don't have to be helpless against them."

Bobby had had no intention of making small talk. After a few less than subtle yawns, he had been shown to a spare bunk, in which he had lain, feigning sleep and listening to the snores of the people around him, feeling surrounded. Eventually, when he had heard no sound from outside the room for over half an hour, he had got up, dressed hurriedly and slipped away.

The base had been built whole inside the warehouse: solid steel walls lay between Iceman and the boarded-up windows he had seen from the outside. He didn't dare look too hard for another way out, and so he had eventually found himself back in the atrium. He had been disappointed, if not surprised, to find people at four of the workstations, and two sentries at the airlock door. He had not recognized any of them—the watch shift must have changed—but they had known who he was. He had claimed to be feeling restless, and they hadn't seemed to mind him pacing the room and inspecting its contents.

The sentries held rifles, and heavy bolts were drawn across the white, circular door itself. Bobby's powers had returned to him, but he hadn't been sure how much good they would do him. He could have taken out the guards, but the door would have cost him precious time and he didn't know what resources the people at the workstations had. More hi-tech weapons like their sonic sphere, perhaps? Even if he could have escaped, the alarm would have been raised and the humans would surely have come after him. They wouldn't have let a 'genejoke' expose their presence here.

Bobby had hovered in the atrium for some time, looking and waiting for anything that might give him an advantage. Perhaps one of the guards would take a rest break? Perhaps something would happen to send all the watchmen scurrying outside again? But the night had dragged on uneventfully, and he had only become more tired. He had surrendered at last, consoling himself with the thought that he might get a better opportunity tomorrow when he was refreshed.

His hopes were confounded, however, as he returned to the atrium to find it buzzing with activity. There had to be at least forty people present, rushing this way and that, getting under each others' feet. Two women had dismantled a blaster weapon of some sort; a pair of legs protruded from beneath one of the workstations; a crudely drawn map had been tacked to the wall, and a small group had gathered around it. Hendrickson was moving from monitor to monitor, taking reports and nodding to himself. Bobby glanced longingly at the door, but it was more out of reach than ever. He stood alone and tried to work out his next move, until a figure emerged from the confusion and approached him.

He recognized the young woman called Debs from last night. What he hadn't realized then, in the darkness, was how attractive she was. Her heart-shaped face was framed by buoyant brown-black hair shaped into a bob, and her eyes were blue and friendly.

Her expression was open and guileless—deceptively so, Bobby felt sure.

"Morning," she said cheerfully. "Had any breakfast yet?" Bobby hadn't, and he couldn't deny that he was hungry. Debs offered to take him to the mess. "We don't have much, I'm afraid," she confided, "but I'm sure we can find you a tin of something."

The square tables and benches in the mess were empty, but Debs stayed with Bobby as he heated up baked beans on an electric hob in the kitchen alcove. To his discomfort, she kept asking questions. He answered with as few words as possible, careful not to betray his contempt for everything she stood for, hoping that she would get the hint and leave him alone. Lying awkwardly, he claimed to have worked as a foreman at the mines outside Hammer Bay until he was driven out of his home by mutates. He had meant to say "genejokes," but he hadn't been able to spit out the insult. He felt as if he were being tested, like his every word was subject to the utmost scrutiny.

"No wonder you wanted out," said Debs, spooning powdered milk into two cups of instant coffee. "Magneto talks a lot about mutant rights, but what about basic human rights? That's what I want to know."

"The mutates had it bad for a long time," said Bobby. It was all he could do to keep his tone civil. "They were treated like slaves."

He regretted the words as soon as he had spoken them. He expected Debs to issue a sharp retort, to denounce him as a traitor to his kind, to summon her colleagues. Instead, she said: "I know. But does that mean we all deserve to have to live like this?"

"Mr. Wagner."

Something about the Priest's baritone voice gave Nightcrawler an unnatural chill. He turned, and looked up into the tall man's intense blue eyes. The Priest's thin lips were set into a grim line. Crooking a long finger to indicate that the X-Man should follow him, he strode away, apparently confident of his obedience. Kurt's first thought was that the Priest had been told about his conversation at breakfast, that his suspicions had been aroused. With a quick glance back at the sleeping Wolverine, he crossed his fingers behind his back and followed. He felt even colder as he was led into the chapel area, trying to avert his eyes from the winged sculpture atop the makeshift altar.

The Priest indicated that he should take a seat at the front of the room. He remained standing himself so that he now towered over Kurt, glaring down at him hawk-like from behind his protruding nose. "Are you not a religious man, Mr. Wagner? Do you not believe?"

Kurt started. "As it happens, my friend, my faith is the most important thing in my life."

The Priest raised an eyebrow. "And yet, we did not see you at prayer this morning."

Kurt swallowed hard. He wanted to tell this man, this false prophet, exactly what he thought of him. As far as he could see, the Priest had taken advantage of the mutates' vulnerability, inducting them into his false church when they had been confused and disoriented. He had used their need to believe in a higher power to manipulate them, to set himself up above them. But his power over them was undeniable, and Kurt couldn't challenge it; not while Wolverine still needed his bed here. "At Carrion Cove," he said instead, "our prayers were a private matter, conducted away from the ears of our oppressors."

The Priest held his gaze for a long, nerve-wracking moment before he accepted his story with a solemn nod. "We are proud of our faith here, Mr. Wagner, and we will not be persecuted for it. We gather again at six-thirty to give thanks to our Lord and pray for a better day tomorrow. We can expect to see you there?" His words had the inflection of a question but the tone of an instruction.

Kurt's only answer was a tight smile, but fortunately this appeared to suffice. With any luck, he and Logan would be long gone before the service began. He felt bad enough that he was effectively denying his own God, if not explicitly then at least by omission. He couldn't have joined in a prayer to Magneto, he just couldn't: the words would have choked him.

The Priest pulled back a chair and sat beside him, now adopting an almost conspiratorial manner. "I visited the infirmary again earlier. The condition of your travelling companion is, I fear, not improving. He may need more help than we can give him."

"I thought the power of Magneto flowed through you," said Kurt brazenly.

The Priest's eyes flashed. "But some are not deemed worthy to receive it."

"Logan is a good man!" the X-Man insisted, containing his anger.

"As you claim to be yourself—and yet you have lied to us."

Kurt narrowed his eyes and tried not to show how worried he was. "How so?"

"You claimed your friend was injured by humans. His wound, however, could only have been inflicted by an animal—or by a man with the characteristics of one."

Kurt nodded and sighed. "We were attacked by mutates," he admitted.

"Where?" asked the Priest sharply.

He thought quickly. "I don't know the name of the village. A few miles to the east of here. They looked like a band of scavengers. They thought we were stealing their food. We couldn't reason with them. We ran."

The Priest shook his head sadly. "It pains me to hear of brother mutates living in such conditions. I can only pray to our Savior that he will end their troubles soon . . . " Then his expression hardened. "This does not explain why you deceived us!"

"We'd been on the run for days. We didn't know who we could trust."

The Priest's eyes bore into Kurt. It seemed that, with each lie, he became more reluctant to believe the outsider. But he hadn't been able to trip him up. Yet. "Your friend does not wear a skinsuit," he observed, casting his eye slowly up and down Kurt's holographic costume as if he could see it for the illusion it was.

"He had the bonding process reversed as soon as he was able."

"A brave decision. I understand the operation is not without its risks."

"Logan is a brave man, and proud. He refused to wear the clothes of a slave for any longer than he had to."

"And with what abilities has Mr. Logan been blessed?"

"Enhanced senses—and he can extend claws from the backs of his hands."

"Claws—like those of the mutate who wounded him."

Kurt nodded. He didn't know where this was going, but he had his suspicions.

"Only I am beginning to fear that his attacker did more than simply wound him," said the Priest. "He is feverish."

"He may have blood poisoning—or his wound may have become infected."

"And there is a rattle in his chest."

"As I said, we have been on the run for days. We have hardly slept. It is a miracle that we have not both come down with colds."

"Hmm." The Priest cradled his chin in one large hand, and nodded thoughtfully to himself. Then, finally, he got to his feet and smoothed down his white robes. Kurt took this as a cue to stand too; he was anxious to get out of here. "I will pray for your friend," promised the Priest. "I trust you will do the same. Our Lord may yet choose to bestow His favor upon him."

He turned away, then, and Kurt sensed that the audience was over. He scurried back down the aisle, trying not to make his haste too evident. He was brought up short by the Priest's booming voice behind him. "Until this evening, then, Mr. Wagner."

Kurt didn't answer. He forced himself to start walking again, although he could almost feel the Priest's hawk eyes burning into his back.

It was with some relief that he finally put a cellar wall between himself and his inquisitor. The sensation didn't last, however: he had too much else to worry about.

He had guessed the reason for the Priest's questions as soon as he had asked about Wolverine's abilities. He had been looking for evidence to support what he suspected. It hadn't been hard for Kurt to deduce as much, given that he was beginning to share the same awful suspicion himself. That was why he had not mentioned Logan's healing factor. He hadn't wanted the Priest to know that, whatever was wrong with his friend, it was having a direct effect upon his mutant gene. He hadn't wanted him to know just how serious the situation was. He thought he had succeeded in throwing him off the scent for now, but he knew that he had gained only a temporary respite.

And he knew that, if his fears about Wolverine's condition proved well grounded, then the reaction of the Priest would be the least of his problems.

"So, what's all the activity about?" asked Bobby, pushing his tin plate away from him. He felt much better with hot food inside him, and he had been talking to Debs for long enough to feel that he could slip a few important questions into the conversation. It was time he found out more about what was going on around him, started working on an escape plan.

Debs sat across the wooden table from him, sipping her coffee. "Preparations. We found a nest of mutates in the village a few days ago. Hendrickson wants to take it out—tonight."

Bobby's stomach sank, and he almost wished he hadn't asked. His distaste must have shown, because Debs leaned forward and said: "You don't seem too happy about that."

Fumblingly, he tried to retrieve the situation. "I don't see how it's going to solve anything." For good measure, he added: "Haven't we lived through enough violence?"

Debs accepted that with a shrug. "Sometimes, we don't have a choice."

"You could stop," he said pointedly.

She shook her head. "You don't understand. We've lost four people to these particular mutates in the past week. I don't like it any more than you do, but it's kill or be killed!"

"That's what your friend said last night," said Bobby, staring morosely into his cup.

"She was right. You've seen it for yourself, Bobby. You don't think those GUMPs were trying to take you alive, do you? They'd already turned you back from the border, but they still came after you. They wanted blood!" That wasn't entirely true, but Bobby couldn't argue the point without giving himself away. "And they're just the acceptable face of Magneto's army: at least he keeps them under some measure of control. The ones you really have to watch out for are the terrorists and the street gangs, the ones who harbor a grudge against all humans. They'd see us all dead just because our genes are a little different to theirs!"

Bobby stared at her, speechless. He had heard that bitter sentiment expressed many times in his life, but never by a non-mutant.

Debs let out a weary sigh. "I suppose I was stupid. I should have run like all my friends did when the United Nations sold us out to Magneto. But Genosha is my home, damn it. I'd sat tight through the civil war and I was just beginning to feel comfortable here again. I even thought that a new ruler might improve things for everyone. I thought Magneto might actually care about making peace between the two races. Pretty naïve, huh?"

"What happened?" asked Bobby.

"They took my job first. I was a data processor, and I was good at it—but my company was forced to employ mutate labor, and I was laid off. I mean, I know we need to get more mutates into employment, but don't I have a right to earn a living too? Magneto says he's keeping humans in Genosha for our skills—but as soon as one of his own kind can be trained to replace us, we're thrown onto the scrap heap!"

"You couldn't find another job?"

"As a street sweeper, maybe. Or a refuse collector or an office cleaner."

"All the work the mutates used to do," said Bobby.

Debs smiled wryly, his implication not lost on her. "I know they have good reason to hate some of us. When I think of what the genegineer and his people did to them . . . "

"But we all turned a blind eye to it."

"I know," said Debs, "but you must remember what it was like before the uprising. The mutates, they were just . . . just there, you know? We used to walk past them in the street and not pay a second thought to them. We didn't ask ourselves if they were happy, because to us they had no emotions. They weren't . . . weren't real people!"

"Because their minds had been tampered with!" protested Bobby.

"We know that now, yes," said Debs, "but at the time, we thought they were just . . . well, born that way. As if they'd been put on Earth to serve us. I remember, we used to have a maid call at our house regularly. I saw her three times a week for the first eighteen years of my life, and I don't remember ever once saying a word to her. And I feel ashamed of that now, of course I do, but it's just . . . it's just how we were brought up, isn't it? It's how we were told the world worked, what we were led to believe. It wasn't our fault!"

Bobby could have argued the point, but he felt he had said too much already. Fortunately, Debs showed no sign of becoming suspicious. She seemed to believe that his concerns were born of nothing more than liberal guilt. A guilt that she apparently shared.

Perhaps he had misjudged her. Perhaps she was a good person after all, her only crime one of inaction. He couldn't blame her for that: had circumstances been different, had Bobby Drake had a choice, then he too might well have kept his head down and lived a normal life. He certainly wouldn't have volunteered to become a target in a war between species.

He shook his head firmly. He wouldn't let himself be won over like this. No matter how good a sob story Debs gave him, only one thing mattered. "I still don't see why anyone has to die," he said. "No matter what the . . . the mutates have done to me, I'm not about to march out into the street and slaughter the first one I see. I just can't do it!"

"I'll second that!" said Debs with feeling.

He blinked at her, confused. In turn, she peered at him questioningly, then her face softened into a broad smile. "I knew you were worried about something! You thought we expected you to go out and fight tonight?"

"You don't?"

"Of course not! Oh, Hendrickson will ask you—and he won't be too pleased when you turn him down—but I won't be going, and nor will about half the people in this base."

"So, what are you even doing here?" asked Bobby.

"I was turfed out of my home."

"By mutates?"

"By the government. I had too much space for one person, apparently, so they moved in a mutate family from the old settlement zone. Oh, they found me another place to stay: a bed in a flophouse, sharing a dorm with three other women. It wasn't exactly in the most up and coming area, if you know what I mean. I went to sleep every night scared that I wouldn't wake up again. When I heard about this place . . . well, it seemed like it was my best hope of staying alive. So, you see, we're in the same boat, you and me."

"Are we?" Bobby persisted. "I'm not sure I could put up with what Hendrickson's doing."

Debs grimaced. "I know, I know, I'm 'turning a blind eye' again. But he and the others say they're only fighting in self-defense, and I wouldn't know how to stop them even if I was sure it was the right thing to do. And I don't know what *is* the right thing to do any more."

Bobby felt he ought to have responded to that—but he was disconcerted to find that he couldn't think of a word to say.

"How are you feeling now, *mein freund*?"

Wolverine was getting used to seeing Nightcrawler looming over him: his concerned face seemed to greet him every time he woke up. "Better'n I was," he mumbled. It was a lie. He felt as if he had the mother of all colds, his muscles ached and all he wanted to do was sleep. The gash in his side still burnt as if his blood had turned to acid.

Kurt wasn't fooled by Logan's bravado, but he gave him some water and made the usual reassuring small talk. He told him he was safe, that he just had to rest a little more, and promised him that he would be up and around, back in the bad guys' faces, in no time.

Wolverine interrupted him. "Are we alone?" he asked. He didn't have the strength to lift his head from the pillow and see for himself.

Kurt glanced around. "We have as much privacy as we will find here, I suspect."

"Have to tell you something." It was hard for Wolverine to say the words, and not only because his throat felt like sandpaper. "Been doing some thinking, and I reckon I know what . . . what's wrong with me."

The light in Kurt's eyes dimmed, and Logan guessed that he too had been harboring unvoiced suspicions. Wolverine had always been a realist, never one to fool himself. He had to face this. So, why then did it seem so much more difficult than any fight he had been in?

"When that . . . that mutate woman . . . when she scratched me. . . ." He took a deep breath. "She did a lot more just tear my skin."

Kurt nodded gloomily. "You think she infected you."

"And not just any infection."

"We don't know that, Logan," insisted Kurt. "Until we can get you to a proper medical facility and run some tests . . ."

Logan shook his head grimly. "It all fits," he said. "The cold-like symptoms, the fact that my mutant gene's packing up on me—and let's face it, elf, what's the most common bug doing the rounds in Genosha at the moment?"

Nightcrawler lowered his eyes and stuck out his lower lip sullenly. Wolverine could tell that he didn't want to believe it, but he had no choice.

"Maybe it was just bad luck," mused Logan. "Her blood mingled with mine. Or maybe that was her power—to cultivate the virus and transmit it to others. Maybe the old genegineer gave her that ability . . . a way to keep the other mutates in line. . . ."

"Don't give up, Logan," said Kurt. "If anyone can lick this, you can." He took one of Wolverine's hands in his own: his white glove felt uncommonly warm against Logan's palm.

He didn't feel like talking any more. He was too tired. He let his eyes close, but he couldn't stop thinking about the alien cells that had invaded his body, of the wound that hadn't yet closed up because his system was too busy waging a war to keep him alive.

He remembered discussing this scenario with the Beast, not long ago, when it had still been comfortably hypothetical. Hank McCoy, of course, had been exploring another avenue in the quest that had come to dominate his life; he had run a battery of tests on Logan to ascertain if his unique biology might provide a much-needed breakthrough. "Theoretically," he had concluded, "your body ought to be able to deal with the Legacy Virus. Unfortunately, the precise action of said virus is unpredictable, and its converse effects upon your mutant gene are an unknown quantity."

"In plain English, Doc," Logan had said, "my healing factor should be able to zap that sucker—but only if the virus doesn't get to it and screw it up first, right?"

"That is an accurate summation," Hank had conceded. A week and many more tests later, he had reached the conclusion that, even if Wolverine could shake off a dose of Legacy, there was no way to isolate his healing factor and pass on the benefits to other sufferers. His research had reached another dead end. He would probably have considered it ironic, thought Logan, that his theory was being put to the test anyway.

He must have drifted off to sleep, but the first he knew of it was when he was peeling his eyes open and looking at Kurt Wagner's concerned face again. "What's the matter, elf?" he asked with a weak smile. "Ain't you got a home to go to?"

"There's something else you ought to know, *mein freund*," said Kurt gravely.

"Don't tell me—more good news?"

"If you do have this virus, then the mutates here must not learn of it."

"Don't take kindly to sharing their living space with plague victims, I take it?"

"They don't understand, Logan. Every one of them has lost friends to the Legacy Virus, but they don't even know how it's transmitted. They're terrified of it."

"Can't hardly blame them. So, what do they do with their sick—put them out of their misery, I suppose?"

"Out on the streets, at least. They call them 'the unclean'—although according to the mutate Priest, Magneto has set up facilities for them in Hammer Bay and the other major cities."

"I can just imagine his face if I turned up there asking for treatment. Don't suppose there's even much hope of getting a bed incognito: Genosha's mutates are all individually numbered, aren't they?" Logan's moment of good humor was spoilt by a painful coughing fit.

"By all accounts," said Kurt, "these so-called field hospitals are little more than quarantined camps anyway. Half the mutates are more concerned with keeping the infected penned up away from them than they are with their health. They believe that Legacy is a punishment inflicted upon the unworthy by . . . by their deity."

"I thought Maggie had the cure. That's why we came here, isn't it?"

"If he does, Logan, then I've yet to see a single sign that anyone has benefited from it."

"You think we might be on a wild goose chase after all?"

"I've heard rumors, but nothing concrete. Magneto might still be testing the serum—and I suppose it would take some time to mass produce it." Kurt looked doubtful.

"Or maybe," rumbled Wolverine, "Charley Xavier was right to be worried. Maybe old Bucket-Head has higher priorities for that cure than distributing it to the needy."

CHAPTER 8

AS Cyclops returned slowly to consciousness, his first instinctive thought was to check that he was wearing his visor. To his relief, he could feel it, cold against the skin of his face. But something nagged at him all the same. Something was wrong.

He could feel a rough, lumpy surface at his back and nothing beneath his feet, but his sense of equilibrium insisted that he wasn't lying down. He was attached to something, sprawled across it at a thirty-degree angle. His limbs were pinned, one arm twisted almost behind his back. He had fought Magneto, he recalled—for all of about ten seconds. He didn't know exactly what had happened—it had all been so quick—but he could guess.

It wasn't until he was fully awake that Scott realized what was needling him. His eyes felt different. The pressure behind them, so familiar that he rarely noticed it any more, was no longer there. He opened them, and felt nothing. No burning sensation as raw power erupted through his retinas and strained against his ruby quartz lens for release.

And Jean was gone.

He couldn't feel his wife through their telepathic link. The realization sent a stab of panic into his heart, but he calmed himself with logic. Something had taken his mutant power from him; it wasn't unreasonable to assume that the same thing had happened to the rest of his team, Phoenix included. She was still alive, still with him, but psi-blind.

He was attached to a hulking metal sculpture, facing a blank wall. Turning his head as far as it would go, he could just make out a large blue, clawed foot at his ear. It could only have belonged to one person. "Hank?"

"Ah," came the familiar voice of the Beast, "our esteemed leader finally extracts himself from the tenacious grip of the sandman. I was beginning to wonder for how much longer I would remain the only one of our number cognizant of our predicament."

"Are the others here?" asked Cyclops. "I can't see."

"If I extend my neck muscles, I can avail myself of a glimpse of Jeannie's red hair—and I believe I may have heard our resident weather elemental stirring a few moments ago."

"You're still in your Beast form."

"So it would appear—but I've been testing the limits of my strength and have found myself decidedly enervated. Am I to infer from your inquiry that you are likewise impaired?"

"Something must be nullifying our powers."

"I have visual contact with a probable culprit," said the Beast. "A young lady whose skinsuit identifies her as a Genoshan mutate."

No matter how he strained, Cyclops couldn't see who his teammate was looking at. The metal that held him wouldn't give: when he tried to break it, to pull his hand away from the twisted sculpture, it only dug into his wrist and drew blood. "What is she doing?" he asked.

"She is immersed in a rather tawdry form of literature. I have attempted to attract her attention, but she has steadfastly ignored my overtures toward her."

"I'm open to suggestions, Hank."

"Bereft of our paranormal abilities, and unless we can muster the physical power to break our bonds, I would conclude that we are helpless."

"That isn't what I wanted to hear," sighed Cyclops.

Storm came round next—and, after she had been filled in on the situation, she asked if the others had any memory of breathing in chloroform. Cyclops hadn't, but he didn't doubt the evidence of Ororo's senses. The revelation worried him, and made him redouble his futile efforts to break free. He had assumed that he had been out for an hour or two at most—but if he had been anaesthetized, then who knew how much wasted time had passed? The room had no windows, and he had no way of knowing the time. The X-Men had been on a tight deadline from the start; what if Magneto and Shaw had put their plan, whatever it was, into action? What if it was already too late to stop them?

Scott was as relieved as he was apprehensive, then, when a door opened and footsteps marched into the room. At least he might learn the worst of it now; he would know what he was up against. To his frustration, he was facing the wrong way to see the newcomers: by his estimation, there were at least four of them. However, there was no mistaking the voice of the X-Men's oldest and most intractable foe: deceptively laid back and tinged by world-weariness, but with a threatening undertone.

"Our guests are awake, I see."

"I still say we should kill them." Cyclops guessed that the unfamiliar voice belonged to Lady Mastermind. He had glimpsed her in the ballroom, realizing who she was even as Phoenix had taken her out. Surprised as he had been to see her at Sebastian Shaw's side, it made a certain kind of sense. The original Mastermind had been affiliated with Shaw's first Inner Circle; clearly, Regan Wyngarde intended to follow in her late father's footsteps in more ways than one. Scott felt a painful mixture of anger and sadness as he remembered what she had put him and Jean through. He had to tell himself that the experience hadn't been real, that the emotions weren't relevant.

"I think we can afford to be magnanimous in victory," purred Magneto.

"You know better than that, Lensherr," said Cyclops, clenching his gloved fists. "You'll never defeat the X-Men until every one of us is dead!"

"You impress me as always, Scott," said the man once known as Erik Magnus Lensherr. "Even in the face of such overwhelming odds, you retain your characteristic bravado. One day, perhaps, I will take your hollow boasts at face value and dispatch you and the rest of Charles's misguided students. Not today, though. We stand on the threshold of a new world order, my friends, and I want you to experience it."

"You have made such claims before," said Storm.

"Indeed," said the Beast. "Were I to indulge in a little armchair psychiatry, then I might diagnose an over-inflated confidence in your own capabilities."

Cyclops felt the metal shifting at his back, and he wondered for an instant if the master of magnetism had lost his temper and intended to crush his tormentors. He was powerless to resist as he was swung around to the front of the insane sculpture. Now, he was hanging vertically, his arms spread above him, his feet not quite touching the floor. The Beast hung to his left, Phoenix beyond him, and Storm settled into a similar position to Cyclops's right.

He could see his enemies now, through the faint ruby haze in which the world was washed by his protective lens. Magneto had swapped his robes for a black suit and tie, and he was accompanied not only by Lady Mastermind but also by Shaw and Tessa. In the corner of the room, by a wooden chair on which lay a battered paperback novel, stood a blonde, teenaged girl in a pink and black skinsuit. Lurking nervously at her side was a tall, wiry male mutate in black and green, with a shaved head.

"I never thought Magneto would work with the Hellfire Club again," commented Storm.

"A temporary alliance, I assure you," said Magneto, "but one that serves us both well."

"In my native Africa, we have a saying: 'If the tiger sits, do not think it is out of respect.'" The words were ostensibly directed at Magneto, but Ororo was looking at Shaw.

Magneto nodded graciously, but chose not to respond. "Allow me to introduce two of my fellow countrymen." He beckoned the mutates forward with a coiled finger. "Miranda, as you have no doubt deduced, is responsible for your current weakened state. Her control over her ability is excellent: she can maintain her power-dampening field around you with minimal effort, whilst ensuring that my allies and I are not affected."

"So, if any of you so much as twitch," said Mastermind icily, "you had best be prepared to face your most terrifying nightmares."

"Until recently," Magneto continued as if irritated by the interruption, "Miranda was kept on a leash and used against her own kind; those who had mind enough to rebel. Raul here has spent most of his adult life working in mines in intolerable conditions. Now, they have become free, equal and productive members of our burgeoning society."

"OK," said Phoenix quietly, "you've made your point." Cyclops was overjoyed to hear her voice again, to know that she was awake and well.

"Oh, but I'm not sure I have, Jean."

"The mutates may think you've improved their lives," said Cyclops, "but what happens when you show them your true colors? What happens when they realize that their sovereign is a fanatic; a man who will abuse anyone and anything to further his own cause?"

"Most of the mutates don't yet know half of what I have done for them," contested Magneto. "Take Miranda and Raul, for example. Not so long ago, they could have counted the remaining days of their lives on their fingers. I have restored them to full health."

"Then the Legacy cure is effective," surmised the Beast, and there was a hint of excitement in his voice despite the situation.

"It has eradicated the virus from their systems—and they will be the first of many to benefit from it. I have a team of scientists working to duplicate the cure. Oh, they had difficulty at first—the alien composition of the super-cell we extracted from your blood defies analysis—but they soon found that, given the right conditions, the cell was only too quick to reproduce itself. The poor, disease-ridden mutates of Genosha call me their Savior, and that is precisely what I will become."

"Your friend Shaw stole that cure from us," snarled the Beast. "We would have ensured that everybody had access to it."

"And how would you have done that, Henry? By handing it to your government? By waiting as they performed months, years, of product testing? A mutant disease is hardly at the top of their political agenda, is it? And what then? Distribution through one of your pharmaceutical companies at a price that my country cannot afford? No, my friend, my way is better."

"And what of the mutants outside Genosha?" asked Storm. "Will you be making the cure available to them too?"

"Not to mention the baseline humans to whom the disease has spread," added the Beast.

"Well," said Magneto, "that rather depends on a few conditions."

"Such as?" rapped Cyclops.

"Or need we ask?" said Storm coldly. "Magneto's goals are the same as they always are. The same as Selene's were. He wants to control other people, make them think as he thinks—and how better to do that than to wield the power of life and death over them?"

"You do me an injustice," said Magneto. "My plans are more grandiose, further-reaching and ultimately more beneficial to the world than those of that soulless vampire."

"Beneficial?" Phoenix's voice was still quiet, but it carried an angry intensity. "Is that what you call spreading Genosha's epidemic further? Is that what you call infecting hundreds of millions of innocent people with a terminal disease?"

Alarmed, Cyclops craned to see his wife's face. "What is it, Jean? What do you know?"

Phoenix didn't look at him. She was glaring at the Black King, her eyes burning with contempt. "Why don't you tell them, Shaw? Tell them what I saw in your mind."

"If you insist." Shaw stepped forward, his habitual smirk on his face, apparently unfazed by Jean's challenge. He addressed all four of the prisoners. "As you already know, the Hellfire Club will celebrate tonight's solstice with a worldwide pyrotechnic display. However, as you must also have suspected, there is an ulterior motive to the celebrations. Our fireworks contain an unusual payload. As midnight strikes and our trident symbol lights the night in each time zone, we will be spreading a great deal more than just seasonal joy to the masses."

Cyclops's stomach tightened, but he stopped himself from speaking. Shaw and Magneto were both in talkative moods—they had come here to gloat—and he needed to learn all he could from them.

"For the most part," said Magneto, "the Legacy Virus has spread slowly. Only the Genoshans have suffered in great numbers: perhaps the operations performed upon our mutates by the previous government made them somehow more susceptible. However, in the course of their study of the virus, the scientists at our Kree facility in the Pacific Ocean found a way to change that."

"It's quite simple, really," said Shaw. "All we have to do is piggy-back Legacy onto a common cold virus, and release that hybrid into the upper atmosphere."

"At first, we had no practical use for such a discovery. We would not have been able to control its effects. But now—"

"Now, you can infect as many people as you like," snapped Cyclops, unable to hold his silence any longer, "and treat only those who swear allegiance to your twisted ideals."

"The rate of transmission will increase exponentially," confirmed Shaw. "My dear?"

He looked at Tessa, who responded obligingly: "I estimate that there will be almost a hundred thousand new cases of Legacy by the New Year. By the end of January, the figure will be closer to a million. Within a year, it will be almost impossible to avoid infection."

"Most satisfying of all," said Magneto, "the virus will no longer discriminate between humans and mutants. In fact, I must confess to enjoying one rather poetic irony of the situation. Our cure was evolved from the Beast's mutated blood cells. I am told that, when injected into human sufferers, it may well activate any dormant mutant genes in their own DNA. Any human who wishes to survive this plague, then, will not only have to rely upon the blood of his sworn enemies, but will risk becoming a mutate himself."

"And, of course, he will have to come crawling to you first," said Phoenix.

"Of course. But I do not intend to be unreasonable. Only a small number of people—those who have shown their intolerance of our kind—will be denied the cure. The rest will be given an opportunity to prove that they deserve it."

"You're talking about cold-blooded murder!" spat Cyclops.

"I am talking about making those who have power in this world accept their responsibilities—for if they do not, then their successors will. I am giving them an incentive to do the right thing. We will start by demanding new anti-discrimination legislation."

"Along with greater power for yourself and your associates, I presume," said the Beast.

"We will never have equality until mutants are represented at the highest levels of society," said Shaw. "That is an ideal to which my Inner Circle has always subscribed."

Magneto smiled. "You could even say that, by weeding out the perpetrators of anti-mutant hate crimes, we will be helping evolution to take its natural course."

"There is nothing natural about germ warfare," snarled Cyclops, "especially not when your weapon is a man-made virus."

Magneto drew closer to the X-Men's field leader, an eyebrow raised in mock surprise and a twinkle of amusement in his eyes. "Always so disapproving, Scott—but don't you see? I am about to create a world in which mutants need not fear, need not hide their very natures. That is the much-vaunted dream of your precious mentor, is it not?" He clapped a hand on Cyclops's shoulder, like a benevolent father. Scott wanted to recoil from it, but he was held too fast, and so he settled for showing his distaste in his features instead.

"We may be fighting for the same thing," he said, "but Professor Xavier would never tolerate your methods—and nor will I!"

"You cling to the belief that humanity can be persuaded to improve our lot. But for how long have your X-Men fought that lost cause, and what have you gained? I have tried it your way, Scott—Xavier's way—and it does not work. The humans hate us, as the Nazis hated the Jews. They know that we are destined to replace them, and they fear their passing."

"And people like you only give them all the more reason to hate and fear. Your plan won't change that, it will only make things worse!"

The good humor drained from Magneto's face, and now his eyes burnt with a white fire. Suddenly, Cyclops was reminded of what a formidable opponent this aging, gray-haired man could be. "What do I care for the opinions of a miserable, stunted species that will die out within a few generations anyway? My only concern is that we are free from their mindless persecution—and if they must be coerced into leaving us alone, then so be it. They started this war—and it was their choice, not mine, to fight it with deadly force!"

"You're wrong," said Cyclops quietly. There was nothing else to add. He and Magneto had had this argument many times—but it wasn't in his nature to stop trying, to say nothing in the face of such overwhelming hatred.

"A shame, then, that your opinion no longer matters." Magneto turned on his heel and strode toward the door. "I am leaving now for Genosha, from where I will coordinate the release of the Legacy Virus. When next we meet, it will be in a better world—and you will thank me for what I am about to do, one day."

"We'll get out of here," Cyclops shouted after him, "and we'll come after you. Even if you release the virus, we can still take the cure from you!"

Magneto paused on the threshold and looked back at the captive X-Men. "Do not strain yourselves. My associate will release you himself in two or three days. By then, the cure will have been distributed to Genosha's mutates, and I will be more than adequately defended. Be warned, my former allies: anyone who dares violate the boundaries of <u>my country</u> from that day forth will face the wrath of a vengeful nation."

He left then, and the mutate called Raul scurried uncertainly after him. Lady Mastermind threw a lopsided smirk in the X-Men's direction before following. As the Black King made to do likewise, however, Storm stopped him in his tracks with an angry bark of "Shaw!"

He turned to face her slowly, his expression placid. Tessa frowned. Miranda, who had been about to retake her seat, hesitated.

"You may be a snake, Shaw," said Ororo hotly, "but I thought better of you than this. I cannot believe that even you would go along with Magneto's insane scheme."

"As my colleague said," said Shaw evenly, "it will benefit all mutants, myself included."

"And ultimately," said the Beast, "it will bring about a world in which non-mutants have no place. Over whom would you laud your enhanced physical prowess then?"

Cyclops waited to see how this confrontation would play itself out. This was why he had brought Ororo and Hank to Sydney, after all: because they had both had recent dealings with the Black King. They had each been forced to work with him. They knew him better than either Cyclops or Phoenix did, and they knew how to get under his skin.

"Oh, I'm sure Sebastian has everything worked out," said Storm with a hint of contempt in her voice. "His strength will be of little use to him once he has achieved his life's aim. What has Magneto offered you in exchange for poisoning your world, Shaw?"

"The Presidency of the United States, perhaps?" suggested the Beast. Shaw smiled at that, then said, "Much as I would enjoy that role, I have set my sights a little higher."

"Sebastian will control the world's business transactions," supplied Tessa. "Nothing will be built, no contract signed and no fiscal policy passed without his authorization—and he will tolerate no inefficiency, no waste, no weak-minded liberalism."

"You intend to make the world over in your image," stated the Beast.

"I intend," said Shaw, "to ensure that history remembers my name."

"Oh, I don't doubt that it will. It will not forget your part in the instigation of a bloody interspecies war. Future generations will vilify the man who helped to reduce our civilization to ruins. Against that, I don't imagine your efforts to rebuild will count for a great deal."

"You are forgetting," said Tessa, "that history is written by the victor—and Sebastian Shaw will be the most powerful man in the world, and the richest."

"The *second* most powerful," said Storm pointedly.

"Ah, therein lies the rub," said the Beast. "It does not sound like the self-styled Black King to subsume his ambitions to those of a transient ally."

"Do not presume to know me," growled Shaw, "either of you."

"Unfortunately for you, Shaw," persisted Storm, "we *do* know you. As does Magneto. He knows that you would not wish to live under his rule any more than we do. However and whenever you plan to betray him, he will be prepared."

"You fought alongside the X-Men before," said the Beast, "when circumstances necessitated it."

"But this time," said Tessa abruptly, "the game remains under

Sebastian's control. The introduction of extra players to the board would only complicate matters."

"Your lapdog is doing a lot of talking for you, Shaw," said Storm. "But remember this: Magneto plays the game well too, and this time the stakes are dangerously high."

Shaw smiled, and his eyes glistened darkly. "Why else would the game be worth playing?"

It was evident that the Black King had his own agenda, and that he wasn't about to discuss it. Cyclops almost wished that Phoenix had read more of his thoughts when she had had the chance—but she would have intruded as little as possible, even in the mind of an enemy.

Shaw turned to his assistant. "Miranda is to keep them helpless," he said. Tessa must have passed the instruction on telepathically because, a moment later, the young female mutate nodded obediently and sat down on the wooden chair.

"I'm afraid I too must take my leave of you now," Shaw addressed the X-Men. "After all, I have a party to organize this evening—and it is past six o'clock already."

He looked directly at Cyclops as he spoke, a malicious grin on his face as if he knew the effect that his words would have. Scott gritted his teeth, determined not to betray the icy fear that formed in his stomach and spread to encompass his entire body.

It was the Beast who put that fear into words, once Shaw and Tessa had left the room. "It appears that time is rather shorter than we might have hoped."

Phoenix called over to Miranda—and, undeterred when the girl did not respond, she talked to her in a gentle, reassuring tone. She sympathized with the hardships from which the Genoshan mutates had been rescued, but asked Miranda if it was right to make other people suffer as she had suffered. She met with no more success than the Beast had. The girl remained infuriatingly silent, occasionally turning the pages of her book.

"I am beginning to suspect," said the Beast, "that young

Miranda is not merely unwilling to listen, but incapable of same."

"I think you're right," said Cyclops. "Remember how Tessa had to instruct her telepathically?" He strained at his inflexible bonds again. "We need ideas, people, and we need them fast. We have a lot of work to do, and we've got just under six hours to do it. As soon as that first firework goes up at midnight tonight, Magneto and Shaw will have won!"

CHAPTER 9

HE closer Rogue drew to the center of Hammer Bay, the more building sites she passed and the more busy people she almost ran into. Magneto had obviously decreed that Genosha's reconstruction should begin with his immediate environs. Perhaps it would be easier to believe his work done once the poverty, disease and strife that were endemic to his country had been pushed out of his sight.

Worried at first, Rogue had tried to take back roads and alleyways, but it was impossible to avoid being seen. She was comforted, however, by the fact that nobody had spared her a second glance. Why would they? She could probably have taken to the air, she thought, without raising an eyebrow. Most of the site laborers were mutates, after all. Many of them could stretch or fly, reaching difficult areas without having to erect scaffolding. Welders could do their jobs without the benefit of expensive machinery, using their own bio-energies, and hod-carriers could lift three times the load of their human counterparts. It occurred to Rogue that the mutates had been bred precisely for this type of work, and she shuddered.

She had found a woolen sweater left unattended by the side of one site, and had taken it gratefully, disposing of the half-melted jogger top that could only have drawn attention to her. The sweater had a roll-neck, and it was baggy enough for the casual observer to imagine that she wore a skinsuit beneath it. Emboldened by her apparent anonymity, she ventured closer than she might otherwise have dared to the command center: a former magistrate base, which now served as the seat of the newly formed government. She observed it from all angles; at one point, she walked right past it with the assured gait of one who had somewhere to get to. She pretended not to be interested in the mutate guards, members of—what were they called again?—the Genoshan Unified Military Patrol.

The last time she had come here, an ally had teleported her into the main control room. But then, her intention had been to confront Genosha's new sovereign. This time, she hoped to keep Magneto unaware of her presence.

She thought about flying to the top of the tower and trying to pry open a window, but she would probably have been seen, if not from inside then certainly from without.

Finally, she took a deep breath and ran up to the relatively secluded back door of the building. Two guards brought up their rifles suspiciously. "You've got to come quick," Rogue panted, clutching her side as if injured. "They're killing us back there!" She tugged at the sleeve of one of the mutates, but he didn't move. "Humans," she elaborated, "with magistrate technology. They've attacked my building site. We need reinforcements, fast!"

The mutate blinked at her impassively. His lips were thin, his nostrils pinched. "Didn't you hear me?" she cried, her desperation only half-feigned.

"I have already notified Command of the situation," said the mutate.

"We cannot leave our post," said his female colleague with an equal lack of emotion.

Well, thought Rogue, it was worth a shot. But on the whole, this was why she usually left the big plans to Cyclops. Not that it was exactly her fault that one of the guards had turned out to be a telepath—and at least she had had the foresight to work out a backup plan.

She had already removed her gloves in preparation, which was just as well. She could feel an itch in her brain, and the male mutate's brow furrowed as he came up against her unusually strong psychic barriers. Rogue clapped her hands to his cheeks before he could probe further or raise the alarm. It was lucky for her that his magistrate gas mask was slung around his neck, leaving his skin exposed.

She held on to him until he sagged and fell away from her; longer than she would normally have risked, but she had to be sure that she was leaving him unconscious. Everything that he was, *she* was now. Her name was Aidan Morgan, and she could feel the hole in her life, the years she could barely remember when she had been brainwashed into trailing around after human magistrates, warning them of rebellious sentiments in her fellow mutates. She felt sick as she saw herself standing over one of her fallen masters, ignoring his pleas for mercy, reaching into his mind and *twisting* it until the pain killed him. She felt pride that *she* wore the uniform now, she had taken control. Most of all, she felt Aidan Morgan's burning passion for revenge. And then, as his telepathic abilities—*her* abilities, now—kicked in, she felt her mind invaded by a million stray thoughts, until finding her own thoughts, finding her self, was like searching for a single voice in a cacophony.

And she couldn't breathe. She didn't know why. She didn't even know who or where she was any more, but an emergency signal was banging away in the back of her head, and every time her lungs tried to take in air, she found her mouth and nostrils blocked. She tried to fight it, tried to find the neural pathways that connected her brain to her arms and legs, and lashed out with all her strength.

It was one of her worst struggles yet. But finally, Rogue emerged whole from a world of noise and confusion—to find herself spread across the Genoshan sidewalk.

It was as if her entire skeleton had dissolved, leaving her a fleshy sack without structure. She fought down the urge to panic, to scream. She told herself that this couldn't possibly be real, it had to be a bad dream. Somebody else's bad dream. But she was in control again now, and the world fell back into place around her as she sifted out which of her recent experiences had been her own and thrust the others into a dark recess inside herself from which she prayed that they would never emerge.

Somehow, she knew how to peel herself off the floor and reshape herself. Her bones were there, she realized, but they bent and stretched like rubber. Humanoid once more but feeling giddy, she looked down at the mutate guards, both of whom were unconscious. The woman had splayed herself out to three times her normal width, and lay almost flat against the floor. So, that was where Rogue's unexpected pliability had come from. The mutate must have wrapped herself around the X-Man and tried to suffocate her, not realizing what would happen when she touched her. No wonder she had been so confused. Indeed, now that she could tune out the distracting telepathic voices—at least to an extent—Rogue felt the woman's additional presence inside her. Her name was June.

The voices disturbed her. They reminded her of her nightmares. Sometimes, she felt as if she held onto a part of everybody she had ever absorbed, kept them locked up in a prison cell in the back of her mind. Sometimes, at night, she heard their voices screaming at her and she woke up in a cold sweat, fearing that they might break free and overwhelm her.

She felt unsteady on her feet, unsure of herself as if she weren't quite here, weren't quite controlling her own actions. She tried to ignore the sensation, concentrating on the matter in hand. She dragged the two guards inside the building. They would be missed soon, if only by the mutates whom they had sent to an imaginary disturbance. Rogue had to move fast.

She accessed June's memories and found her knowledge of the command center's layout. Magneto, she learned, had installed a team of scientists in a basement laboratory, where they were working on a top secret project. She smiled. Things were going her way at last.

She hurried along a deserted hallway and down a flight of stairs. With luck, she thought, she could find the lab, snatch the cure to the Legacy Virus and be out of this place before anybody else saw her.

Bobby Drake glanced nervously around the tiny, empty storeroom. Having given up hope of leaving the magistrates' base through the main door, he had plucked up the courage to search a few more rooms for an alternative exit. He had bumped into several people as he had explored, but fortunately nobody had seemed interested in what he was doing. He hadn't really expected to find anything, but now here he was, staring up at an inviting hatchway in the ceiling and wondering what lay on the other side of it.

He was on the topmost level of the base—at least, he could find no stairs to take him higher. Was it possible that the hatchway led outside? It made sense, after all, for the magistrates to have had an emergency escape route.

He peered out through the storeroom door and, seeing nobody, closed it gently. The walls of the room were lined with dusty shelves, and he tested one to see if it would take his weight. Then, he climbed upward and reached out across the ceiling until he could take hold of the hatch's locking wheel and turn it. It spun easily, and the thick, circular hatch fell inward and away from him with a heavy clang that made Bobby wince. He was horribly aware that, if anybody caught him here, he would have no explanation for his actions.

The hatchway didn't lead to daylight, but nor did it lead to another section of the white-lit base. The space beyond it was dark, and it smelt faintly of wet rot. Straining his muscles, Bobby reached up until his fingers found the lip of the hatchway. Then he swung out across the room and hauled himself up through it.

He found himself on the flat roof of the base. The surface beneath his feet was steel, but he was standing among the timbers of the surrounding warehouse. The ceiling of the old building was barely a foot above his head—and his heart skipped with delight as he saw dust motes dancing in a vertical shaft of light. He hurried toward the filthy skylight and operated its clasp, but it was locked.

He made to smash the glass, reasonably sure that nobody could hear the sound from below—but closer inspection showed that it was reinforced. He formed a crowbar out of ice instead, and forced it into the narrow gap between the skylight and its frame. His first attempt to lever the window open ended in the shattering of his makeshift tool—but he repaired it, making it stronger this time, and tried again. The window began to give, just a little.

"I wouldn't do that if I were you."

Bobby started, dropped his crowbar and whirled around to find Debs standing behind him, wearing a magistrate's padded uniform and aiming a magistrate's rifle at his chest. He cursed his own stupidity: he had become too absorbed in his task, in thoughts of freedom, to hear her sneaking up on him.

"This isn't what it looks like," he said lamely.

"Oh? Then I didn't just see you create that thing out of thin air?" Debs drew closer to him, the rifle shaking a little in her hands. "The only thing around here that 'isn't what it looks like' is you, Drake. You lied to me. You're a stinking gene freak!"

"I'm a mutant!" snapped Bobby.

"Same difference. I suppose you were going back to your friends, were you? Now that you've found us, you were going to lead them all back here to kill us!"

"No!"

"I trusted you, Bobby. I thought you were different. You said you didn't want to fight."

"I don't!" he insisted. He was waiting for his moment, ready to ice up. The rifle's armor-piercing bullets could almost certainly penetrate his frozen shell, but he could take Debs by surprise, hit her with the world's biggest snowball and disarm her before she had time to react. But he hesitated, seeing something in her expression: something to suggest that the situation wasn't hopeless, that she wanted to believe him. He held out his hands in appeal, and said: "Look, I may have been born a mutant, but I'm not a Genoshan. I'm an X-Man, if that means anything to you. When you found me last night, I wasn't trying to get out of the country, I was trying to get in."

Debs peered at him through narrowed eyes. "Go on," she said.

"OK, so maybe yesterday I might have sided with the mutates if it had come to it," admitted Bobby, feeling that total honesty was now the best policy. "I know what they've been through, and I was ready to blame all the Genoshan humans for that. But you reminded me that everybody's different, that I can't blame an entire race for the actions of a few people. I hope you can see that too."

"What are the X-Men doing here?" asked Debs, still suspicious.

"We think Magneto might be about to threaten the world again. We're here to find out what he's planning, and to stop him if we have to."

"Will you get rid of him for us?"

Bobby shook his head sadly. "If we could. Look, Debs, this mission is important—and I'm grateful to you and your friends for saving me from the border patrol, but I have to get out of here! Will you let me go? I promise you, I don't have any contact with the mutates."

"And if you do? If you run into them outside?"

"I wouldn't tell them about this place. I don't want to be the cause of any more deaths."

"And the attack tonight?"

"I . . ." Bobby almost resorted to a lie, but he was sure Debs would see through it. "I don't know. If it came to it . . . I think I might warn them. . . . Hendrickson's planning a massacre!"

Debs kept the gun trained on him for a moment longer, then she lowered it and nodded. "OK. I'm going to let you go, Bobby. My instincts tell me you're a good person, and you're right—I shouldn't change that opinion just because of the makeup of your genes."

Bobby smiled wanly. "If only there were a few more people like you . . . "

"But you can't go out this way. The skylight's wired up to a silent alarm. Hendrickson would have troops out front before you could hit the ground."

Bobby grimaced. He had been so close.

"Come with me," said Debs, sounding sure of herself again. She flicked on the rifle's safety catch, tucked the weapon under one arm and dropped lithely through the open hatchway into the storeroom below. Bobby followed her, dismissing the paranoid suspicion that she might be leading him into a trap.

They hurried down several flights of stairs and emerged into the main atrium, where they were greeted by an impatient Hendrickson. "Where have you been?" he asked Debs. "The rest of the party is all ready to go; they're only waiting for you."

Bobby found himself holding his breath as he waited for Debs to answer.

"I've been showing Bobby the ropes," she said. "I thought he might come out with us."

"Are you crazy?" retorted Hendrickson. "Do you want him dead?"

"It's a simple reconnaissance mission," said Debs. She half-turned to Bobby, and explained: "We're checking out the village building by building. Sometimes, we find food. Sometimes, we find equipment."

"And sometimes," said Hendrickson, "you find genejokes. Or they find you."

"There'll be half a dozen of us—and we know where their main base is now; we can steer clear of it. Anyway, the mutates hardly ever attack in broad daylight!"

"Drake isn't ready. You saw what happened last night—he almost got himself killed!"

"I can look after myself," protested Bobby.

"Not without the right equipment you can't," shot back Hendrickson. He shook his head decisively. "No, you're staying put for this one—but I'll take you down to the armory and get you kitted out." He clamped a strong hand on Bobby's shoulder and guided him away. The X-Man cast a forlorn look back at Debs, who threw a tiny, helpless shrug in his direction before moving to join her colleagues at the door.

"It's just that I get claustrophobic," babbled Bobby as he was led from the atrium. "I'm starting to feel hemmed in. I think I need some fresh air."

"We'll try you out on the hardware," said Hendrickson gruffly. "If you're good enough, you can come out with us tonight. Did Debs tell you? We've got a mutate nest to burn out!"

Bobby swallowed hard, fell into step beside the heavyset man and said no more.

The laboratory was unguarded, but it was sealed by a reinforced door with a locking pad. Rogue scowled at the numbered keys, searching the fading memories of Aidan and June but finding that neither of them knew the combination.

She hadn't seen anybody on this underground level. Had she had more time, she could have waited in hiding until somebody came this way and opened the door for her. As it was, she was beginning to think that brute force was her only option. She would lose the element of surprise, though—and if Magneto was around, perhaps her life to boot.

Then, a third option occurred to her. She still possessed Aidan Morgan's telepathic powers, and his knowledge of how to use them. She let her mind drift from her body, shuddering at the weird, giddy sensation of disconnection. She felt like a ghost, tentatively feeling her way around a psychic landscape that corresponded to the shape of the building above her. She skirted around Magneto's throne room, knowing that his psychic defenses were prodigious. If her mind brushed against his, he would surely know about it.

A parcel of thoughts called to her with its familiarity, and she steered herself toward it. She recognized Jennifer Ransome: a mutate whom the X-Men had once liberated, now Magneto's chancellor. Rogue found herself looking through Jenny's eyes, thinking her thoughts—and somewhere, her own body drew a sharp intake of breath at the sudden change of perspective.

Rogue/Jenny was standing in a corridor, talking to a young man with short, brown hair and rugged, unshaven features. "I can't believe you're being so cynical about this," she said. "If you'd seen those two people . . . the Legacy cure saved their lives!"

"I don't doubt it," said the man, "but if Magneto plans to do nothing more than end the epidemic, then why does he need this 'Hellfire Club'? And why all the secrecy?"

Rogue/Jenny pouted. "Perhaps he doesn't want to raise our hopes until he's sure."

"He's keeping things from his own government!"

"Then perhaps he doesn't trust some of us. He has good reason!"

"And don't you think it's some coincidence that he's doing all this while his son is out of the country? Pietro wouldn't have let him lie to us."

"What's wrong with you, Phillip?" snapped Rogue/Jenny. "Do you *want* the mutates to keep suffering? Perhaps you want to follow in your father's footsteps after all!"

Phillip Moreau blanched, and Rogue felt Jenny Ransome's immediate contrition, and her love for this man. Phillip's father had been the infamous genegineer, whose surgical procedures had facilitated the oppression of a race—but Phillip himself had been instrumental in changing all that. When he had seen the magistrates taking Jenny away, when he had learned his family's evil secret, he had stood up and spoken out against the old regime.

"I'm just worried that Magnus is becoming too powerful," he said quietly. "When he came here, he promised to end the fighting in Genosha. If that's still his goal, then I'm behind him all the way. But I've heard how he talks about human beings, even those of us who work with him. I don't know what he'll do when he doesn't need us any more."

"I know," sighed Jenny with an apologetic half-smile. "I've wondered about that too."

Rogue had been riffling through the young mutate's memories, and now she found what she was looking for. She withdrew her psychic presence even as Jenny and Phillip fell into an affectionate hug. She had invaded their privacy enough, she felt.

"I just don't want us to go back to how it was before," said Phillip, "with one race victimizing another."

And then, Rogue was alone again, back in the basement and back in her own body. She hurried over to the lab door and used the last vestiges of her dissipating telepathy to scan beyond it, to see if she could expect a reception committee. To her disappointment, the lab must have been psi-proofed, because she couldn't sense anything at all within its walls.

"All right, girl," she muttered to herself, "here goes nothing!"

She tapped the four-digit combination into the keypad and stepped back, ready for anything as a mechanism whirred and the door finally slid open.

She swore under her breath as a figure stood revealed.

At seven feet tall with shoulders almost half as broad, he more than filled the doorway. His colossal bulk could be attributed to his containment suit: Rogue knew that inside the gold-plated armor existed a creature of pure energy, massed around a human skeleton. Behind a perspex chest plate, his ribs could sometimes be glimpsed through an atomic furnace. The plate connected to an equally transparent domed helmet, from beneath which a skull leered at her. Much to her regret, she had encountered this hulking engine of destruction before.

His name was Holocaust.

Bobby squinted along the sights of a rifle, his gaze tracking across a field of two-dimensional buildings. A figure appeared on a rooftop: a cardboard cutout of a mutate in a skinsuit, an orange flash of energy in his eyes. Gritting his teeth, he squeezed the trigger, and the gun whined as it fired a thin beam of light. The beam hit a sensor in the figure's head, and it fell backward. Bobby heard another cardboard target popping up to his right, and he shifted his aim and fired again. A third mutate appeared in a window, and then the figure on the roof was back. Next, a door flew open to reveal a woman in a magistrates' uniform; Bobby jerked his rifle around to cover her but, tempting though it was, he managed not to fire.

He had scored nine hits with nine shots, when suddenly his tenth target sprang out from behind a trashcan, much closer than he had expected. He leapt back, startled, as it hurtled toward him, carried by a concealed rail in the ground. The cutout was brought up short with a heavy clang, just a foot or two in front of his face, and he stared at it speechlessly as the main lights came back on and dispelled the red-tinted gloom of the practice range.

Hendrickson applauded as he stepped out of the shadows behind Bobby. "You did well," he said. "Very well indeed."

"I've always had a good eye," mumbled Bobby, still staring at the final target. In fact, he had spent many long hours in the Danger Room, the X-Men's hi-tech training facility, honing his reflexes and sharpening his aim. Of course, he was more accustomed to bombarding his targets with snowballs and ice darts than with bullets, but the principle was the same.

The only thing that had slowed him down was the bulky body armor beneath his dark green combat suit. He was used to having more freedom of movement.

"And don't worry about that last one. It takes most people by surprise. Just think of it as a warning: out there in the field, some of the mutates will be coming right at you."

"Thanks," said Bobby, grateful that Hendrickson hadn't guessed the true reason for his miss. He *had* been surprised, but not only by the target's sudden appearance: the Danger Room sprung tricks like that on him all the time. The reason he had hesitated, the reason he had been unable to fire, was that this target was more detailed than the others. And more familiar. Painted onto the cardboard was a rather good likeness of his teammate, Wolverine.

Tearing his eyes away from the worrying effigy, he asked: "So, do I get to go out with you tonight or what?"

Hendrickson smiled. "You're keen. I like that."

"And?" prompted Bobby.

"You're in. Frankly, you're too good to leave behind. Briefing at 1800 hours."

"And we leave at half past, right?"

"1830 prompt."

"I'll be ready."

Bobby tried to sound enthusiastic, but his insides were in turmoil. He had come to the conclusion that the fastest way out of this place was to go along with Hendrickson: the raid on the mutate "nest" was to take place earlier than he had expected. "Those freaks have the advantage at night," its orchestrator had explained. "Half of them can see in the dark, can't they? Anyway, according to our intelligence, they have some kind of evening gettogether. We can hit them when they least expect it, trap them in their own lair like rats!"

His plan was to abscond from the raiding party as soon as he could; with luck, he could still reach Hammer Bay by sunset. But where would that leave the people of this village; the mutates who were about to be slaughtered, and the humans who would die fighting them? He had been able to avoid thinking about it before. He had told himself he had more important things to worry about, that this was none of his business. But now, he felt involved. He felt as if he ought to do something—if only he knew what.

Hendrickson took the practice rifle from him and dropped it into a rack. "Now, let's see about getting you something a bit more useful, shall we?"

He led the way down another corridor, stopped at a heavy, triple-locked iron door and produced a bundle of keys from his belt. Most of the shelves in the armory were bare, but Hendrickson found an old rifle and dropped it into Bobby's hands. The X-Man stood quietly, feeling numb, as an ammunition belt was slung over each of his shoulders and a small silver grenade pushed into one of his belt pouches. "For emergencies only. We don't have too many of these left. They're like smaller versions of the sonic sphere: they let out a high-pitched shriek, which makes it impossible to concentrate. It'll stop the genejokes from using their powers for a minute or so—just long enough for you to make a run for it."

Further down the corridor, Hendrickson bobbed into a small storeroom and emerged with a magistrates' mask and cap, which he tossed to his new recruit. "Good fit?" he asked as Bobby donned them reluctantly.

"Not bad," said Bobby, his voice distorted by the mask's speaking grille. The skin of his face was prickling beneath the cold, hard metal.

"As soon as we get outside, you put that mask down, right? Those monsters will throw everything they can at you: fire, acid, all kinds of weird energy. You need to protect your skin—and there's a ventilator in there to deal with gas attacks. One of the local mutates can turn herself into a vapor and suffocate you—so you need the protection, believe me."

As they moved on, they passed a window in an office door. Bobby caught sight of his own reflection in the glass, and hardly recognized himself. He remembered what Wolverine had said before, about a mutate in magistrates' clothing. He had allowed himself to be turned into a symbol of oppression. Disgusted, he tore the mask from his face and let it hang from its strap around his neck. But what else could he do?

As they approached the main atrium again, Bobby heard voices raised in alarm, talking over each other. Hendrickson frowned and quickened his pace.

Debs's reconnaissance party had returned—at least, four of its six members had. Bobby almost bumped into one in the doorway as he was carried through by two other men, his arms draped over their shoulders. His combat suit had been shredded, he had lost his mask, his face was pale and dirty, and his eyes were closed. The other three were slumped against the consoles in the atrium, exhausted and probably hurt, surrounded by concerned colleagues.

Hendrickson's voice cut clearly across the babble. "What happened here?"

The answer came from several people at once. "Mutates!" "Gene freaks!" "They were ambushed!"

One member of the ill-fated expedition levered herself to her feet, although she was clearly in pain. "We lost Mark. They killed him. And . . . and David . . . he's hurt bad. . . ."

"And Debs?" Bobby stepped forward. He couldn't help himself. "Where's Debs?"

The woman met his yearning gaze for a second. Then, she lowered her eyes and shook her head despondently.

"What's happened to her?" The question emerged as an imploring cry.

"She went down," said a middle-aged man with dark hair and a moustache, who was sitting on the floor, his back propped up against a console, his rifle lying carelessly beside him. "Hit by an energy beam. She was alive, but we couldn't reach her. The gene-jokes must have her!"

"And you just left her?" Bobby made for the airlock door. "We've got to get back out there!"

Hendrickson placed a restraining hand on his shoulder. "Not yet, son. We've got a plan, remember? We attack at 1830. If we go off half-cocked before that, we'll just lose more good people—and we'll throw away everything we've worked toward."

"But Debs!" he protested hopelessly. "They've got Debs. What if they hurt her?"

Hendrickson shook his head sadly. "There's nothing we can do for young Debra just now, son. If the mutates have her, then she's almost certainly dead already. We have to accept it!"

If Rogue had learned one thing in the Danger Room, it was that hesitation could be fatal. She threw herself at Holocaust even as he was turning and stooping to fit his bulk through the doorway. She didn't—couldn't—think about how powerful he was, about the fact that he and a colleague had once given even Earth's most powerful team of super heroes, the Avengers, a run for their money. She cannoned into his golden armor, but it was like colliding with an ocean liner. She felt as if she had put her shoulder out.

Still, she must have taken Holocaust by surprise, because she got past him. Either that or he thought he would have more room to fight her in the huge, white, brightly-lit laboratory than in the narrow corridor outside. Rogue was still unsteady on her feet, still hardly aware of her new surroundings, when a mighty, metal-encased fist struck her from behind. She fell to the ground beside a lab bench, and Holocaust extended his left arm toward her. In place of a hand, he had a huge, dome-shaped attachment dotted with holes. Bright energy roiled inside it: the essence of Holocaust himself. His containment suit allowed him to channel his very being through this appendage, turning it into a devastating weapon.

"I am honored," said Holocaust mockingly, in his crackling, sizzling voice. "One of the X-Men themselves has come to challenge me. Any more of you lurking out there?"

"Just little old me, sugar," said Rogue, scrambling out from beneath his blaster. Holocaust didn't fire: he was toying with her. She had to take advantage of that. She vaulted over the bench and ducked down behind it. She heard her foe's footsteps pounding toward her, but she tried not to let that unnerve her. She slipped her fingers beneath the heavy wooden block and, with a strain, she lifted it and threw it. It shattered as it hit Holocaust, glass beakers smashing on the floor and papers fluttering everywhere.

That gave Rogue a second to get her bearings and glance around the room. There were shelves and cabinets everywhere, and all manner of equipment—most of which she couldn't even name—spread around the perimeter. She flew at the nearest cupboard and yanked open its doors, revealing rows of chemicals in vials. She batted the first rank aside, letting the vials fall and break where they may, but she couldn't see anything that looked like a cure. As if she would recognize it anyway, without a clear label.

She hadn't forgotten Holocaust. He had waded through her obstruction by now, and raised his weapon to fire. Rogue took to the air just in time. There was a tremendous *foosh* of energy, which seemed to set the world alight. And suddenly, the cupboard was burning, its spilt contents igniting easily, and that was one avenue of exploration lost to her.

Holocaust couldn't do that too many more times; not without a recharge. Even so, Rogue was no physical match for him. She had to keep out of his reach, keep baiting him, make him fire again and again. With each blast, he would become weaker. Unless, of course, he hit her. Then, he would replenish himself by absorbing her fading life force.

"You're working for Shaw again, right?"

"I'm working *with* Shaw."

"And here I thought you'd decided not to be anyone's poodle any more."

Holocaust came at her like a runaway tank. Rogue took to the air instinctively, but there wasn't enough clearance between his head and the ceiling. He filled her field of vision.

She threw a punch at him, aiming for the transparent part of his containment suit over his chest, hoping to crack it. The blow didn't seem to hurt him, but it forced him to take a step back. Rogue saw clear air beside him and hurtled into it. She wasn't the most maneuverable of the X-Men, but in his cumbersome armor, Holocaust wasn't quick enough to catch her.

She took shelter behind another lab bench, but he blew it apart with an energy blast. He was losing patience, thought Rogue. Either that was very good or very, very bad indeed.

"I was the heir apparent to a world once," he roared as he bore down upon her again. According to the X-Men's files, Holocaust hailed from an alternative version of Earth, although the details were sketchy. He had been the protégé of the man who had ruled that world, a powerful being known as Apocalypse. "I will have that again!"

"Sure," Rogue mocked him, "just as soon as you find the right set of coattails to ride to the top, huh?"

Holocaust's enormous fist left a dent in the wall behind her as she twisted past him again. But this time, he was ready for her. He caught her with a sideswipe from his arm, and she went into a tailspin and collided with another cabinet. Holocaust picked her up by the front of her sweater before she could get her breath back, and he batted her across the face with such force that it felt as if her neck were going to snap. She writhed in his iron grip, but she couldn't break it. He swung her around and threw her into a set of shelves. Rogue heard glass breaking behind her as, winded, she slid to the floor.

And then, Holocaust had her pinned, one giant foot resting on her chest, his hollow eye sockets seeming to glow as his lipless mouth twisted into a sneer and he brought up his weapon arm, slowly, tauntingly, and leveled it between her eyes.

"One less person in my way now," he growled.

And Rogue's vision was seared by a tremendous explosion of heat and light, for an instant before the world went dark.

CHAPTER 10

NEIN!" exclaimed Nightcrawler. *"Under no circumstances!"*
"Listen to me, elf," croaked Wolverine urgently, reaching up to squeeze Kurt's hand. "I've lost all track of time in this sickbed, but I know we've been here more than a few hours."

"It's almost five PM, local time," mumbled Kurt.

"Right. That means it's getting on for nine in Hong Kong, and—what?—eleven in Sydney. All points east of here, the Hellfire Club parties are already in full swing."

"I know," said Kurt, nodding ruefully. "Whatever Shaw and Magneto are planning, it could begin at any moment. But—"

"But nothing! You've got better things to do than nursemaid me."

As if to undermine his argument, Logan was gripped by another convulsion. His body went rigid, his spine arcing. Kurt's heart ached for the pain he must have been going through, but there was nothing he could do. He had watched this happen three times before, and the attacks were getting closer together. "Looks like this is it," Logan had said after the first convulsion. "The fight's stepped up a gear in there. Kill or cure, it'll soon be over."

He lay back now, panting, his face glistening with sweat. But as soon as he got his breath back, he continued as if nothing had happened: "Rogue and the kid might have reached Hammer Bay, or they might not. I'm still in no condition to hit the road again. You could be our last hope."

Kurt sighed. "I know you are right, *mein freund*—but the mutate Priest is suspicious of us already. If he finds I've flown the coop, he'll turn his attention to you."

"I can deal with old Skull-Face—and I won't let this damn virus take me out either. I'm a fighter, Kurt. I'll still be here when you get back."

Kurt forced a bittersweet smile. "You'd better be!" But he couldn't escape the nagging fear that he was talking to his best friend for the final time.

He felt he ought to say something more. A last goodbye, just in case? But Logan withdrew his hand, and said gruffly: "Go on—get out of here!" Kurt nodded gratefully, an unspoken affection and understanding passing between the two men.

And then, he heard the searing sound of an energy discharge, and a scream.

Rogue was teased back to consciousness by a smell like ozone and an insistent buzzing in her head. Opening her eyes, she gasped to find a familiar face in front of her: Magneto, dressed in his full battle robes and helmet. He must have shocked her awake.

For a second, she saw her old foe in a new light. Magnetic force rippled around him, almost visible and quite intoxicating. And she knew he would wield that force against anyone or anything that dared threaten his people. He was the only man who could protect her.

She realized that a lingering trace of Aidan Morgan had resurfaced inside her, distorting her perceptions, and she fought it down with a shudder.

"Fancy . . . running into . . . you here . . ." she murmured weakly.

Her face felt as if it had been sunburned. She didn't know why Holocaust hadn't killed her: whether he had been under instructions not to, or whether he had simply not had enough power left. Either way, she was grateful. She was in a small cell with a heavy door, which stood open behind Magneto. Her arms and legs had been spread behind her and clamped to the wall by thick metal tubes, leaving her to hang in an uncomfortable X shape.

"I did not spare your life to engage in small talk," said Magneto tersely. "I suspected, when I saw that only four of Xavier's children had made the journey to Sydney, that I would find more of you here. How many X-Men have invaded my country?"

"Actually," lied Rogue, "this is a solo mission. The Professor must have thought I was best placed to talk a bit of sense into you."

Magneto's eyes flashed. "We have discussed this tiresome subject before. You think we share a history, but we do not. You are thinking of another man."

"The man you used to be."

"That man has gone forever."

"Oh, I don't doubt that, sugar. I've seen into your mind, remember? I've seen how twisted, how screwed up with hatred, you've let yourself become."

"Think yourself lucky," Magneto growled, "that you—like my naïve doppelganger—have never had to witness the horrors I endured, never had to bathe in the fires that tempered me."

Rogue rolled her eyes. "Oh, here we go again! I'm sick of hearing how you can't be blamed for anything, how one bad experience in your childhood gives you the right to murder and maim as you please!"

Magneto's expression was incandescent. He slapped Rogue hard across the face, then tore back his sleeve to reveal a number tattooed on his arm. She winced at the sight of it. "You call this 'one bad experience'?" he blazed. "Do you think we should just forget that one race attempted to commit genocide against another?"

"I'm sorry," said Rogue, bowing her head. "But," she insisted, "it was normal human beings who fought against the Nazis and beat them!"

"And yet they continue to slaughter each other over land disputes, grievances so old that they don't even remember the causes and don't understand, or simply in the name of so-called 'ethnic cleansing'! No, we must never allow ourselves to forget humanity's potential for destruction, Rogue—for that way lies extinction!"

"And you think mutants are so much better?"

"We are a higher form of life, that much is unquestionable."

Rogue shook her head. "You don't think Apocalypse is as bad as any human war criminal? What about Stryfe, the mutant who released the Legacy Virus? Or Selene? Or for that matter, your new friend Shaw, a man who builds mutant-hunting Sentinels for the government? I've been in enough scrapes in my time to know that scum comes in all shapes, sizes and colors."

"Our kind has been systematically mistreated since we began to emerge. We have each had to fight back in our own way. You are not so different yourself."

Rogue was wrong-footed. "What's that supposed to mean?"

"You belonged to the Brotherhood of Evil Mutants, did you not? A group of freedom fighters—some would say terrorists—which I myself founded and christened ironically."

"I . . . I was young, then. I didn't know better. Mystique . . . "

"You were a victim of circumstance," said Magneto triumphantly, "a product, as we all are, of your upbringing. You experienced only hate, and you gave it in return."

"Until I chose to take responsibility," said Rogue. "Until I went to the X-Men."

"You had no choice," laughed Magneto scornfully. "You needed their help to control your abilities. And Charles Xavier indoctrinated you just as surely as Mystique had."

"That's not true!"

Magneto's face softened into a confident half-smile. "We shall soon see who is right and who is wrong. Oh, I don't imagine I can solve all our problems overnight—you are right about that much—but it will be interesting to see how our race develops without the weight of human prejudice upon us, don't you think?"

Rogue narrowed her eyes, feeling ice in her stomach. "What are you planning?"

"Let us simply say," said Magneto, "that I will not see another generation of mutants shaped by abuse!"

The mutates had captured a human being.

She was young and slender, with short, brown-black hair and a heart-shaped face. She was wearing a magistrates' uniform, but her weapons had been taken from her. A livid burn stood out on her temple from where, Kurt gathered, she had been winged by a blast of bio-energy while trying to break free. She was not struggling any longer.

They were taking her to the end cellar—a whole crowd of mutates, so thick that their captive was virtually carried aloft on the tide. As one woman said to Kurt, with a chilling certainty, "Our Priest will tell us what we ought to do with her."

Kurt tagged along with them as they poured into the chapel, because he had a very bad feeling about this. The Priest, already standing behind his altar, received his visitors with a serene expression, as if he had foretold their arrival. Not that it would have been at all difficult to hear them coming. The woman was pushed to the front of the crowd to allow the Priest to examine her. Despite her injury and his imposing height, she straightened her back and looked him mutinously in the eye.

"They were sniffing around Jasper Street," offered one of the mutates.

"Six of them, there were—all armed to the teeth!"

"But they ran like cowards when they saw us."

Everybody was talking at once now, offering their own version of events, and Kurt couldn't hear what anyone was saying. He began to make his painstaking way through the throng, slipping into gaps where he saw them. He had to be near the front. In case he was needed.

The Priest held up a hand for silence, and the clamor ceased immediately. He walked around the altar and drew closer to the prisoner, looming over her, his thin lips twisting into a smirk.

"So, young lady," he said in a quiet but threatening voice, "what is your name?"

She spat in his face.

A few people gasped, but the Priest's expression didn't flicker. He turned away and wiped his cheek with a white sleeve. "It hardly matters anyway," he said, "except perhaps to your next-of-kin. We know you well enough. We call you Oppressor. We call you Murderer. We call you War Criminal!" His tone sharpened further with each insult—and by the time he had finished, he was back behind the altar, his blue eyes as cold and hard as ice. "And soon, in the eyes of the Great Lord, our Savior, we will call you Dead."

"What has she done?"

Kurt Wagner's question cut across the general murmur of approval, and turned it into whispers of discontent. The Priest glared at him, his eyes narrowing as his brow furrowed. The front two lines of mutates parted to allow Kurt forward, and he found himself by the human woman's side. She looked at him quizzically, perhaps even hopefully.

"What has she done," he repeated, "to deserve execution?"

"If you were truly from Carrion Cove as you claim," rumbled the Priest, "then you would not ask such a question. You would know how the humans have treated our kind."

Kurt forced himself to ignore the ominous reaction behind him. He looked the Priest squarely in the eye as if challenging him to prove his suspicion. "Not all humans," he contested. "From what I hear, it was our people who struck the first blow in this case."

"We walked into an ambush!" the woman spoke up, obviously unwilling to let Nightcrawler do all her talking for her. "We were looking for food, and for that a good friend of mine was killed in cold blood! How dare you try to paint *me* as the murderer here!"

Her tone of righteous indignation did not sit well with the mutates. "Jasper Street is ours!" somebody made himself heard over the general hubbub. Somebody else added: "You walk into a mutate area, you deserve everything you get!"

"Since when did Magneto start divvying up streets?" the woman spat back at them. "I didn't see any signposts or fences out there!"

She was only riling them further. Kurt tried to calm things down. "Magneto doesn't want our two races to fight," he reminded the mutates reasonably. "Those days are over. He wants us to work together to rebuild Genosha."

He felt he might have got through to some of them, had it not been for the Priest. "And yet, this woman wears the uniform of a magistrate!" he announced with theatrical intonation. "She carries the weapons with which her people once subjugated and beat us!"

"For self-defense!" the woman protested angrily, but her words were lost beneath the roars of the crowd.

The Priest's raised voice, on the other hand, carried easily. "The Savior has forgiven many flatscans, that much is true. So long as they show repentance, He allows them to work for our country's greater good. But there are those who still feel nothing but contempt for our kind—and to those sinners, Magneto would have us show no mercy!"

The mutates were pressing forward now, gathering around the woman as if they intended to kill her there and then. Nightcrawler was left with no choice. He flung an arm around her, visualized the street above him and teleported. There was a moment of nothingness. Then, Kurt reappeared in exactly the spot he had just left. Beside him, the woman fell to her knees with a sickly groan. He was feeling the pain of another tandem 'port himself, but it was nothing compared to his horror at the failure of his ability, at finding that he was still surrounded by baying mutates.

"You are forgetting, Mr. Wagner," said the Priest, "that I channel our Savior's powers. He allowed me to detect your movement through the magnetic lines of force and, by redirecting them, bring you back to us."

"Traitor!" somebody shouted, and Kurt felt hands tearing at his hair from behind.

He fought back, but the mutates took the Priest's silence as a taciturn approval of the attack. They piled on top of Kurt, punching and kicking and spitting—and when he tried to teleport out from beneath them, he only returned to his starting point again. He doubted that the Priest was a match for his so-called Savior, but his magnetic powers were certainly formidable. Little wonder, then, that these people held him in such reverence.

And then, somebody's intrusive fingers found a pouch in his clothing—a pouch that couldn't be seen but could be felt—and dislodged the image inducer from within. As the device was ripped away from Kurt, the illusion of his blue and red skinsuit blinked out.

A collective gasp rose from the mutates as they pulled away from their victim, the better to see what they had just revealed. With malicious satisfaction, the Priest said: "My suspicions about Mr. Wagner were justified, I see. He is not one of us."

"I'm not the only person here without a skinsuit," said Kurt, but his cause was already lost.

"You are the only one who thought to conceal the fact," replied the Priest smoothly. "And what of your aspect? Is this too a deception? A disguise? Could these grotesquely distorted features be a human attempt to mock us, to hold us to ridicule?"

"I'm a mutant," said Kurt sullenly. "You know that. You've seen what I can do."

"Ah. A mutant but not a mutate?"

"My abilities evolved naturally. I am not from Genosha."

"Indeed not," said the Priest triumphantly, exposing his tombstone teeth. "This costume—" He ran a disparaging eye up and down Nightcrawler's red tunic. "—betrays your true nature."

"We still have much in common!" Kurt addressed the crowd imploringly.

"I hardly think so," said the Priest tartly. "You are an enemy of our Savior, are you not? An X-Man! A mutant terrorist who has pledged to overthrow Magneto's rule of Genosha."

"Th-that's not true," stammered Kurt, but his denial was met by hoots of scorn and derision. "I mean, I *am* an X-Man," he admitted, "but . . ." Nobody was listening any more.

"And he's brought the rest of his team with him!" shouted the human woman, to Kurt's surprise. She was standing again, her fists clenched defiantly. "I've already met one of them. You can do what you like to us, but it'll do you no good. The X-Men are going to bring that tinpot little dictator you call a Savior to justice! It's all over for you, you gene freaks!"

"Enough!" snapped the Priest, and there was silence again in the chapel. "The guilt of this man and this woman is only too evident," he continued after a suitably dramatic pause. "And there is more. I have been unable to heal our other new recruit, and now the reason why has become clear. He too is an X-Man, undeserving of our Savior's grace. Indeed, he has already been dealt the just fate of the heathen."

A ripple of fear passed through the Priest's attentive audience. He raised his voice. "Yes, Mr. Logan has the Legacy Virus—and Mr. Wagner here deliberately kept that fact from us. He brought his cohort here to us the hope that his filthy pestilence would spread. But he reckoned without the strength that our faith gives us, the protection that Magneto extends to the pure of heart and the true of deed." The Priest bowed his head and placed his hands flat on the altar before him. "I must meditate now. I must commune with our Savior, through the power of the magnetic fields, and learn what He would have us do with these sinners."

The Priest closed his eyes, and Kurt realized that this might be his last chance. He couldn't teleport, but he still had his natural agility and his other abilities. It was a long shot, but perhaps he could snatch the woman, leap to the ceiling and be out of here before any of the mutates could use their own powers against him. But even as he tensed himself, ready for action, he felt the air around him crackling and he was unable to move a muscle. The Priest, far from communing with anybody, was manipulating his magnetic field, paralyzing him.

The Priest's bald head jerked back up, and his eyes snapped open. The mutates waited breathlessly for his pronouncement. A bead of sweat trickled down the side of Kurt's neck.

"Our liege is pleased with us," said the Priest. "Through our diligence, we have confounded his enemies. Kurt Wagner will receive Magneto's personal attention: he is to be taken to the command center in Hammer Bay on the morrow. His friend has already been judged, and will not be allowed to pollute our clean air any longer. He will be sacrificed."

"You'd kill a man just because he's sick!" cried Nightcrawler. "How does that make you any better than the magistrates?"

The Priest ignored him. "The human woman has demonstrated her intolerance. She cannot be redeemed. We will not suffer her to live a moment longer."

The woman swore at him, but she didn't move. Kurt realized that she was held fast too. And then, the Priest turned to glare at her, and his blue eyes looked as if they were on fire. The woman's face turned pale and she bit her lip. She was in pain, but trying not to show it. The mutates backed away from her in awe, and Kurt could sense the charge in the atmosphere, could almost see the forces that were gathering to tear her internal organs apart.

He yelled his throat raw, appealing for reason, for mercy, to no avail. He strained to reach the Priest, just a few feet away from him, but he couldn't so much as move his hand. He couldn't even turn away, but he closed his eyes and offered a silent prayer Heavenward as the woman finally let out a piercing, gargling scream, which was abruptly curtailed.

A tear teased its way through Nightcrawler's eyelashes and welled onto his cheek.

Three strands of barbed wire had been strung across the end of Jasper Street, wrapped around streetlights on each side. Resting against the barricade was a wooden board on which somebody had scrawled "HUMANS KEEP OUT" in white chalk. And bound up in the wire was a bedraggled corpse, its magistrates' uniform in shreds, a bloody hole in its chest. A warning of a more graphic kind.

The man's name was—had been—Mark Jameson. His friends had come here, despite the danger, to see that he received a dignified burial. Everybody had agreed that, uncivilized as they were, the mutates would not have provided one. Hendrickson had been reluctant to send a rescue party out so close to his briefing, but feelings had run high and he had had little say in the matter. There were tears now, shudders of revulsion and dark mutterings about vengeance. One woman bowed her head and said a quiet prayer.

Iceman felt out of place, as if he were intruding upon their private grief with his combat suit and his rifle and his secret. He looked away, sickened, as Mark Jameson's friends began the painstaking process of detaching him from the barbs.

Bobby's job was to cover them as they went about their task. He lined up alongside another eight stoic sentries in an arc formation, and watched the lengthening shadows. "The genejokes will expect us to retrieve the body," Hendrickson had warned, "but they're unlikely to turn up in force. They know we'll be mob-handed, and they won't want to risk a major confrontation. They're cowards at heart." Even so, Bobby had been warned against the danger of a lone sniper. He wore his gas mask for protection. He wondered what he would do if he saw a mutate. His gun had no 'stun' setting. Could he bring himself to use it? He resolved to fire a warning shot first: he could always claim to have aimed for the target and missed. If that didn't work . . . then what?

He had no right being here at all. With time running out, he had finally overcome the biggest obstacle between him and his goal: he had found his way out of the humans' fortified base. He should have been halfway to Hammer Bay by now. He had had more than one chance to slip away on the short journey across the village.

But he couldn't stop thinking about Debs. She had been good to him, all things considered. He had liked her. He couldn't leave her to die. He had even tried to persuade Hendrickson to bring the attack on the mutates forward. The X-Men would have gone in now, however much it compromised their plans, because a life was at stake. Not that he could have said as much, of course. Nor had he been able to refute the cold logic of Hendrickson's argument. He had considered going after Debs alone, but it would have been suicidal—even if he could have sweet-talked somebody into telling him where the mutates' base was.

"It's good to see such fire in you," Hendrickson had said—a little patronizingly, he had thought. "Hold on to that, Drake. You'll need it against those genejokes tonight!"

That was when Bobby had realized what he must have sounded like: so eager to embark upon a mission which, not so long ago, he had been dreading. A mission alongside armed non-mutant human beings. A mission with the stated intent of killing their genetically gifted cousins. A mission against his own kind.

"All I care about," he had said just forty minutes ago, "is getting Debs away from those freaks before they hurt her!" In his anger, he had let the insult trip off his tongue. He hadn't thought about what he was saying, what the words meant. He felt ashamed.

And he didn't know what he would do next: when he had saved Debs—if he could—but in the process had become caught up in Genosha's civil war. When he tried to think about it, it felt like a black hole looming over his future, in which he could see no light. He felt helpless and afraid and frustrated at the senselessness of the whole situation.

But, for all his training, he couldn't think of a single way out of it.

Raul Jarrett was standing alone outside Magneto's throne room, wondering what he was doing here. He felt light-headed, and a pain was growing in the pit of his stomach—too little food and too much tension over the past two days, he supposed—but he didn't know what else to do.

Magneto hadn't said a word to him since Sydney. Perhaps Jarrett had incurred his disfavor somehow. He thought he had performed well enough when he had reported finding nothing in Shaw's rooms, when he had deceived his leader—but Magneto was the Savior, all-powerful, and Jarrett still couldn't shake the fear that he could see into his heart and mind.

Perhaps the Savior had seen his doubts. Perhaps he had seen how the revelation of his plans had disconcerted him. Perhaps he was disappointed in his subject.

Magneto, Jarrett told himself, knew what was best for the mutates. It was not his place to question his wisdom. But he remembered how he had suffered with the Legacy Virus, and it seemed cruel to inflict such suffering upon others. Not that some of the humans didn't deserve it—particularly those ex-magistrates and politicians who had fled Genosha before they could be punished—but many had done nothing wrong. It was likely that they only wanted to live in peace, but Magneto was about to drag them into a war. Raul Jarrett knew how that felt.

He had not expressed his opinion, of course. He had followed the Savior wherever he led—and, when Magneto had strode into his throne room without dismissing the wretched mutate, the door swishing shut behind him, he had thought it best—perhaps safest—to wait. In the absence of further instructions, however, he was beginning to feel tired and foolish.

He was glad to see the friendly face of Jenny Ransome, his former nurse, as she turned into the corridor. She frowned at him as she reached the throne room door, and asked what he was doing here. He explained, falteringly, as best he could, and she thought for a second before drawing him conspiratorially to one side.

"You've been spending a lot of time with Magnus, haven't you?" she said. It felt odd to hear the Savior referred to in such a familiar way. Jarrett nodded dumbly, and Jenny asked: "Has he said anything to you? Did he tell you what his business was in Sydney?"

"Um . . . well, he didn't say anything *to* me. . . ."

"But you do know?" she asked urgently.

Jarrett felt his blood freeze. Was she trying to trick him, to prove Magneto's suspicions about him? She was a member of his government, after all; surely she knew what was going on? But his gut instinct said otherwise—which, in some ways, was worse. He had already betrayed his leader for Sebastian Shaw, now he was being asked to do so again.

"I . . . I don't . . ." he stammered, glancing reflexively at the closed door.

"Come on Raul," she said, smiling sweetly. "You wouldn't be telling just anybody, would you? You know you can trust me."

"I don't know if I . . . the Savior . . ." He longed to tell her, to share his concerns with somebody who could reassure him and make things better. But all he could think of was the four X-Men who had dared to oppose Magneto, trapped in the metal sculpture.

"I know he's mass-producing the Legacy cure—but there's something else, isn't there?"

Tears pricked at the backs of Raul Jarrett's eyes. "Please don't make me . . ." he whimpered.

And then, the door slid open, and Jarrett jumped and almost cried out as Genosha's sovereign towered over his chancellor, his expression grim. "Do you have something to say to me, Jennifer?" he asked in a cold voice.

"I . . ." She hesitated. "Yes, Your Eminence. Yes, I do."

Magneto nodded curtly and stepped aside to allow her past. As the shadows of the throne room swallowed her, he turned to regard Jarrett with dispassionate eyes as if wondering what he were still doing here. "I have no further need of you, Raul," he said finally. "You may return home."

"I . . . I don't have a home, my liege."

"I see," murmured Magneto. Then, out loud, he said: "See Mr.

Moreau. He will arrange accommodation for you. And Mr. Jarrett?"

He stiffened, his heart beating fearfully.

"I can rely on you, I hope, to forget anything you may have seen or heard recently?"

"Y-yes, my liege," stammered Jarrett, nodding enthusiastically as he backed away.

As soon as the throne room door had closed again, he turned and ran. But he didn't get far.

The muscles in his legs were aching, and he wanted to be sick.

Nightcrawler had been taken to a dusty cellar corner, almost walled in by high shelves. Here, his wrists had been bound behind his back with sturdy cord, and attached to a set of pipes which led to an old boiler. His image inducer had been destroyed and his hidden comm-set taken from him. Then, the Priest had lowered a dome-shaped metal helmet onto his head, and Kurt had winced as he had felt slender needles piercing his scalp.

"An old magistrate device," the tall man had said in his baritone voice. "I never imagined I would find a need for it, but we live in strange times. It blocks certain nerve signals. It will prevent you from using your special abilities or, indeed, removing the helmet itself." With a smile, he had added: "After all, I cannot give you my undivided attention all night, can I?"

Kurt had made another plea for his friend's life, but it had failed as he had known it must. "Do not worry," the Priest had sneered. "You will have an opportunity to bid farewell to Mr. Logan. You will be our guest at this evening's service, during which the purification of his soul will take place. In the meantime, Louise will take care of you. She's a telepath, you know. So, be assured that I will know immediately if my presence here is required."

Louise, it transpired, was the gray-haired woman with whom Nightcrawler had spoken at breakfast: the one with the baby, although she must have left Magnus with somebody else while she was on guard duty. She took her assignment seriously: she sat straight-backed in a wooden chair at the point where the shelves gave way to the rest of the cellar, and she stared fixedly at him.

When Kurt's stomach rumbled to remind him that he hadn't eaten all day, he cast a wan smile in her direction. To his disappointment, she blanked him completely.

He cleared his throat. "That woman probably had a family, you know."

Louise said nothing.

"Brothers and sisters. Parents. A child, perhaps. Or a husband."

Still no response.

"I wonder how they're feeling now. I wonder if they're waiting for her to come home. Jumping at every sound. Beginning to fear the worst, but still hoping against hope."

Her silence might have been a good thing. Her jaw was clamped shut, and she had shifted her gaze to stare past him. As if she couldn't allow herself to hear him. As if she feared that his words might have an effect.

Kurt went in for the kill. "Is that how you felt when Michael was killed, Louise?"

Louise's eyes flicked toward him, just for an instant before she forced them away again. She drew in a deep breath.

"That was his name, wasn't it? Your baby's father. You must miss him very much." Kurt wondered how much time he had. The evening service was at half past six; it had to be some way past five now.

He had made his point. It was time to try another tack. "I've met Magneto, you know," he said casually. This time, Louise's eyes remained upon him. She didn't quite believe him, he could see that. "Many times, in fact. He was an ally once."

"You are lying!" she snapped.

"Our goals are not so very different. The X-Men, like Magneto, want equality for mutants. It is only over our methods that we disagree. He thinks to achieve peace through the use of deadly force, but history tells us that he can never be successful. There is a fine line, *mein liebchen*, between a freedom fighter and a terrorist."

"Magneto knows what is best," she said automatically. "He is the Savior."

"He is a man, Louise, that is all. A mutant."

"No!"

"He may have great powers, but that doesn't make him a deity."

"He was put on this Earth to end our suffering! You're lying! You're lying!"

"I'm telling you the truth, Louise. Magneto's origins are the same as yours and mine."

She shook her head furiously, her hands over her ears. "I will not hear this blasphemy!"

Kurt shouted at her, angered by her unwillingness to listen: "His name is Erik Lensherr. He is a survivor of a Nazi death camp, scarred by his experiences. The X-Men first encountered him when he launched an unprovoked assault on a military base in America. The last time I saw him, he had caused almost irreparable damage to Earth's electromagnetic field, threatening all life on the planet. You're a telepath, Louise. Look into my mind, and tell me then that I am lying to you."

There were tears in Louise's eyes now, but her glare was mutinous as she jumped to her feet. "I don't care what you say," she shouted back, "and I don't need to read your thoughts. I know the truth!"

"You know what your Priest has told you—but he's using you, Louise. He'll say whatever it takes to maintain his own power over the mutates. Why can't you see that?"

"If it weren't for Magneto, I wouldn't have my son!"

"He controls magnetic fields," scoffed Kurt. "He can't create life!"

"He is our Savior, and I won't let you persuade me otherwise!"

"Are you so narrow-minded that you won't even consider another point of view?"

Louise's expression hardened, and she scowled at Nightcrawler with a steely determination that he hadn't imagined she could possess. She drew herself up to her full height, and said primly: "I am not narrow-minded, Mr. Wagner. I simply have faith!"

The words hit him like a crossbow bolt to the heart.

He had lost his temper with her, frustrated by her stubborn insistence on clinging to her own worldview in defiance of all reason. But how would he have reacted himself in her position? Could he have constructed a logical rationale for his own religious beliefs? Of course not: his faith was an instinctive thing. He couldn't prove the existence of his God—but he would have refuted to his dying breath the suggestion that Jesus Christ was just another man.

"The difference between my God and yours," he said quietly, "is that mine wishes me to not to kill, especially not in his name. There is no greater sin."

"It is people such as you and the humans who cause all the suffering and death in the world. Magneto only exacts divine retribution. He brings justice."

"He has blood on his hands," said Nightcrawler, "as will all the mutates if you stand back and let your Priest murder my friend." But it was hopeless. He knew now what he was up against, that this was an argument he could not win.

And from that moment on until the Priest came for him, he said nothing more.

CHAPTER 11

MOST people thought of her as efficient and ruthless, without conscience or feeling. But those people didn't know the real her. Nobody did. She had worked hard to build a façade around herself, and to maintain it whatever the circumstances, whatever the cost.

If anyone had read her mind now, if they could have seen her agonizing uncertainty, they wouldn't have recognized her. They would have wondered what she was doing, standing alone in this corridor with her ear pressed up against a closed door. She could hear nothing from the room beyond. The X-Men had been prisoners for many hours now, and they had run out of things to say to each other. She could sense their presence, though. Her mind brushed against theirs—just a light touch; nothing that they, without the powers of Phoenix, could have detected—and she knew they had given up hope. They couldn't escape the trap in which Magneto had placed them. Not without some form of outside intervention.

She wondered if she could help them.

Her name was Tessa. She had no surname: she had left it behind a long time ago, along with her old life, when she had joined the Hellfire Club.

She had been a teenager, then. She had spent most of the inter-vening years at the side of Sebastian Shaw. She had come to know him as nobody else did, as few ever had. Away from him, she had no existence. And in turn, she had earned his rare trust. She hadn't used her psychic powers to manipulate him—she hadn't dared be so overt—but she had been able to read any suspicions in his mind and act to quell them. Shaw had never realized quite how power-ful a telepath she was. She had had to be. Her own mind had been probed several times by Hellfire Club members such as Selene, Emma Frost and Madelyne Pryor. She had always been able to conceal her true self from them. Sometimes, she had had to bury it so deeply that she had become, in thought as well as deed, the woman she pretended to be.

She had had to make many tough choices. In order to prove her loyalty to Shaw, she had done things of which she wasn't proud. But she had known, when she had accepted this assignment, that it would be difficult. And lonely. Not even the X-Men knew that their founder had also recruited Tessa, and sent her on a mission deep undercover. Charles Xavier had foreseen a time when the Hellfire Club would become a major threat to the world. Her job had been to keep him appraised of its activities—and, only when it was absolutely necessary, and when she could do so without jeop-ardizing her cover—to intervene.

Tessa had saved the X-Man Psylocke from the organization's clutches, but she had been unable to do the same for Phoenix. She hadn't known about the original Mastermind's plans for Jean Grey until it had been too late. If she had been able to anticipate the outcome of those plans—the accidental unleashing of the creature known as Dark Phoenix—she would have acted sooner. She didn't want to make the same mistake again.

But things had changed recently. She didn't know why, but her relationship with Shaw had felt strained ever since his trip to the future. It had been a subtle shift in his manner, at first, and the odd stray thought. She had hoped it was unimportant but, without knowing exactly what he had seen, it was impossible to be sure.

She had considered probing his mind, but he had built up his defenses to the point where that would have been extremely dangerous.

And then, he had challenged her about Emma Frost—as if he had expected her betrayal, her passing of his secrets to the erstwhile White Queen. He had appeared to accept her explanation this time, and he had said nothing more about the matter. But his trust in her had been eroded, and that made her position increasingly untenable.

It would have been easy for Tessa to do something. Almost too easy. She could steal into the mind of the young mutate Miranda, and alter her perceptions. Miranda would believe that she was maintaining her dampening field around all four prisoners, but in reality it would have shifted just far enough for one X-Man to regain his or her abilities. A month ago, she could have done it, and Shaw would never have suspected her involvement. The X-Men's escape would have been blamed on a momentary lapse on Miranda's part. Now, it was likely that he was watching her, waiting for her to prove to him what he already suspected.

He had not confided his plans in her. In itself, this was not unusual, but it presented Tessa with a problem. Storm and the Beast had been right: she had no doubt that Shaw planned to turn on Magneto somewhere down the line. Perhaps he had the situation in hand, in which case she would be foolish to risk exposing herself. But what if he intended to wait until after the Legacy Virus had been spread and lives imperiled? What if he made his move only for Magneto to second-guess and defeat him?

And what if he was counting on Tessa to free the X-Men behind his back? The Black King considered himself an expert reader and user of people, and that was just the sort of game he might play. Perhaps that was why he hadn't appeared too concerned when she had brought the mutant heroes into play in the first place. Perhaps this was a test for her: a test that he expected—and needed—her to fail.

It would have been easy for Tessa to do something.

But what if she made the wrong move?

The party had been in full swing above Cyclops's head for at least two hours. A regular drum beat and the sound of conversation, muted by the ceiling, had lulled him into a fitful doze. As he surfaced now, chiding himself and wondering how he had been able to sleep no matter how tired he had been, he realized what it was that had coaxed him awake.

He could sense Jean in his mind again. He smiled at her loving telepathic touch. *You're back,* he said to her without speaking.

I don't know why, she confided, *and my psi-senses are still weak—but at least I can feel them again.* She sounded overjoyed; Scott realized that, for her, having her mind imprisoned in her own body must have been like being blinded.

My optic blasts aren't working, he reported. *The dampening field must still be in force, it simply isn't affecting you. Are you strong enough to deal with Miranda by yourself?*

I don't think she even realizes what's happened yet. I'm going to try stimulating her sleep centers. She probably won't read that as an attack, in which case she might not think to rectify whatever it is that's gone wrong.

Good plan!

Cyclops waited tensely as a minute passed, and then another. He could still hear the beat of the music upstairs, like a clock ticking down the seconds until midnight. They had to be approaching the final hour now. But in this small, well-lit room, nothing seemed to happen.

Then, finally, Miranda's head began to nod, and she let her book fall into her lap and took a deep yawn. She looked over at the captive X-Men, and for once, Cyclops was glad of his visor because it concealed the fact that he was staring at her intently, willing her to succumb to Phoenix's psionic manipulation.

The Beast, hanging between Scott and Jean, must have noticed something or picked up on a change in the atmosphere, because he threw a questioning glance in his leader's direction. Miranda, fortunately, did not appear suspicious. She yawned again, and her head nodded onto her chest. She probably thought she could rest her eyes for a moment—but Phoenix had other plans, and soon the loudest sound in the room was that of Miranda's rhythmic breathing.

A minute later, Cyclops's eyes began to burn again.

"Well done, Jean," he breathed. He twisted his head to look up at the band of metal that held his left arm in place. His wrist was bloodied and his sleeve torn from his previous attempts to break it. He aimed carefully at the manacle and closed his fingers, tapping a palm stud to activate his visor. He opened it only a fraction, allowing a pencil-thin beam of energy to escape but concentrating all his power into that beam. At first, he feared it wouldn't be enough, that he was still too weak. But the beam grew in strength with each second away from Miranda's influence, and it began to cut through the metal like a laser.

It took Cyclops another five painstaking minutes to free first his left leg and then his right arm. He was able to drop the short distance to the floor now, and stoop close to his remaining trapped limb. At such close range, he could risk a wider-angled blast, and he made short work of the thick loop of metal that encircled his leg above the knee. By now, the Beast had removed a constricting band from across his chest, and one from around his arm, his restored strength augmented by Phoenix's telekinesis. Ignoring the shooting pains of pins and needles in his hands and feet, Scott helped them to finish the job. It took less than two minutes, after that, for the combined efforts of the three X-Men to pry Jean loose.

Once they had stepped away from the sculpture, Storm could act at last. Three forks of lightning stabbed through the air, targeted precisely to explode her bonds at their weakest points. Anyone still touching the conductive metal would have been electrocuted; anyone but her. A beatific expression settled upon the weather elemental's face as she soared free, and the smell of ozone filled the small room.

"What now?" asked Phoenix.

"Now," said Cyclops, "I think it's time we brought an end to the festivities."

He led the way through the corridors of the Hellfire Club building, relieved to find them empty. Music still played in the ballroom, but most of the well-heeled guests had spilled out onto the verandah and down toward the harbor. The trident display, Phoenix had learned from Shaw's mind, was to be set off from the roof, so she and the Beast headed up there to stop it. A grandfather clock told Cyclops and Storm that it was half past eleven: time enough to deal with the situation here, but what about the other parties across the world?

They created a stir as they raced out into the warm night, Storm spreading her black and golden cloak and taking to the air. Some people didn't notice them at first—or, filled with alcohol, were slow to react to their appearance—but others gasped, and more than one glass was dropped. Cyclops shouldered his way through the crowd, faster than it could part for him: he had to find Shaw and Tessa before they knew what was happening.

Fortunately, from her vantage point, his teammate had already spotted one of their targets. A powerful updraft caught Tessa's old-fashioned black ball-gown and lifted her into the air, where Storm was waiting for her. The trick to dealing with the Black King's assistant was to keep her off-balance, unable to concentrate to use her telepathic abilities. Her physical strength was no greater than that of any normal human being: now that Storm and Tessa had closed in hand-to-hand combat—and in the air, at that—the battle would be brief and the outcome in no doubt.

Cyclops knew where to head now: it was unlikely that Tessa would have strayed too far from her employer. Sure enough, he soon spotted Shaw being hurried away by concerned guests, along with a man and a woman who must have been members of Sydney's own Inner Circle: non-mutant members, hopefully. In a sea of monkey suits, the anachronistic finery of the fleeing trio was hard to miss.

As he went after them, some people tried to intercept him. He handed off the first three with ease, but their example inspired others to find their courage. A wide but low-powered burst of energy from his eyes shocked, discouraged and scattered them.

Cyclops caught up to his prey even as Shaw reached the front of the Hellfire Club building. He waded through the Black King's would-be bodyguards, spun him around, seized him by the ruffled front of his shirt and slammed him against the French windows, an arm across his throat. The expression on Shaw's face was thunderous.

"Go on," growled Cyclops in his ear. "Fight back! Show these good ladies and gentlemen what you can do. Let them know that their precious club is really run by mutants. And give me an excuse to wipe the floor with you!"

Shaw glared at him for a long moment before composing himself and readopting his familiar smirk. "I do not intend to fight you, Mr. Summers," he said. "However, I am afraid I cannot speak for all my associates."

Without relaxing his grip on the Black King, Cyclops turned his head to find Lady Mastermind behind him. He unleashed an optic blast, which struck her in the chest—but as she fell, she metamorphosed into a stunned partygoer in an elegant white frock. An illusion. And now, because he had fallen for it, the crowd was beginning to panic.

He cast around for a glimpse of his true foe—and saw her, striding unhurriedly toward him. She was wearing a black gown: the same one, Scott realized, that Tessa had been wearing. And she was carrying Storm, slung unconscious across her shoulders. The onlookers drew away from her, unsure who she was and what she was about to do. If this was an illusion, then everybody could see it this time. Even so, Cyclops held his fire, his fingers hovering over his palm stud, until he could be sure. He couldn't risk hurting another bystander.

Lady Mastermind stopped a few feet in front of him, and dropped his teammate. "Poor, confused Storm thought she had picked up Tessa," she smiled. "Imagine her surprise when I switched the concepts of up and down in her mind. She saw the ground coming toward her, and tried to pull up. The result was quite spectacular. Fortunately, her body gave me a soft landing."

"Whatever you do to me," said Cyclops, setting his jaw determinedly, "I'm ready for it. I'll know it's not real. I won't let go of Shaw."

Lady Mastermind laughed. "So sure of that, are you, X-Man? So sure you know what is real and what is not?"

And suddenly, Cyclops could feel the manacles around his wrists and the ache in his muscles again. "No . . ." he whispered to himself as a cold realization enveloped him.

"Oh yes," she said, "I'm afraid it's true. You never escaped from Magneto's trap. You're still there."

And he could see it now: the plain walls of the room breaking through what he had thought of as reality. He could feel the metal at his back, see Miranda at her guard post again. Shaw, the Hellfire Club building and the late-night revelers faded away, and the only thing that remained constant was her: Lady Mastermind, regarding him with malicious glee. "Did you really think you could escape us? I have enjoyed toying with you, X-Man; giving you false hope only to snatch it away. But now, the time for games has past."

"Are you all right, Scott?" asked Phoenix, still trapped as he was. "What did she do to you? What did she make you see?"

"Whatever it was," lamented the Beast, "I fear it will pale in comparison to the real-life horrors about to be unleashed."

Cyclops's eyes widened. His throat felt dry. "What time is it?" he croaked.

"Midnight," said Lady Mastermind with satisfaction.

And even as she spoke, Scott heard the dull crump of an explosion from somewhere above him, and knew what it had to be. The first trident firework. The first Legacy bomb.

A door loomed ahead of the Beast, but he could already hear the bolts on its far side being drawn back: Phoenix had employed her telekinesis without breaking her step. Likewise, Hank shouldered his way through the obstruction as if it weren't even closed, and the two X-Men burst out onto the flat roof of the Hellfire Club building.

They were greeted by the true face of the organization: the face that most of its members never saw, but with which they were only too familiar. The uniformed agents, a dozen in all, were concealed from the guests below by a waist-high parapet. They were gathered around a rocket-shaped firework, four feet tall, held vertical by an A-shaped metal frame. A long fuse dangled ominously from its lower end.

As the heroes had hoped, their sudden entrance had taken the mercenaries by surprise: they were scrambling to their feet, still reaching for their guns, when the Beast threw himself at them, tucked in his arms and legs and barreled through them like a bowling ball.

I'll keep the goons occupied, Jean telesent to him as he landed nimbly beside the A-frame. *You see to the rocket.*

She was gesturing with her hands, causing rifles to spring from their owners' grasps or their barrels to bend back upon themselves. But some of the agents had set their sights on the Beast. He delivered a roundhouse punch to one, toppling him into the man behind him and avoiding a retaliatory strike with a deft handspring, which also gave him the opportunity to plant his foot in another man's face.

"Excuse me sir," he said, catching sight of an agent with a tool belt slung around his waist, "but could I trouble you for a short loan of your screwdriver?" The agent swung the butt of his bent rifle at the X-Man, but Hank ducked beneath it and plucked his prize from its pouch. "Thank you," he said as he straightened and sent the bemused technician reeling with an uppercut to the jaw, "and goodnight!" Two more men tried to rush him, one from each side—but he dodged their blows, planted his hands on their shoulders, pushed himself upward and bounced off their heads, somersaulting over the rocket to land on its far side.

Thus distanced from the melee, Hank began to disassemble the pyrotechnic device, using his claws to pry loose its plastic shielding and the screwdriver to disconnect the circuit boards within. The rocket had an onboard processor: Shaw and Magneto had spared no expense to ensure that the evening went with a bang, so to speak. It was a delicate task—he couldn't afford to upset the rocket's payload, nestled in its plastic heart—and not for the first time, the Beast cursed the big, clumsy hands that his mutant gene had given him.

He tried not to let the sound of gunfire distract him, even though he heard an awful lot of it. There was a limit to how many bullets his teammate could deflect until, exhausted, she failed to see one coming in time. Nevertheless, he also heard a satisfying number of male grunts and cries, and the smack of flesh against flesh, as Phoenix kept her foes off-balance and hurtling into each other. Even those who were able to reach her were doubtless learning that, for all her psionic prowess, she had not neglected her physical training.

It was when the agents *stopped* firing, Hank supposed, that he would have cause to worry.

He could see a test tube now, so small and slender. He threaded two of his clawed fingers through the workings of the rocket and gingerly took hold of it, willing himself not to tremble, not to place too much pressure on the fragile glass. The tube looked empty, but its invisible contents were deadly. He realized that he had begun to sweat. Holding his breath, he manipulated the tube until he had dislodged it from its molded cavity.

All he had to do now was draw it back toward him.

And then, a Hellfire Club agent came flying through the A-frame, splintering it. The rocket fell one way, and the Beast the other as a head cannoned into his stomach.

Sorry, came Jean's abashed telepathic voice. *Slip of the mind. No harm done, I hope?*

Lying on his back, Hank felt the tube in his hand, and lifted it to his eyes. He felt as if his heart wouldn't beat again until he had dared to look at it—but, miraculously, it was intact and still stoppered. Relief washed over him.

Until the fallen mercenary kicked his hand and sent the test tube flying out of it.

The Beast let out a horrified cry as it described an arc toward the edge of the roof. Pushing his muscles to their limit, he practically leapt into the air from a lying start, but the mercenary tripped him. Perhaps he didn't know what he was doing. Or perhaps he thought that, if the trident firework couldn't spread the Legacy Virus into the atmosphere, then at least it could be released at ground level. Perhaps he expected to gain Shaw's approval for his quick thinking. Perhaps he would even be granted a measure of the vital cure.

In the end, the agent's motives didn't matter. It took the Beast a second to get past him—and that was a second too long.

He reached the parapet, looking out over the lights of the harbor. Closer to him, and two stories below, he saw the heads of Shaw's guests—and the test tube, disappearing between them. Time seemed to have slowed down, the tube dropping in slow-motion; even so, there was no way to reach it before it shattered on the flagstones.

And then, incredibly, its fall was reversed. The tube sprang back up toward Hank as if attached to an elastic cord, and he reached for it, but it sailed past him and into Phoenix's hand. She was standing at the parapet beside him, and she flashed him her radiant smile. Behind her, he saw that the last Hellfire Club mercenary had fallen.

And then, from below, he heard Cyclops's voice: an agonized howl of "Noooo!"

The X-Men's field leader was almost directly beneath the Beast, at the building's French windows. His arms were spread out behind him, and his knees slightly bent as if something were restraining him. To one side of him was Sebastian Shaw; to the other was Lady Mastermind—it took Hank a moment to recognize her out of costume—with Storm lying unconscious at her feet. Clearly, she was the cause of Cyclops's distress.

The Beast vaulted over the parapet without stopping to think twice. He slowed his descent with a somersault and made to land lightly on his feet. But he hit the ground an instant before he expected to, unprepared for the sudden impact, which jarred his bones and made him lose his footing. Later, when he had a moment to think, he would realize that Mastermind had seen him coming and cast an illusion, making him believe that the ground was further away than it was. Right now, he was just grateful not to have broken a leg. He was still trying to get his breath back when he became the target of ten or more party guests, emboldened by his fall. They leapt upon him, punching and kicking and spitting racial slurs. He kept his head covered with his hands until he saw a way through them. He propelled himself through one man's legs, tripping him in the process and bringing down three more like dominoes.

While the Beast was still on his hands and knees, somebody hit him from behind with a walking cane. He winced and turned on the culprit, seizing the weapon on its next downward stroke and using it to pull himself to his feet before knocking it aside contemptuously. He was still a little shaky, but the mob were a lot less gung-ho now that their target was no longer on the ground. Hank bared his fangs, hoping to bluff them into keeping their distance. Two of his erstwhile attackers simply turned tail and fled.

And then, he felt an explosion inside his head, and before he knew it, he was on his knees again. It was a supreme effort to prop his eyes open, to keep himself from toppling onto his face. Somebody had invaded his mind.

And, looming over him, he saw her, a smile on her lips and a sadistic glint in her eye.

It was Tessa.

Shaw spun Cyclops around and punched him in the face. The X-Man staggered, looking bewildered as if he didn't know where he was or what was happening to him. He was obviously still in Lady Mastermind's thrall, trying to reconcile what he was feeling to what he could see and hear. Shaw punched him again, obviously relishing this show of force, and Cyclops went down.

Watching from above, Phoenix narrowed her eyes and formed a field of psycho-kinetic energy around the Black King, lifting him away from her husband. Now, it was his turn to be confused as his feet pedaled air and his arms waved helplessly, not knowing what to do to maintain his balance. By the time he was level with her, however, floating on the far side of the low parapet, he had adjusted to his situation. He clenched his fists and glared at Phoenix furiously, but there was nothing he could do.

"Why don't you try your luck with someone who can fight back, you loathsome little man?" she snarled.

"Gladly, my dear," he growled in return, "if you would only put me down."

"I might just do that," she said, "and faster than you expect."

Shaw said something else, but Phoenix wasn't paying attention. She was talking to Cyclops through their telepathic link. He was just getting to his feet, but Mastermind had him believing that he was surrounded by a dozen past and present members of Shaw's Inner Circle. He raised his hands slowly, but Jean could read his thoughts as he worked out who was the weakest member, the one to target as he made his break.

Scott, listen to me! she urged him. *Whatever you're seeing, whatever you think is happening, I want you to fire a half-strength optic blast at ten o'clock . . . now!*

He didn't hesitate for a second. He snapped his head around to the ten o'clock position and unleashed the power of his eyes. A scarlet energy beam thudded into Lady Mastermind's chest, taking her by surprise, and she was thrown backward to land in a crumpled heap.

Most of the guests had dispersed now, terrified as the violence had escalated, and Phoenix could hear police sirens approaching. She turned her attention to Tessa, but Storm had already woken, and a lightning bolt struck the ground beside the novice telepath. Startled, Tessa leapt back and lost her psi-grip on the relieved Beast. He jumped up and dispatched her with two quick blows, catching her as she fell and laying her down gently. As Storm carried Cyclops up to the roof, Hank scaled the building himself, finding toeholds in the window frames and brickwork.

By the time the police arrived, the four X-Men had relocated to another dark rooftop, several blocks inland. Phoenix had dragged a reluctant Shaw along with them, and he scowled mutinously at each of them in turn as they encircled him.

"We've disarmed your bomb, Shaw," said Phoenix triumphantly, displaying the seemingly empty test tube. "We'll be taking this back home with us to dispose of it safely."

He responded with a deliberate shrug. "There are many more."

"We should return to the Blackbird," suggested Storm, "and contact Professor Xavier. He can send reserve teams to find and dismantle some of the other devices, while we deal with the ones nearest to here."

"You can't possibly reach them all in time," sneered Shaw.

"He's right," said Phoenix. "There's less than twenty minutes to go before midnight."

"But the time difference gives us an advantage," said Cyclops. "The fireworks are meant to form a chain between Hellfire Clubs across the world, from east to west. The next one must be at the branch in Hong Kong. Midnight won't strike there for another two hours. In the Blackbird, we could make that deadline with time to spare."

"At the risk of dampening your optimism," said the Beast, "the

Hellfire Club also has headquarters elsewhere in that time zone: in Perth, in Western Australia."

"And Hong Kong is Shaw's home base," said Phoenix gloomily. "He's unlikely to have left it unguarded." She glanced sharply at the Black King, but his face gave nothing away.

"We still have a chance," insisted Cyclops. "Even if we can't reach all the devices in time, we can deal with most of them."

The Beast shook his head. "Regrettably, it would not ease our predicament. This particular strain of Legacy was engineered to be highly contagious. If a single capsule is released into the atmosphere, then the consequences will be no less certain, albeit slower to ensue, than if they all are. Unless the United Nations were both willing and able to place entire countries in quarantine, the infection would spread worldwide."

"It hardly bears thinking about!" said Phoenix.

"And presumably," said Storm, "even if we could reach all the devices in time, there's nothing to stop Magneto from releasing the virus another way?"

"Indeed not," said the Beast. "He would merely have to break open a capsule such as the one that Jeannie is carrying—and he could do so tomorrow if he wished, in any city that took his fancy. We would have robbed the Hellfire Club of its grandiose gesture, its macabre joke upon the world—and we might have slowed Magneto down—but no more than that."

"Then there's no other option," said Cyclops. "We have to take back that cure. If Magneto doesn't have sole possession of it, he can't use it to blackmail anyone. Perhaps he'll even forget this mad scheme altogether."

The Beast looked at Shaw. "I don't suppose he left a sample of the serum with you?" The Black King's lips tightened into a thin line. "No," sighed Hank, "I didn't *think* that sounded like our old and trusting friend."

"Shaw can still help us though," said Cyclops.

Shaw raised a quizzical eyebrow. "And what makes you imagine I would want to? I think I know you well enough to dismiss any intimations of violence toward my person."

"Nevertheless," said Storm, "the X-Men could do a great deal of harm to your reputation, and to both the Hellfire Club and Shaw Industries, were we to put our minds to it."

"But let's skip the threats," said Cyclops. "You'll come to Genosha with us because you intended to turn on Magneto all along—and, whatever your plans were, we've put a spoke in your wheels. If you want to stop him now, you'll have to do it our way."

Shaw inclined his head slightly as if in agreement.

"What's the plan?" asked Phoenix.

"We fly out in Shaw's private jet: it's almost as fast as the Blackbird, and it should get us into Genoshan airspace without being attacked. After that, we take everything Magneto can throw at us—and we get that cure from him, whatever we have to do. With any luck, our team on the ground might also have learned something we can use."

"We know that, when they arrived in Genosha last night, Magneto wasn't present," said the Beast thoughtfully. "Perhaps they were able to make some headway—or even discover the whereabouts of the cure—in his absence."

"Perhaps," said Cyclops grimly, "but I used my comm-set to contact the Blackbird's onboard computer on the way over, and they haven't radioed in. Until we hear otherwise, we have to assume that we're on our own."

Tessa had a headache, but the detective wouldn't stop asking questions. She squirmed impatiently in Sebastian Shaw's seat, behind his desk, as the thickset man with short, graying hair appeared to copy her every word into his notebook in tortuous longhand.

She had recovered consciousness just as the police cars and an ambulance had arrived, and she had immediately sent a telepathic instruction to the leader of Shaw's squad of mercenaries to keep his men hidden. She had assured an anxious paramedic that she needed no treatment, driving home the message with a gentle mind-push when he had proved infuriatingly insistent. She was on the verge of resorting to such methods again.

"How many more times do we have to go through this, Sergeant Grace?" she sighed. "I don't know where the mutants came from, and I don't know what they had against the Hellfire Club, if anything. They appeared to be fighting each other; perhaps we simply got caught in the middle of an internecine squabble."

The policeman nodded. "I can see that, Miss, er . . . Tessa, but I'm still worried about these reports from some of your guests that a . . ." He referred to his notes, slowly leafing back two pages. ". . . Sebastian Shaw—your employer—was carried away by one of these mutants."

"I told you," she said tersely, "I saw Mr. Shaw myself after the attack, and he was perfectly unharmed. Your men were already on the premises—I'm surprised you missed him."

"I would still like to speak to him, Miss Tessa," said Grace, "just to tie up my notes."

"He had urgent business to attend to. He was forced to leave."

"At midnight?"

"The Hellfire Club is an international organization, Detective Sergeant. It is still morning in New York. I will ask Mr. Shaw to call in at your station as soon as he returns. In the meantime, he has authorized me to answer your questions." Tessa got to her feet impatiently. "So, unless there is something else . . . ?"

Grace remained stubbornly seated. "You must be able to contact Mr. Shaw?"

She was about to give him a tart answer when the door to the office opened, and Regan Wyngarde strode in. Tessa's eyes widened in alarm at the sight of her, brazenly wearing her combat leathers—but the policeman smiled and stood to shake her hand.

"There will be no need for that, thank you, Tessa," she said. "I have been able to reschedule my appointments. Under the circumstances, I thought it best."

"Sebastian Shaw, I assume," said Grace—and Tessa smiled to

herself as she peered into his mind and saw the fiction that Lady Mastermind had created for him.

Grace asked a few more questions, and Tessa fed the answers to Lady Mastermind telepathically, ensuring that they tallied with her own—and, just as importantly, that they were short and to the point. She breathed a secret sigh of relief when Grace finally acceded to being escorted out of the building by the person whom he believed to be Sebastian Shaw. She had better things to worry about than an inquisitive policeman.

By now, Cyclops, Phoenix, Storm and the Beast were no doubt on their way to confront Magneto. She only hoped that they could stop him from committing an atrocity, and that their escape hadn't hindered any plans on Shaw's part to do likewise. Encouraged as she was, however, by this turn of events, she couldn't help but wonder about one thing.

The X-Men, Tessa was sure, couldn't have got free by themselves.

So, if she hadn't helped them—who had?

CHAPTER 12

IN his fever-induced dream, Wolverine was fighting for his life.

He was surrounded by his greatest foes: the feral killer known as Sabretooth; Lady Deathstrike, who had turned herself into a part-machine creature for the sole purpose of destroying him; Magneto, even. The list was endless. They came at him from all sides, punching, clawing, biting—and no matter how many times he hit them, how many times his claws sliced through their flesh, not one of them fell.

The reverse, however, also held true. He was battered and bloodied, his costume and the skin beneath it torn. One of his eyes was half-closed by a purple swelling and at least two of his ribs were broken. But Wolverine fought on.

Dimly, through a red haze, he recognized that the dream mirrored his immune system's real-life struggle against the Legacy Virus—and the knowledge spurred him onward, doubling his determination to be the last man standing.

There was an animal inside the man called Logan, and sometimes it scared him. Sometimes, he felt he didn't belong with the X-Men, couldn't adhere to their simplistic moral code—but it was they who had helped him bring the animal under control. No matter how many times he had thrown their naïve compassion back in their faces, they had not given up on him. Without them, he might have lost all reason by now, given in to his savage side. He had been there, and he didn't want to live like that.

Sometimes, however, the animal was a source of strength—and he gave in to it now. He let his mind sink into a tar pit and his instincts take over. He didn't think about what he was doing, he just put all his heart and soul into the savage fight for survival.

He was only half-aware of being woken, of skinsuited mutates bending his arms behind him. He lashed out blindly as if they were the villains from the dream—and if a tiny part of Wolverine's mind sensed that something was wrong, then it was overwhelmed by his satisfaction as his attackers fell down and didn't get up again.

His triumph didn't last long. His limbs became rigid and his spine snapped straight, jerking his head up. Something propelled him forward until he collided with a wall. He was spread-eagled against it, his face pressed into the wet stone, unable to make his arms or legs move—and, temporarily bereft of reason, he couldn't work out why any of this was happening. He let out a bestial howl, expressing his frustration in the only way left to him. And then, his arms were pulled behind his back again, only this time he couldn't feel any hands upon them, nothing to push against.

He howled again as his wrists were thrust together and he felt cord biting into them. But, at the same time, his body was wracked by another convulsion. Agony sliced through him as his muscles spasmed and tried to double him up but his paralyzed backbone resisted.

Wolverine's eyes rolled back into their sockets, a milky whiteness giving way to the dark.

But he didn't stop fighting. Racing out of the shadows around him were the immortal mutant known as Apocalypse, the armored Silver Samurai, and a hundred other hate-filled faces from his past. He extended his claws, twisted his lips into a snarling, beserker grin and ran to meet them.

Nightcrawler had almost worked his bonds loose when the Priest arrived to collect him. Under his hawkish scrutiny, two mutates refastened the cord around the prisoner's wrists before untying it from the boiler pipes. The Priest took the trailing edge, and Kurt was forced to bite back his resentment as he was led away like a dog on a lead at the head of a ragged procession. With his hands tied behind him, he had to keep up or be dragged along backwards. He thought about making a break for it—even with the inhibitor helmet on, he still had his natural agility—but he had to see Logan first.

He stooped his head to follow the Priest through the hole into the chapel. The smell of the scented candles hit his nostrils, their smoke blurring his vision. And as he straightened again, his heart skipped at the sight of an unconscious Wolverine splayed across the altar on his back. His teammate's wrists and ankles had been bound to the legs of the sheet-covered table, and thick straps lay across his shoulders, stomach and hips, leaving his bare chest exposed.

"He put up quite a struggle, your friend," said the Priest out of the corner of his mouth as he walked slowly up the central aisle, the mutates filing in and finding seats behind him. "He killed one of my flock and injured three more. They have been placed in quarantine, of course, lest Mr. Logan has spread his unholy infection to them."

"And what will you do if he has?" asked Nightcrawler bitterly. "Will you kill them too?"

"The Legacy Virus only takes hold in the infidel. My people, I am confident, will pass this test—but those who fail will be cast out. Nothing is more contagious than sin, Mr. Wagner."

They had reached the end of the aisle now, and the Priest stooped to lash Nightcrawler's cord to a front table leg, just below Wolverine's limp hand. "The best seat in the house," he murmured with a ghoulish smile.

Kurt glared at him, but the Priest returned his hostile look with equanimity as he took his place behind the altar. "You didn't tell me that Mr. Logan's skeleton is laced with metal," he said in a conversational tone. "It would have saved me a certain amount of inconvenience had I known earlier. It certainly made him much easier to control than I expected."

"That's all you're really interested in, isn't it?" said Kurt. "Controlling people. You and Magneto are much alike in that regard."

"Thank you," said the Priest.

"It was not a compliment."

"I am sure it was not. I know about this group of yours, Mr. Wagner, these X-Men. I know that, in your own way, you even believe that you are furthering the cause of mutantkind."

"Then why—?"

The Priest's voice hardened. "Because you do not have the vision to do what must be done—and in opposing those who do, you cause as much harm as the most ignorant flatscan."

"And you're doing all this to 'further the cause of mutantkind,' are you?" said Kurt hotly. "These people are as enslaved to you and this so-called religion you've imposed upon them as they once were to the human government."

"Think yourself lucky, Mr. Wagner, that you do not share your friend's fate. In Magneto's eyes, you are not yet beyond redemption. He has not infected you. When I take you into His presence, you would do well to fall to your knees and thank Him for His mercy."

"Yes," murmured Nightcrawler, regarding the Priest through narrowed eyes. "That's what this is all about, isn't it? Your triumphant arrival in Hammer Bay tomorrow. Magneto will certainly be interested to know that you've killed one X-Man and taken another captive. You'll come face to face with your God at last. And what will you ask of him, I wonder?"

"I share his knowledge of the power of magnetism, and today I have proved myself worthy to wield it. I will sit at the Savior's right hand as his trusted lieutenant."

Kurt saw the zealous fire in his foe's eyes, and he realized for the first time that the Priest really believed what he was saying. He responded with a sardonic smile, which exposed his fangs. "Magneto does not have lieutenants, *mein freund*," he said, "only servants."

The chairs had all been taken now, and the last few mutates were climbing into the room and taking up positions along its sundered back wall. At an abrupt gesture from the Priest, the low buzz of excited conversation ceased, and a deathly, expectant hush fell.

He spread his arms wide, tilted his head back and intoned: "My friends: this is a special day for us. As we gather here to give thanks to our Savior, we have been granted an opportunity to prove ourselves worthy of His love. This mutant—" He glanced down at Wolverine, his thin features twisting in contempt. "This X-Man," he spat, "has already been marked out as a sinner. He has been made unclean. It is our duty now to dispatch him, to disperse his spirit upon the magnetic force lines that it can be born anew." He reached into his white robes and pulled out a polished dagger. Its wooden handle had been carved into the shape of Magneto's winged symbol, and painted in blood red. As the Priest raised it above his head, candlelight glinted off its wicked blade. Nightcrawler tensed. Bound and powerless as he was, he had no chance against the Priest, let alone his followers—but he couldn't stand back and do nothing.

"Let the touch of metal purify this tainted soul!" bellowed the Priest.

And as he began his downward stroke, Nightcrawler sprang, the cord around his wrists snapping tight and forcing him into a backward somersault as his legs swiped sideways across the altar and his feet caught the Priest in the stomach. A gasp rose from the congregation, and several members jumped up as their spiritual leader fell back, winded, and dropped his weapon. Kurt, meanwhile, landed awkwardly back where he had started, and saw the ceremonial blade on the floor. He tried to grip its handle between his toes, but the cord stretched to its limits and he couldn't quite reach it.

And then, the dagger was snatched from the floor by a Priest incandescent with fury, still not able to stand quite upright but advancing upon the X-Man with a murderous expression. Nightcrawler twisted out of the way of his first thrust, and managed to trip him. But, as his foe picked himself up again, he found himself paralyzed as he had been before, caught in an unbreakable magnetic grip.

"Kill me," he said in a strained voice, "and you lose your audience with Magneto."

The Priest was shaking, struggling to contain his fury—but he appeared to win the battle. He let the hand that held the dagger drop to his side, and he closed his eyes and took deep, calming breaths. Then, without another word, he strode back into position to complete the sacrifice—and as the mutates settled back onto their chairs, sweat beaded Kurt Wagner's brow and he realized that he couldn't delay the fateful moment any longer.

He would have to watch Wolverine die as he had watched the human woman die, helpless, literally unable to lift a finger to stop the murder of his best friend.

But at that moment, an explosion resounded through the mutates' base, and startled most of the congregation out of their seats again. Even the Priest must have been taken by surprise, because Nightcrawler felt control of his own body returning to him. For now, he bided his time, sub-vocalizing a quick prayer of gratitude for the timely intervention.

The Priest recovered quickly. "My friends," he cried, rounding the altar and brandishing his dagger, "we are invaded!" And the explosion had indeed seemed to come from the base's main entrance in the centermost cellar of the long row. "The heathens choose this holy time to attack us, thinking to disrupt our prayers—but it is precisely because we have the blessing of Magneto already that they will not defeat us!"

Galvanized by his words, the mutates roared in agreement and began to pour out of the chapel, squeezing through the entrance hole two and three at a time.

The Priest stood and watched them go, offering his encouragement and the blessings of their earthbound deity, but he made no move to join them. For the moment, however, he had his back to his two captives and appeared to have forgotten about them. Nightcrawler looked desperately for a way to capitalize upon this temporary respite, but saw nothing.

Until, to his surprise and delight, he heard a familiar *snikt* sound, like a pair of knives clashing together, and he turned to its source.

Wolverine hadn't moved. He looked as if he were still unconscious, his skin pale and his breathing shallow. But from the back of his right hand—the hand nearest to Kurt—he had extended a single adamantium claw.

Quickly, Kurt shifted around so that the Priest, if he turned, wouldn't see what he was doing. He pulled his wrists as far apart as he could and felt for the claw behind him, resting the taut cord on its sharp point. And he began to cut himself free.

There were butterflies in Iceman's stomach as he waited, along with a thirty-strong raiding party, at the door of a mid-terraced house in a narrow street. Hendrickson had slipped into the building, and he attached a disc-shaped explosive device to the cellar door before returning to the entrance and counting down the seconds with controlled impatience.

The explosion deadened Iceman's ears: he hadn't expected it to be so fierce. Clearly, Hendrickson had wanted to make a statement. He had blown the door from its hinges, well and truly announcing the humans' arrival. And, even before the smoke began to clear, he was plunging forward and shouting to the others to follow him.

They clattered in single file down a flight of wooden steps, some of the keener and more athletic among them vaulting the banister rail to reach the floor faster. There were no mutates in the cellar, but—as Hendrickson had conjectured in his briefing—the walls to each side had been knocked through into other basement rooms. The humans split into two groups, taking up positions around each of the rough-hewn doorways. Bobby went to the left, and strained to see into the shadows cast by the dingy light of bare bulbs. Even as his eyes were adjusting, as he became convinced that there was nobody in the next cellar either, he heard footsteps behind him, and Hendrickson's voice: "Here they come!"

And the magistrates' rifles began to bark. "Like shooting fish in a barrel," somebody commented.

Hendrickson had been right again. The mutates must have been gathered in a room somewhere to the right of the main entrance. As they rushed to investigate the explosion, they were easy prey for the humans, who were already in position, well covered and waiting. They couldn't all crowd around the hole at once, but their onslaught was nevertheless relentless: as one person emptied his magazine, he rolled out of the way and let somebody else take his place while he reloaded. Most of Bobby's group crossed the cellar to join their colleagues, but he stayed put. He didn't want to shoot anybody. A lump formed in his throat as he listened to cries and screams that he couldn't do anything about. He began to wonder what he was doing here, and the only way he could answer that question was to fix an image of Debs's face in his mind.

The mutates had the measure of the situation now, at the expense of several lives. They had found their own defensive position, behind the next wall along, and they returned the humans' fire across the intervening cellar. Bobby jumped as a blast of red bio-energy ricocheted from the brickwork beside him. But, at a nod from Hendrickson, three humans hurled teargas grenades, and smoked their foes back out into their sights. Bobby was grateful for his mask as some of the gas drifted back toward him, tinting the air green.

Suddenly, Hendrickson was by his side: even with his mask in place, his heavyset form, the stripes of rank on his uniform and his gruff voice were unmistakable. "Nobody this side?"

"No sign of activity, sir," reported a woman next to Bobby.

"Four of you, get down there. Make sure the place is cleaned out from here to the far wall. I don't want any of those freaks sneaking up behind us."

Bobby volunteered for that duty, because it got him away from the front line and allowed him to explore half the base. Perhaps he would find Debs. Along with three of the humans, he advanced cautiously through the next cellar and the next, probing each corner but finding nothing. His colleagues were rather more enthusiastic about the search, overturning furniture and breaking the legs off tables and chairs with their rifle butts. They dashed cups and plates to the floor, beat the stuffing out of mattresses and tore any clothes they found.

In the third cellar, behind a row of wine shelves, they found four beds. Bobby's stomach tightened as he saw that the furthest two were occupied. Two bodies were covered from head to foot with white sheets, which—compared to those found elsewhere in the base—were clean and fresh. He approached the first one on his tiptoes, heart pounding in his ears. Nudging the sheet aside with the barrel of his rifle, he revealed a mutate corpse. It was a middle-aged man with ridges across his forehead, and Bobby felt bile rising in his throat as he saw that he had been crudely eviscerated as if by the claws of a wild animal.

"We're wasting our time," said a woman behind him, her sudden voice making him start. "It's a mutate morgue. We should get out of here before we catch their filthy disease."

"This man didn't die from the Legacy Virus," snapped Bobby. "It looks more like he was killed by one of his own." Or one of *our* own, he thought. But how was that possible?

"Who cares? So long as the freak's dead!"

Bobby took a deep breath and bit his tongue as the woman marched away. A third member of the quartet followed her, but a young man—about Bobby's age, as far as he could judge through the combat uniform—hesitated. Bobby threw him a grateful nod, glad to have his back covered as he approached the final bed. He had to see who lay beneath its sheet. He had to see if it was Debs.

But even as his fingers brushed against it, the sheet was flung back, and Bobby let out a startled cry as a short woman with black feathers all over her body sprang out from beneath it. She hit his chest with both hands, hurling him into the wall, and he tried to bring up his rifle, not intending to fire but hoping that the threat would be enough. But something knocked the weapon from his hands and sent it skittering across the floor—and an instant later, he felt the blow of an invisible fist to his head.

He looked for his remaining colleague, but he too had come under attack. A wiry mutate in an orange skinsuit had been clinging to the ceiling above him, half-concealed by a support beam. Bobby was just in time to see him land on the young man's shoulders, wrapping his supple legs around his chest and his arms around his throat, and clinging tight.

And then, his first opponent came at him again, screeching like a bird of prey, her talons slashing across his chest and making him thankful for his body armor. Reflexively, he covered his face with his hands and tried to fight his way through her. She gave ground with surprising ease, and Bobby saw for the first time that she was bandaged around her stomach and that a spreading stain was darkening the white dressing. These people must have been patients here. They had hidden when they had heard his group approaching. He felt a pang of guilt: by exposing them, he had forced them into a fight that they hadn't wanted.

Hacking at her foe again, the bird-woman cut through to his skin. Out of the corner of his eye, Bobby saw his own rifle being raised as if by telekinesis and turned upon him. There was no time for regrets; nor could he disguise his true nature any longer. If he didn't fight back with everything he had, these people would kill him.

He formed a hard shell of ice around his magistrate costume, just in time to protect himself from another swipe of a talon. He bombarded both his foes with a fine hail of snowflakes, momentarily blinding the bird-woman and revealing the feminine outline of his invisible assailant so that, even as her first shot went awry, he was able to locate her and knock her down. He whirled around, intending to deal with the flexible mutate next—but even as he did so, his young colleague slumped to the ground, his neck broken.

And at that moment, the other two humans rounded the end shelf, and skidded to an astonished halt as they took in the tableau before them.

"It's Drake!" the woman screamed. "He was a stinking genejoke all along!"

And they brought up their rifles and fired indiscriminately into the infirmary. Iceman threw himself to the floor between two beds as the invisible mutate was hit by a bullet that hadn't been meant for her and flopped beside him, losing her transparency in death. The bird-woman screeched in fury, shrugging off a shot to the shoulder as she flew at her attackers, talons outstretched. And the flexible mutate avoided the bullets altogether, taking a prodigious leap onto the far wall and bouncing off it to hit the human woman from behind.

Bobby didn't know what to do, which side to fight for. All he knew for sure was that every one of the combatants wanted him dead. But then, as he lay there on the dirty stone floor, he realized what lay beside him, beneath the final bed in the row: another sheet-wrapped corpse. And he reached for it with trembling hands, feeling a hammer blow to his heart as he unwrapped it and found himself staring into Debs's blank, dead eyes.

Several seconds passed before he could think again, before it occurred to him that the battle had ended. All he could hear was the not-too-distant sound of shouting and gunfire from the main entrance. It sounded as if the mutates had broken through to the central cellar, taking the fight to their attackers. Looking under the row of beds, Bobby saw the shapes of motionless bodies, but he couldn't identify them all.

His rifle lay beside him, dropped by the invisible woman, and he picked it up and rose to his feet cautiously. To his surprise, nobody tried to kill him.

He counted five corpses. It took him a second to realize who was missing—and when he did, he looked up in alarm, even as the flexible mutate dropped toward him from the ceiling. He reacted with well-honed reflexes, clubbing the mutate with his rifle and throwing him off-course. The orange-clad man twisted in midair to land on his feet, and sprang for his enemy with lightning speed. He wasn't strong, but he was fast: he landed punch after punch, but somehow managed to wriggle out of the way of every one of Iceman's own blows. It was all the X-Man could do to keep the mutate's questing hands from his throat.

And every time he threw a punch, he was doing it for Debs, picturing her dead eyes in his mind—and with each miss, he became more and more frustrated, a fiery pressure building in his chest and demanding release.

Somebody had let off a sonic grenade. Hendrickson's group must have been in trouble. Even at this distance, the piercing shriek drilled into Iceman's head and threatened to drown out his thoughts. Everything but the image of Debs. He gritted his teeth and fought on, sweat dripping into his eyes—or was it tears?—as he abandoned any attempt to think faster than his foe, and just lashed out at random and hoped for the best.

To his immense surprise, the mutate was suddenly wrapped around his gloved knuckles. Perhaps the sonic attack had distracted him too, made him careless. Whatever the reason, Iceman had the upper hand. He consolidated his success with a good head shot, and the mutate toppled backward and fell like a wet sack. Momentarily, Bobby wondered if he had hit him too hard, but in that hate-filled instant, he really couldn't have cared less.

He stood astride his fallen, dazed foe and jammed the end of his rifle into his head as the world around him became one endless, agonizing scream and he was barely aware of anything else. "You killed her, you bastards!" he yelled over the relentless siren. "You killed her!" There were tears on his cheeks, and his hands were shaking.

And the mutate was looking up at him with saucer-wide eyes full of fear.

And then, the siren broke off, but the silence that replaced it seemed somehow louder as if reality were crashing back in around Bobby Drake's ears. And he realized what he was doing, and it filled him with horror and revulsion.

Shuddering, he flung the rifle as far away from him as he could, and helped the suspicious mutate to his feet. "Go on," he mumbled, unable to meet the gaze of his erstwhile adversary. "Get out of here, and keep running. Go!"

The mutate didn't stop to question his change of heart. He ran. And, when a weary and emotionally-drained Iceman rounded the end of the wine shelves a moment later, he was just in time to catch a glimpse of an orange back heading away from the main entrance. He frowned. Was the mutate looking for a hiding place deeper into the base? Or was there a way out down there? So far, the entrance to every cellar he had been in had been well and truly sealed—but it made sense that the mutates would have left themselves an emergency exit.

He made a decision. With Debs gone, he had no reason to be here any more. He would do what he should have done hours ago, when he had first had the chance.

The sounds of battle from the entrance had lessened. Either the fight was coming to an end or the humans had pulled back to regroup on the street as per Hendrickson's contingency plan. The two sides were determined to tear each other apart, each blaming the other for their rotten lives, and the tragedy of it was that neither of them was right or wrong. Iceman could even understand, now, how they had been driven to this. But, whatever the reason, he knew that nothing he could do would stop them.

So, reluctant as he was to do so, as miserable as it made him, he turned his back on them.

And he walked away.

* * *

Wolverine's enemies lay dead around him.

He didn't remember felling them, but it didn't matter. It only mattered that he had won. He stood in the darkness and watched as their bodies faded back into the shadows from which they had come. He was panting and flushed from his exertions, and his rational self was resurfacing. He was able to think again, to be aware of his situation beyond the immediate need to kill or be killed. Sometimes, it seemed that every time he gave in to his animal side, his real self faced a harder climb to reestablish dominance. Sometimes, it seemed that the animal must be his real self after all.

He needed to rest now, to let the darkness swallow him. But not for too long. There were other battles yet to be fought. Out in the real world.

He felt hands at his shoulders, coaxing him awake. He felt as if he had slept his deep, healing sleep for many hours, but it had probably been only minutes. He opened his eyes, and smiled to find his best friend there again, undoing the straps that held him down. He could hear fighting, not far away but not too urgent.

"Don't try to move," said Nightcrawler. "Go back to sleep. I'll get you out of here."

He smiled. "Think you can lug my metal-reinforced carcass about, elf?"

"As far as I must."

"No need. Check out the war wound."

Nightcrawler glanced at him as if he thought he might be delirious. Then, gingerly, he peeled back the bandage from his side. Wolverine lifted his head just far enough to see the expression of delight on Kurt's face. *"Unglaublich!"*

"Closed up, huh? I figured as much," he said triumphantly. He had been able to feel that his healing factor was working again, but it was good to have it confirmed. "Looks like this old body still has some fight left in it after all. We won this one."

"By the skin of our teeth. How are you feeling?"

"Exhausted, and weak as a kitten—but fantastic!" He tried to stand, but his stomach muscles felt like over-stretched elastic. He grimaced. "Might need a hand getting up, though."

"*Sehr gerne,*" said Nightcrawler, "on condition that you do something for me in return."

"The headgear?"

"I can't remove it myself. As soon as I reach for it, I lose control of my arms."

Wolverine closed his eyes and fought down a dizzying head-rush as he was hauled to his feet. He lifted the dome-shaped metal helmet from Nightcrawler's head, then he leaned against the altar and took in his candlelit surroundings. His gaze alighted upon the mutate Priest, who lay facedown in the aisle, and he turned to his friend with a quizzical look.

"Much as he might like to believe otherwise," said Kurt, "he is far from being another Magneto. Our old foe could not have been taken by surprise as he was. He would have sensed my approach through his magnetic field."

Wolverine saw something on the floor beside the Priest's bald head: a heavy, golden ornament in the winged shape of Magneto's helmet logo. He grinned wryly.

At that moment, a short, thirty-something woman with gray hair stumbled into the chapel, a wailing child in her arms. Her face was blackened, her eyes red and puffy, and she was coughing fiercely. She carried with her a whiff of teargas, which made Logan's nose wrinkle. She was halfway up the aisle before she saw the unconscious Priest, at which point she stopped dead and turned pale with fear.

"Louise!" exclaimed Nightcrawler.

"What have you done to him?" she cried. "I need him. My Magnus needs him!" The woman's concern for her baby seemed to override her fear of the X-Men: she hurried forward and fell to her knees at the Priest's side.

Kurt bounded up to her, his face a picture of concern. "Let me see him."

The woman recoiled. "Get away!" she screamed. "I don't want you infecting him."

"I don't have the Legacy Virus, Louise," said Kurt evenly. The woman glanced suspiciously at Wolverine. "And nor does my friend, any more."

"She doesn't want our help," growled Logan, "fair enough. Let's get out of here!"

But Kurt was kneeling beside the woman, reaching out to her imploringly. "He isn't breathing, Louise. Give him to me. I can help him."

She hesitated for long seconds. She looked down at the Priest, but it was obvious that he wouldn't be stirring for some time. She looked into Nightcrawler's yellow eyes—and, although she didn't hand Magnus over, nor did she resist as Kurt took him and laid him on his back across a wooden chair. She brought her knees up to her chest, weeping, as the X-Man breathed into her baby's tiny mouth.

"I left him in his crib," she sobbed, "just during the service. I didn't think he'd come to any harm. I didn't know the flatscans would attack. I couldn't reach him! If they've hurt him . . ."

"*Gott sei Dank!*" breathed Nightcrawler, throwing his head back with a relieved grin. Wolverine could see that the baby's chest was rising and falling again.

Kurt handed him back to his mother, who wrapped her arms around him, tears still flowing. "He was so special. I thought he was blessed. A little miracle. How could the Savior turn his back on a child? He's so young—what could he have done to deserve this?"

"He breathed in a little teargas, that's all," Kurt tried to console her. "He should be fine now." But his words didn't seem to have an effect. "You should get him checked out at a hospital," he persevered, "just to be sure. You do have hospitals here, don't you?"

Louise shook her head miserably. "They can't help us."

And suddenly, Wolverine thought he knew what she was crying for.

She turned to him and, hesitantly, as if afraid to hope, she asked: "Is it true? Are you really . . . clean now? Can you make him clean too?"

He shook his head sadly, and watched the light in her moist eyes die.

"How long have you known?" asked Kurt quietly.

"He's had the sniffles for a week. And . . . and last night, I noticed a rattle in his chest. I . . . I tried to deny it at first. I kept telling myself it was only a cold. I should have brought him to the Priest, I know, but I thought he . . . I was scared he might. . . ."

"Every kid gets a runny nose from time to time," said Wolverine gruffly.

"Logan's right," said Nightcrawler. "You mustn't assume the worst."

"Would your God see this happen, Mr. Wagner?" asked Louise with sudden clarity. "Would your God allow an innocent child to suffer and die?"

It was a question that Kurt couldn't answer. Logan saw the pain in his expression, and had some idea of what was going through his head—and his heart.

"Don't wait for the Priest to wake up," said Kurt finally. "Take Magnus to a hospital. They can test him for the virus and treat him if . . . if the worst happens."

Louise nodded, tears welling from her eyes again. "I know my faith hasn't been strong enough, and perhaps I am being punished for that. But if Magneto can only spare my child, if he can take me instead, I swear I will never doubt Him again."

Wolverine stepped forward. "Listen, darling—" he began. But Nightcrawler silenced him with a gentle hand on his arm.

"Don't take her faith away from her Logan," he said softly. "It's all she has."

They teleported away, then. Not wishing to materialize out in the open, Nightcrawler took them to the end house in the row: the one into which the mutates' emergency exit led. He had checked it out before, surreptitiously, fixing its location and layout in his mind. As brimstone-scented smoke dissipated across the deserted hallway, he clutched a pained hand to his stomach. "I have *got* to stop doing that!" he gasped.

"You're not kidding me, elf!" Wolverine was leaning against a gray-plastered wall to get his breath back. The tandem 'port had taken a greater than usual toll upon him: worrying proof that he hadn't yet fully recovered from his trauma. "Tell me there's a way out of this place that doesn't involve churning our guts up again."

Kurt gazed out of a broken window beside the front door. "We'll have to use the back entrance," he said glumly. "They're fighting in the street now."

There were bodies on the tarmac: more than he liked to count. His sole consolation was that both humans and mutates had now pulled back from close combat. They had found cover behind abandoned cars, and in the doorways and windows of houses on each side of the road. The air between them was thick with bullets and energy beams, but with both sides entrenched in their defensive positions, fresh casualties were few. With a little luck, the skirmish would eventually grind to a halt as limbs became tired and ammunition spent.

"Funny!" snorted Wolverine. "I thought this was what Magneto came here to prevent!"

"Give him his due," sighed Kurt. "I suspect he tried."

Logan opened his mouth—but before he could make what Kurt suspected would be a scathing retort, the cellar door flew open, and a man in the mask and combat suit of a magistrate emerged. Wolverine spun around, and let out a curse. Had he been at his peak, he couldn't have been surprised like this: he would have smelt or heard the man's approach.

For his part, the magistrate was frozen in his tracks. Then, unexpectedly, he stepped forward and blurted out: "Wolvie! Boy, am I glad to see—"

But Wolverine had already sprung at him, snarling with rage, determined to compensate for his oversight.

And Kurt recognized the magistrate's voice, muffled as it had been by his mask—but by that time, it was already too late.

Wolverine had buried his claws up to his knuckles in Iceman's heart.

CHAPTER 13

HE cockpit radio of Shaw's luxurious private jet sputtered to life. Through a cloud of static, a female voice said: "Unidentified aircraft, this is Genoshan Air Traffic Control. This country has been closed to incoming flights by order of its sovereign, Magneto. You have two minutes to transmit an authorization code or leave our airspace. Failure to do either will result in your being shot out of the sky. No further warning will be broadcast. Thank you."

"Your move, Shaw," breathed Cyclops.

A knot formed in Phoenix's stomach as the Black King said nothing, continuing to stare ahead into the gray sky with a dark expression. A tense silence fell until, from her position behind the controls of the plane, Storm prompted sternly: "The authorization code, Shaw!"

"I doubt that, even with your hardy constitution, you could survive a missile strike to this conveyance," mused the Beast. "Are you so eager to see Magneto's plan succeed that you are prepared to perish alongside its opponents?"

"Ninety seconds," said Cyclops in a strained voice.

Shaw didn't move. His face didn't flicker. He didn't even blink.

"Oh, he'll transmit the code all right," said Phoenix confidently.

And Shaw half-turned to face her, an eyebrow arching in mild curiosity.

She smiled at him sweetly. "The only question is, will he be in control of his own mind when he does so?" She leaned toward Shaw, and lowered her voice threateningly. "You know I don't want to do this, don't you Sebastian? Please don't force my hand again."

He returned her stare unflinchingly, and she could read nothing in the depths of his eyes.

"One minute," said Cyclops.

Shaw nodded abruptly, and reached past Storm's arm to activate the radio. "Air Traffic Control, this is Hellfire One requesting permission to land." His fingers blurred across a small keyboard set into the instrument panel, and he sat back with a trace of a smile on his lips.

The radio emitted another static burst, and then nothing else for some time. Phoenix's anxiety was exacerbated by the fact that, through her psychic link, she could feel her husband tensed like a coiled spring. What if Shaw had betrayed them? What if he had sent a warning signal? Perhaps she ought to have seized control of him after all, taking the information they needed from his thoughts. The idea disgusted her, but the stakes were too high to risk failure. Wolverine would have told her she ought to be more ruthless.

"Hellfire One," said the voice of Air Traffic Control at last, "you have permission to land."

And the outpouring of relief in the crowded cockpit was almost tangible.

Storm guided them in over Hammer Bay, and a wave of melancholia washed over Jean as she looked at the scarred and pitted landscape beneath them. She felt for the people of this beleaguered country, wishing that the X-Men could do more to help them.

"Incoming," reported the Beast. "Two magistrates at eleven o'clock, flying under their own power: mutates, if you can imagine such a thing."

Jean glanced over. "I've got it."

The magistrates took up positions on each side of the plane, peering suspiciously into the cockpit. The X-Men froze, nobody saying a word, until their temporary escort peeled away again, apparently satisfied. "Well done, Jean!" smiled Cyclops.

"And may I inquire as to what they thought they saw?" asked the Beast.

"Three Hellfire Club agents," said Jean. "And they mistook me for Tessa." The procedure required to disrupt the evidence of the mutates' eyes had been minor, and non-invasive: a simple matter of reordering their surface thoughts. "After all, they might have been suspicious if the Black King had been sighted without his faithful poodle."

Shaw didn't rise to the bait. He didn't even speak as Cyclops placed a gloved hand on his shoulder and gestured to him to stand. "We appreciate your getting us this far," said the X-Men's field leader, tight-lipped, "but I think we can dispense with your services now." Nor did Shaw protest as he was guided firmly toward the rear of the plane. Jean followed her husband quietly, in case of trouble. But only after the Black King had been bound with rope in his own comfortable quarters did he break his self-imposed silence.

"Good fortune!" he said quietly.

Phoenix returned to the cockpit to find Storm already bringing the plane around over Hammer Bay's once-bustling airfield. Within seconds, she was beginning her final approach.

Iceman looked down into Wolverine's eyes, numb with horror. He should have remembered how he was dressed, how it would look— but then, his teammate had not given him a second to explain himself. Even now, he could see no remorse in Logan's gaze, no reaction at all.

He had always heard that, when you were stabbed, you didn't feel the knife. It was like taking a punch—until you felt yourself weakening as every beat of your heart pumped more blood out of your body. He felt like that now. He had seen the claws flashing toward him, had felt the solid blow beneath his breastbone—and now, the knuckles of Wolverine's upturned fist were pressed into his chest as if they could keep his wound sealed. A cold flush had enveloped Bobby, and his legs were beginning to shake. Seconds dragged by like minutes as he waited for that moment of grace to pass, for the pain to hit him. For his life to ebb away.

Then, Wolverine pulled away from him, and Bobby saw that his claws had been retracted. "You got lucky, kid," he growled. "I caught your scent at the last instant."

It had only been a punch, after all. Bobby wanted to say something, to voice a protest: *Is that supposed to be an apology?* But he was too giddy with relief. He could hardly breathe. He tore the mask from his face and hurled it away, taking in great gulps of air.

"Are you OK?" asked Nightcrawler.

"Don't suppose you've seen any sign of Rogue?" asked Wolverine before he could answer. When Bobby shook his head, he scowled and said: "This ain't good. It's past midnight in Sydney, and three-quarters of our strike team haven't even had a sniff of the target. We need to get moving—that is, if we aren't too late already!"

"Perhaps Rogue has dealt with the situation on her own," said Nightcrawler, but he sounded doubtful.

"I've still got my comm-set," offered Iceman.

Wolverine shook his head. "No point blowing our cover now. If the good guys have won, we'll find out soon enough. If not, we'll need surprise on our side."

He led the way into the back of the house, where he forced a locked window. The three X-Men climbed out into an alleyway, and followed it until it met a street. It took them another ten minutes to find an abandoned car that looked fit to drive. Iceman didn't recognize the make—it was a domestic Genoshan model—but, although the windscreen had been smashed, it hadn't been burnt out like most vehicles on the road. Wolverine popped his claws, pried open the gas tank, sniffed at it and grinned. "Should get us where we want to go."

"It will attract attention," warned Nightcrawler.

"A risk we have to take."

Wolverine dropped into the driver's seat and tripped the ignition like an expert. "Which way to Hammer Bay, elf?" he asked. "I wasn't paying a whole lot of attention on the way here."

"I'll drive," said Nightcrawler firmly. "You need to rest." It looked for a second as if Wolverine would argue—but, to Bobby's surprise, he held his tongue. He simply climbed into the back of the car and rested his head on the seatback.

Five minutes later, they had left the village behind them, and were roaring down an otherwise empty country road. The car's engine ground like a hacksaw, and Bobby kept glancing over at the indicators on the dashboard, nervously. However, as the distinctive buildings of Hammer Bay came into view ahead of them, he found he had better things to worry about than the possibility of breaking down.

He didn't hear the small jet at first, the noise of its engines almost drowned out by that of the car. He only became aware of it as it appeared in the windscreen, having passed low over them. It must have been on its final approach—and like them, its destination was the Genoshan capital. Given that the island's borders were supposed to be closed, it didn't take Wolverine's intuition to guess that the plane was important somehow. Squinting, Bobby could just about make out a red trident symbol on its tail fin.

"I take it back," muttered Wolverine from behind him. "Looks like we might just be in time for the fireworks after all."

Phoenix let out a breath of relief as the mutate guards stood aside, and she and her three colleagues marched into the command center. There had been a limousine waiting for them at the airport—but throughout the short journey here, she had had to maintain the belief in all onlookers that Magneto's visitors were really Sebastian Shaw, his personal assistant and two bodyguards. Normally, this wouldn't have been a problem—but it would have taken just one skilled telepath to pierce the X-Men's disguise. In a country with a majority population of mutants, Jean had feared exposure at any second.

The guards had wanted to escort the visitors to their sovereign's throne room, but Cyclops had played the part of the Black King well, dismissing their offer with exactly the right amount of contempt. The quartet swept up a flight of steps, and then, after checking that no eyes were upon them, they slipped into the shadows of an adjoining corridor.

Jean had been scanning the building, and she sensed a familiar set of thoughts. "I've found Rogue," she reported. "She's in a cell on the next level up. No trace of the others yet." The Southern X-Man had felt Jean's telepathic touch too, and she welcomed her into her mind. They didn't converse as such; the exchange of information was much faster than that. Rogue simply allowed her friend to riffle through her recent memories.

Phoenix relayed her findings to her teammates. "Magneto has a laboratory in the basement—and Rogue thinks it's where the Legacy cure is kept. She can take us to it."

"OK," said Cyclops. "It won't be long before Magneto realizes we're here. Hank, your job is to free Rogue and find that cure. As soon as you have it, the pair of you should get out of here. Don't risk coming back for us!" A shadow passed over the Beast's face, and Jean could see that he wasn't entirely happy with his instructions. However, he didn't argue.

"And the rest of us, I assume . . . ?" began Storm.

"Will keep Magneto busy. For as long as we can, at least."

They went their separate ways, then. Phoenix placed an image of Rogue's location in the Beast's mind, and he loped away up the next flight of stairs. The rest of the X-Men raced along the corridor, no longer hiding behind a pretence. Jean hadn't dared scan for Magneto's presence, lest he detect her psychic tendrils—but she had picked up stray thoughts from a few of his minions, which suggested that he was indeed in his throne room.

Cyclops didn't hesitate for an instant when he reached the heavy metal door. He attacked it with a full-strength optic blast, which sent shrapnel flying inward. And the X-Men burst into the presence of their greatest foe.

To find that he was ready for them.

Magneto's metal throne had been shaped out of an old magistrate workstation. It stood in the center of the room, dominating it—but unlike, say, Selene's throne, it was not in any way ornate. Genosha's ruler was not interested in the opulent trappings of power, merely in power itself. His throne didn't even look particularly comfortable. Numerous thick cables straggled across the floor to plug into it, and the arms and back of the chair were festooned with dials and switches. From here, he could presumably override any mechanical or computerized device in the building, and perhaps beyond.

The sloping wall behind the throne was studded with windows, which looked out over the master of magnetism's domain. The setting sun cast a dull red light through the glass. Magneto stood with his back to it, facing the door. He wore his full red and purple combat suit, and his metal gladiator's helmet. His hands were clasped behind his back, and his eyes burnt with white-hot contempt for his three uninvited visitors. The shrapnel from the door hung in midair before him, a cloud of twisted scraps of metal.

"I'm dismayed," he said, "that you apparently think so little of me. Did you really believe I would be taken in by such an obvious ruse? No, I allowed you to enter my country for one reason alone: because you have proven yourselves too dangerous to remain free."

With a nod, he sent the shrapnel flying back toward them with the force of a hundred bullets. But Phoenix had anticipated such a move. It was hellishly difficult to seize so many small objects in her telekinetic grip, but she succeeded in deflecting those that would have caused herself or her friends harm. A telekinetic force bubble would have been more effective—but this way, there was nothing to stop her teammates from rushing to the counterattack even as the metal shards clattered off the wall behind them.

Between them, Cyclops and Storm wielded some of the most powerful mutant energies yet identified—but Magneto had surrounded himself with a barrier of magnetic force, which coped admirably with the combination of energy beams and lightning. Phoenix held back, trying to remain inconspicuous as she probed at the psi-shielding in his helmet. If she could penetrate it, she could take him in a second—but Magneto knew the X-Men's abilities and strategies too well. Ignoring his closer foes, he extended a hand toward Jean and took control of her magnetic field. As she rocketed into the air, she was forced to break off her assault to concentrate on keeping herself from being dashed against the ceiling. Magneto hurled her this way and that, faster than she could apply the telekinetic brakes: it was like playing a furious game of Ping-Pong, with her body as the ball. She cannoned backward into one wall, the impact winding her. Magneto tried to press his advantage by slamming her into the floor, but she caught herself in time.

Cyclops had switched tactics, aiming his optic blasts between his enemy's feet. He blew a hole out of the floor, but Magneto simply levitated himself above it. Still, the distraction was enough to make him momentarily lose his hold on Phoenix. She flashed a quick telepathic message to Storm before trying to overbalance him by pulling his legs, force field and all, out from beneath him. The X-Men's weather elemental applied a well-timed gust of hurricane-force wind—and Magneto staggered back and fell against his throne.

The expression on his face was priceless: a mixture of astonishment and fury. Cyclops hammered at his force field again—and this time, some of his ruby energy penetrated it, and his target flinched as if stung. The X-Men had gained an early advantage, but they couldn't afford to let up. Their opponent was too dangerous, especially when cornered. They hammered at him, hitting him with everything they had, just trying to keep him down.

And then, the throne itself reared up, grinding and screeching as Magneto reconfigured its metal components into the shape of a gigantic fist. It hurtled toward Storm, who tried to fly out of its path—but the fist reacted with the speed of Magneto's thoughts. It struck her in the back, and knocked her out of the air. With a wide-angle blast, Cyclops blew the fist to smithereens—but Magneto simply reformed it, the fragments coming back together as if in a piece of time-lapse photography shown backward. It swooped toward Phoenix next, and she only avoided it by leaping aside and simultaneously giving it a TK push away from her. It thudded heavily into the floor, almost punching through it.

Magneto was back on his feet now. "No matter how many times I spare you," he raged, "you won't learn your lesson. You keep trying to thwart my ambitions!"

"And no matter what you do, Lensherr," contested Cyclops, "you'll never change that. Even if you kill us, people will always rise against a tyrant like you!"

He shoulder-charged Magneto, but rebounded from his field as if he had run full-tilt into a rock wall. Magneto then felled him with three powerful punches in quick succession, apparently relishing the use of his physical strength. Storm came at him again, but she was still groggy and she couldn't get out of the way as the metal fist encircled her, turning into steel bands that pinned her arms to her sides.

Magneto turned on Phoenix, then, and she gasped as she was buffeted by a wave of magnetic energy. When she was able to open her eyes again, she found herself pinned against the wall, her feet not quite touching the floor, Magneto's sneering face an inch from hers. "I ought to be insulted," he said, his anger having lessened now that he had the upper hand, "that you thought it would take only three of you to defeat me. I have fought three times as many X-Men to a standstill."

She could feel him in her veins, controlling the iron in her blood, exerting just enough pressure for her to start to feel the pain. Just enough to remind her that, should he so wish, he could turn that pain into unbearable agony. He could kill her in a heartbeat.

"We've always stopped you before," she said, defiant nonetheless, "no matter the odds."

"Oh, my dear Jean." Magneto shook his head like a disappointed father. "So proud, so stubborn, so strong. I have allowed myself to harbor such high hopes for you. You could accomplish so much at my side, if only you would see the world as it truly is, if you could forget the naïve dreams of your mentor."

He let her go, and she fell to the ground, exhausted and aching inside.

"Of course," he said, looking down at her with a dark smile, "you didn't really *expect* to win this battle, did you? You only thought to keep me occupied for a time. Perhaps you thought I would have forgotten so soon that I encountered *four* X-Men in Sydney. It was a futile gambit. That Legacy cure is important to me, Jean. It is the foundation stone upon which I will build a new, more peaceful world. Henry McCoy will not leave the building with it."

Phoenix summoned all her remaining strength, and tried to hit him with a psi-bolt. She must have reached his mind, because his lips tightened and his nostrils flared—but if she caused him any more than a minor twinge of pain, he certainly didn't show it. His eyes flashed angrily, and he delivered a stinging, backhanded blow to her cheek.

And, at that moment, the windows behind him exploded.

The three missing X-Men rode into the throne room on an ice slide, glass shards flying before them. They were a mismatched bunch—Nightcrawler in his red tunic, Wolverine wearing nothing but a frayed pair of khaki shorts and Iceman dressed in, of all things, a magistrate's uniform—and Jean could hardly imagine what they must have been through to get here. But right now, she would have been hard pressed to think of a more delightful sight.

The cavalry had arrived.

* * *

The Beast put a foot against the wall to brace himself, wrapping both hands around the metal tube that clamped Rogue's arm to that same wall. He strained with all the power of his sinews to tear it loose—but, even with the addition of his teammate's much greater strength, he couldn't make it budge.

"I should have known that matters were proceeding with a suspicious lack of difficulty," he muttered under his breath. Phoenix's directions had taken him straight to Rogue's cell, where he been surprised and pleased to find no guards posted outside. Just as happily, the simplistic lock had yielded to his manipulations after only a couple of minutes. The restraints around Rogue's arms and legs, however, must have been created by Magneto using his control over all things metal. They had no clasps or keyholes, nor even seams into which he could pry his clawed fingers. And they were riveted firmly to the metal-plated wall.

Rogue looked weary, her face streaked with sweat and her striped hair in disarray. Hank wondered how long she had been forced to hang in this uncomfortable position, her limbs splayed out behind her. "I'd suggest you go on without me," she said bravely, "but last time I was there, Magneto's lab was guarded by one of Shaw's watchdogs."

"Anyone whose acquaintance I have previously made?"

"Holocaust."

"Holocaust?"

"Armored bruiser from some alternative dimension or other. Used to call himself Nemesis."

"I'm familiar with him," said Hank, chagrined. "My outburst was prompted rather by the belief that his powers are considerably more than a match for our own."

"We'll see about that," growled Rogue through gritted teeth. "We're X-Men. We don't give in to anyone or anything. Not Holocaust, and not these blasted manacles!"

"On three?"

She nodded. Hank counted down, and they bent their combined

strength to one final supreme effort. To the Beast's satisfaction, it bore fruit; the metal tube was wrenched from the wall, and Rogue's right arm was freed. After that, the left came easier: she could pull at this restraint with both hands, while the Beast supported her so that, still held by the legs as she was, she didn't fall to the floor face first.

"Leave Holocaust to me," said Rogue as they worked together on her final manacle. "I can take him."

"Pardon my skepticism," said the Beast. "I was under the impression that you had put that claim to the test already today—and that this period of incarceration was the result."

"I'll be ready for him this time," said Rogue stubbornly. "I don't have to beat him outright, anyhow—so long as I can keep him busy while you do your part."

The Beast sighed. "Cyclops and the others are pursuing a similar course of action with regard to Magneto." Rogue's left leg came free at last, and he waited patiently while she sat and massaged her feet to restore circulation to them. "I cannot claim to feel entirely at ease," he said, "with a plan that involves so many of my teammates endangering themselves against superior opponents on my behalf."

He didn't tell her the rest of it. He didn't tell her about the nagging guilt he had felt since Emma Frost had brought her news to the X-Men's mansion. Nobody had blamed him for helping Shaw find a cure to the Legacy Virus: his friends had understood his reasons for doing what he had. Nobody had pointed out the fact that, were it not for him, Magneto's plan could not have progressed this far. He had, nevertheless, set into motion a chain of events that had led to this moment. He had ignored the warning signs and taken an extreme risk, in the misguided belief that he could manage the consequences.

And yet, there was an aching hope in his heart too, because there was still a chance that he could achieve everything for which he had aimed. He could retrieve the cure and ensure that it was distributed to the needy. He could save countless lives. The question was, how could he face himself if even one X-Man had to be sacrificed in the process, for his hubris?

"Comes with the territory, sugar," said Rogue, jerking Hank out of his reverie. He looked into her sympathetic eyes, believing for a moment that she must have read his mind. "The important thing is, you get that cure to Muir Island and you save the whole darn world. After that, Magneto can do what he likes to the rest of us— it won't matter!"

"It would matter to me, my friend," he murmured.

Raul Jarrett had had a strange and wonderful dream. A dream in which the Savior of mutantkind had restored him to full health. A dream in which he had visited a distant land at the Savior's side. A dream in which he had spoken to cabinet ministers and foreign businessmen, seen costumed X-Men and been privy to the thoughts of Magneto Himself.

It had been terrifying.

But it had only been a dream, real as it had seemed at the time. In its latter stages, he had even felt his real-life aches beginning to intrude upon his fantasy. He had a distant recollection of waiting outside Phillip Moreau's office, his lungs on fire, gasping for breath and wondering what was happening to him; a moment later, he had woken here, his limbs spread like overcooked spaghetti across a hospital bed as his mutant gene failed him again.

Even now, he was sure—from the glimpse he had taken, before white light had overwhelmed his senses and forced his eyes closed—that he was in the private room in the command center, rather than at the dirty field hospital. But then, his head was buzzing, and he couldn't hold on to a coherent thought for longer than a few seconds. The Legacy Virus was in its final stages, causing him to hallucinate.

He was only grateful that, in one of those hallucinations, he had been afforded some respite from his pain. A few sweet moments of relief before the end.

He imagined that he could hear voices.

"Why didn't you tell me this before?"

"I've only known myself for a few hours, Phillip."

"We only *had* a few hours to stop that maniac!"

"I don't know *how* to stop him!"

"He has to listen to his cabinet, doesn't he? We should call an emergency meeting. If we could get Pietro back here . . ."

"It wouldn't make any difference."

Slowly, Jarrett recognized the female voice as belonging to Jenny Ransome; at least, it had belonged to Nurse Jenny in his dream. Proof, then, that it was not real—that the dream had not quite lost its hold on his waking mind yet—but he couldn't ignore it, couldn't drive it away, no matter how many things it said that his weary brain didn't want to think about.

"You didn't see him, Phillip," she insisted. "He told me about this . . . this scheme of his to spread the Legacy Virus because he knew I couldn't stop him. And he made it pretty clear what would happen if I tried."

"He threatened you?"

"He didn't have to. I shouldn't even have told you about this. But . . ."

There was a long silence, broken only by a soft clink of glass against glass. And then, Jenny spoke again, in a quiet, tremulous voice. "Oh, Phillip . . . the blood test . . ."

"It's positive, isn't it?"

Another silence, shorter this time. Then, Jenny said: "It's worse than we thought. This is more than just a relapse, Phillip. It's as if the virus has evolved to resist the super-cell. It's more virulent than ever. We could try the cure again, with Magneto's permission, but . . ." She dropped her voice to a whisper as if afraid that her patient might be listening. She needn't have bothered. The rest of his body might have given up on him, but Jarrett's hearing was unbearably acute, and her words filled his head. "But I don't think it's going to work. I think we're going to lose him—and in minutes rather than days."

He didn't hear any more voices after that. Perhaps the dream had ended at last—or perhaps it was just that sleep had claimed him again, and a new dream had begun.

Certainly, the image of the Genegineer, his blurred face hovering over Jarrett as he prepared to operate, belonged to his past. Unless, of course, the time since then had been a dream itself: a tortuous, anaesthetic-induced nightmare born from his fear of being mutated, of becoming less than he had been. A non-person. If that was indeed the case—if he was to be given a chance to live the past ten years or more again—then it would be different this time. He would stand up for himself. He would fight back. He would have to—because he couldn't face the thought of another lifetime of being a victim. Of being betrayed by humanity, by fate and ultimately by the would-be Savior who had turned out to be a cruel despot after all.

As the pain drained from his body, however, he knew that his days of being victimized were over at last. He didn't know where he was going, but suddenly he was certain—more so than he had been of anything before—that it was to somewhere better.

He could see his family, but he didn't know if they were a final figment of the life behind him or his first glimpse of the one to come. He swam toward them through the darkness.

And somebody peeled back his eyelid, and white light stabbed into his skull again.

A voice called out his name as if from the end of an infinitely long tunnel. But he didn't want to go back to that place of bewilderment and hurt, so he ignored it.

Raul Jarrett closed his eyes again, knowing beyond doubt that it was for the last time.

CHAPTER 14

WOLVERINE knew from hard-earned experience that there was only one way to deal with Magneto. Fortunately, it was just the way he preferred to fight: hit the enemy hard and hit him fast. Keep him off-balance—otherwise, he would strike out through his superb defenses and win the battle in seconds. Nightcrawler and Iceman knew it too, and the trio took full advantage of the fact that their arrival had taken the master of magnetism by surprise.

As they launched an all-out assault upon his force field, Phoenix—who was down but evidently not out—telepathically updated them on the situation, stressing the importance of keeping their foe busy until the Beast and Rogue had escaped with the Legacy cure. To hell with that, thought Logan. They were fighting the most dangerous man in existence. As if that weren't bad enough, his control over metal made Wolverine particularly vulnerable to him. His thoughts flashed back to the time when Magneto had peeled the adamantium from his bones, and drawn every atom of it out through his pores. The process had taken seconds, but the agony had seemed to last for hours. The eventual operation to replace the metal, while less painful, had taken a great deal longer.

He dismissed the image from his mind, along with the unwanted feeling of apprehension that the memories engendered. The anger and the resentment, he kept hold of. They fuelled him. When Wolverine fought Magneto now, he fought to kill—and he would not be entirely at peace until he had succeeded. It was against the X-Men's code, of course, but they could argue about that later, when the necessary deed was done. What would Summers do about it, anyway? Throw him off the team?

He raised his right arm to strike again, expecting his claws to glance off the magnetic force field but aiming for Magneto's heart just in case. But something prevented him from landing the blow. A familiar sensation. He cursed under his breath as his arm twisted around in front of him, against his will. Now, Wolverine was looking at the points of his own claws, and straining with all his might to keep them from stabbing into his eyes.

Magneto had obviously gotten his second wind. With a hand gesture, he drew billions of microscopic ferrous particles out of the air and caked them around Iceman. Suddenly encased in a dull gray shell and unable to breathe, the young X-Man fell to his knees and clawed at his face. Nightcrawler was teleporting constantly, trying to keep his opponent disoriented by punching and kicking at him from all sides like a one-man army. But Magneto could sense his passage along the magnetic lines of force, and predict where he would appear next—and, inevitably, a hunk of hurtling metal finally found its target.

By now, though, Cyclops and Storm were back on their feet. Wolverine's control of his claws was restored to him as the room was filled with the flash of electricity and the scent of ozone, and Magneto reeled. Cyclops rushed to Iceman's side and freed him with a delicate but well-practiced, highly-focused application of his eye-beams. As Wolverine rejoined the fray, he fancied that he could also feel the telekinetic influence of Phoenix, straining to part the force field in front of him. His claws were penetrating closer to their target than ever.

But Cyclops was already down again, his feet pulled out from beneath him as a metal fragment ricocheted off his skull. Magneto turned to Wolverine, his weathered face twisted into a snarl, and he strengthened his field and thrust outward with it. A spike of magnetic energy punched into Logan's chest and knocked him back.

Recovering in a second, he leapt forward again, adding his strength to Storm's winds and lightning bolts, Iceman's ice boulders and Phoenix's telekinesis.

The pitched battle raged on, wearing down its participants as neither side was able to gain any significant ground. As far as the X-Men were concerned, this meant that they were achieving their objective, giving their teammates the vital minutes they needed.

But, for the frustrated Wolverine, it wasn't anything like good enough.

Rogue waited, tensed for action, at the end of the corridor that led to the basement laboratory, watching as the Beast tapped the combination into the numeric pad. To her relief, it hadn't been changed yet. The locking mechanism whirred into action: its painfully long cycle could almost have been designed to give Holocaust time to get into position beyond it. She flew forward before the heavy door had slid aside, her top rate of acceleration turning her into a hurtling torpedo. For a horrible instant, she feared she had mistimed her launch and that she would smack into the door itself. Then, suddenly, it pulled out of her way and she caught the briefest glint of gold plating as she cannoned fists-first into Holocaust's abdomen.

The hulking creature toppled backward, the satisfaction of the moment dulling the pain of impact that shot through Rogue's muscles. She kept on top of him, pounding at the transparent dome at the top of his armor, ignoring the howl of fury that emanated from his fire-shrouded skull face. A blue blur shot past her—and, under her breath, she murmured, "Go, Hank, go!" For all her earlier bravado, she didn't know how long she could keep this up. Holocaust was already struggling to rise beneath her, bucking and almost throwing her off him. She had been trying to keep his weapon arm pinned with a foot, but he yanked it free and turned its rounded end toward her. Rogue saw bright energy building behind the weapon's holes, and jumped for it, delivering a final kick to Holocaust's head in the process. He fired, and she rolled beneath the explosion, wincing from its heat against her face.

They scrambled to their feet simultaneously. Rogue wanted to duck for cover, but she couldn't take the chance that, if he couldn't see her, Holocaust would target the Beast. She spared a glance for Hank, who was bounding around the large, white room, prying open cupboards and drawers with manic urgency. And she realized that they weren't alone.

A man and two women in white coats were cowering behind a lab bench. Blast it, thought Rogue, she could have done without the innocent bystanders. That was, if they could be considered innocents: clearly, they were doing Magneto's dirty work for him. Of course, like Shaw's scientists, they might not have had the option to refuse him.

She took to the air and buzzed Holocaust, keeping herself out of his grasp but not so far out that he lost interest in her. By drawing him further into the lab, away from the door, she was giving the white-coats a way out. Two of them took it without hesitation; the final woman, to Rogue's chagrin, must have been too scared to break cover.

She had cracked her foe's head plate. She hadn't realized it before, but she saw now that a hair-thin line crazed across the clear surface. Holocaust's energy—his very self—was seeping out through it, leaving an orange vapor trail on the air. Her heart soared. She was winning.

And then, he caught her with a stunning backhand, flinging her backward across a hard bench. She bounced once, rolled and crashed to the floor. Holocaust was upon her again in a second, hauling her to her feet and delivering another solid blow. Rogue slammed into the doors of an upright cabinet, leaving her imprint in the thick metal. Her eyes closed, but she could hear his heavy footsteps approaching again—and her brain was screaming at her to get out of his way, but her muscles weren't responding.

She let out an involuntary groan as she crumpled.

"Get away from her, Holocaust!" yelled an angry voice.

The Beast dropped onto Holocaust's shoulders, sprawling across his domed top and covering his head plate with his arms. Blinded, the creature reached up to dislodge him, but the Beast propelled himself away with a kick of his powerful leg muscles. Rogue realized that he had deliberately targeted the crack in Holocaust's armor: he had widened it, just a little, and the vapor trail was thicker now.

"Hank, don't do it!" she groaned. "You're no match for his strength."

"Parity in that department is not required," insisted the Beast, "as long as our other-dimensional friend fails to lay an armor-clad hand upon me."

Indeed, Holocaust was swiping clumsily at him, but the Beast's amazing agility kept him one step ahead. Rogue could even feel her own strength returning, and she started to lever herself up, leaning on the dented cabinet behind her for support.

"I may not be able to hit you," snarled Holocaust. "Pity you can't say the same about your teammate." Rogue froze as he aimed his weapon arm at her again—and, with an anguished cry, the Beast threw himself at the swollen limb, trying to deflect it. That, of course, was what Holocaust had hoped for: with a gleeful cackle, he batted the blue-furred X-Man aside.

Rogue had no choice. She flew at him, even though she hadn't yet fully recovered from her beating. If she could just widen that crack. . . . But she never reached it. Holocaust smashed her out of the air. She hit the same cabinet again, causing it to rock and almost topple. And then, she was staring helplessly up at her foe's lopsided sneer and his leveled weapon arm.

So much for learning from experience, she thought bitterly. So much for her grand plan. This round had ended even quicker than the first, and in exactly the same way.

"That déjà vu is a bitch, isn't it!" cackled Holocaust. "This is goodbye, Rogue. You had your chance. You don't get taken alive twice."

The Black King stood on the tarmac of Hammer Bay's small airfield, his hands behind his back and his feet apart, an expression of studied calm on his face as a warm evening breeze ruffled his dark hair. It hadn't been difficult to escape the bonds in with which the X-Men had left him. Because he had not used his strength against them, they had thought him drained—but in fact, he had been conserving his power, biding his time. He had pulled his ropes apart like strands of tissue paper. So far, everything was going well. Even so, Shaw's casual demeanor was a mask for the anxiety that had coiled his nerves tight.

A patrolling aircar passed overhead at last, and he flagged it down. As it came to rest on its quiet antigravity jets, he allowed himself another quick glance at his pocket watch.

He instructed the car's three mutate occupants to take him to Magneto. When they looked at each other uncertainly, he snapped: "Do you know who I am? I am Sebastian Shaw, the head of the most powerful organization in the world. Lensherr *will* see me."

The mutates had obviously heard his name, because it was enough for them. Suddenly, they became attentive—almost sycophantic—toward him. One of them held an aircar door open for him, while another got out of the vehicle altogether to afford him more room. A few minutes later, Shaw touched down in the street outside Magneto's command center, and his pilot offered to escort him to the throne room of the Savior. Declining curtly, he strode into the building. The mutate guards at the main door *did* recognize him—he had been here several times in the past few weeks— and they jumped to attention as he passed them.

He didn't miss the nervous looks in the guards' eyes, and he soon realized what was causing them. He could hear distant thuds and cracks from the direction of the throne room. The mutates had been well trained not to approach their sovereign's inner sanctum, whatever the situation, unless summoned. Magneto liked to fight his own battles.

Shaw smiled. The X-Men were nothing if not predictable. He had taken a gamble, and he had begun to fear that time would run out before it could pay off. The prospect of a lifetime under a dictator's thumb had loomed like a shadow over him: he had thought about his own future self, turned into a cowering serf by the Black Queen, Selene, and he had hoped that he would have the courage to die before he let such a fate befall him.

But, by bringing him here, by occupying Magneto at this critical juncture, the mutant heroes had given him another chance. The game was in its final stages—but there was still time for his plan to bear fruit, for him to move his pieces into a winning position.

He took a circuitous route through the corridors of the center, avoiding the throne room and its brawling occupants. He had almost reached the infirmary when its door flew open, and two figures emerged at a run. He recognized Phillip Moreau and Jennifer Ransome.

"Shaw!" exclaimed Moreau, skidding to a halt.

The Black King raised an eyebrow, and tried not to betray the feeling of impending triumph that welled within him. If he read the situation right, then it was all he could have hoped for. "I was on my way to check the progress of your patients. Nothing has gone wrong, I hope?"

Moreau made to push past him. "We need to speak to Magneto."

He restrained the young man with a hand on his shoulder. "Magneto is busy." With a wry smile, he added: "As I expect you can hear."

With impeccable timing, a tremendous crash resounded from the throne room upstairs. Moreau and Ransome exchanged an uncertain glance.

Shaw smiled, and held out his hands in a magnanimous gesture. "Perhaps I can be of assistance?"

Once again, three X-Men rushed Magneto. Once again, they were thrown back. It was becoming almost a ritual.

Phoenix had linked the six heroes telepathically. They were well used to working in concert with each other, to coordinating their attacks—but this way, each knew for sure what the others were thinking. It gave them an additional edge. Cyclops and Wolverine, for example, concentrated their blows upon the same square inch of their foe's force field, Scott timing his optic blasts perfectly to avoid hitting his teammate. Iceman and Storm worked together to lower the temperature inside the field, forcing Magneto to expend precious energy on exciting the molecules around him if he didn't want to freeze. The onslaught was relentless. As Jean continued to probe the force field telekinetically, she sensed it weakening—but she could also feel Magneto's anger, his determination, like a physical force. The longer he was kept from his laboratory and the cure therein, the more savagely he fought.

He picked up Wolverine and used him as a cannonball, shooting him into Nightcrawler even as he materialized from his latest 'port. Nightcrawler collided with Phoenix in turn, and Magneto devoted a small fraction of his power to keeping Logan pinned down, trapping Jean and a dazed Kurt beneath his reinforced frame. He also redirected one of Storm's lightning bolts to strike Iceman. And, while the X-Men were still reeling, trying to regroup, he drew himself to his full height, spread his arms wide and bellowed: "Enough of this!"

He brought down the ceiling. Phoenix erected a TK bubble around herself, Wolverine and Nightcrawler, and wished she had the strength to extend it to the others. Bombarded by debris, Storm was forced to land and take cover. Iceman was out. Jean could also sense her husband, using a wide-angled blast to pulverize as much of the plummeting ceiling as he could—but she couldn't see him through a billowing cloud of dust.

Magneto was screaming through the chaos: "You only seek to delay the inevitable!"

But he had lost his grip on Wolverine. With the speed of a striking snake, Logan leapt at him, and plunged his claws straight through his weakened force field. Magneto fell back before him, and Jean thought she could see actual fear in his eyes as he stopped his attacker's claws less than an inch in front of his face. She could see the effort that it took him to push Wolverine back, but he succeeded in doing so nevertheless, and in building up enough momentum to knock him senseless against the far wall.

A scarlet energy beam stabbed through the dust haze, catching Magneto unawares. It struck him in the back, and he fell to his knees with a gasp. But Jean knew that Cyclops couldn't press his attack: a heavy timber had fallen across his chest, restricting his movement, and his foe had fallen out of the limited range of his optic blasts. Then, Nightcrawler disappeared from Jean's side and reappeared on Magneto's shoulders. He wrenched the metal helmet from his head, but was felled by a blast of magnetic force for his troubles.

Phoenix seized her opportunity.

Launching a psi-bolt at an opponent was like attacking him with a piece of her innermost self, seeking to overwhelm his very being with a concentrated expression of her own. In the fraction of a second that it took Jean to strike, at the speed of thought, Magneto erected his force field again—but he was an instant too late. She had almost reached him.

She was only dimly aware of her physical body, in its prone position, clenching its fists and gritting its teeth, feeling as if its eyes were bleeding, as she pushed her way through the final inch of the magnetic shield. But her attack had lost momentum, and she still had to contend with Magneto's natural psychic defenses.

Like the X-Men themselves, he had trained his mind to resist outside influences. But his mind was even more difficult to penetrate than any of theirs: Professor Xavier had conjectured that Magneto possessed latent telepathic abilities of his own, although this remained unproven. Whatever the reason, it took all of Jean's remaining energy to push her way into his psyche, and only a ghost of herself made it through at all.

She was kneeling on moist soil, the tang of iron and blood on her tongue, surrounded by mutates with skinsuits and shaved heads. She felt weak, too weak to stand, but she dragged herself to her feet anyway. Magneto was still trying to rebuff her, to dispel her faint psychic presence, and her mind translated his attack into the unpleasant sensation of her muscles straining to pull themselves apart. She was blurring around the edges, but she had to hold herself together. She had to find him, had to locate his essential self—the part of his mind that she had to shut down—in this cluttered psi-scape. She didn't have long. She fought her way through the mutate crowd, none of whom moved either to get out of her way or to stop her. They were like zombies. Zombies with numbers tattooed upon their foreheads.

If Jean had been stronger, more alert, she would have seen it right away. She would have known exactly which part of Magneto's mental landscape she had intruded upon.

Reaching the edge of the subdued crowd, she found herself pressed up against a chain link fence. With a sense of foreboding, she looked up, knowing what she would see. Barbed wire.

Black-uniformed, jackbooted guards surrounded her. They lashed out with sturdy truncheons, and she folded and almost dissipated there and then. They lifted her by the arms and hauled her away, and Jean chose not to resist. Perhaps they were taking her to Magneto. Perhaps he wanted to gloat before he expelled her from his consciousness.

But the gray, cubic, hard-angled concrete building into which the guards dragged her was empty. One look at the bare walls of its single room, and she began to struggle in vain. It was only after she had been beaten again and flung to the floor that she looked up and saw the nozzles that extended from the ceiling like shower heads. And her blood froze, her heart numbed by the very idea that someone could do—*had* done—this to another person. To a whole race. The room was filling up around her, mutates filing in without protest until there was no space left and they were pressed up against the walls. They trampled Jean, but she couldn't rise from her knees. She had to fight, but she had no strength left. No willpower. Her psychic form was clinging to this realm by its metaphorical fingernails.

And, too late, she knew where Magneto had to be.

She looked up into his creased face and his sad, gray eyes, and the number in blue ink on his shaved head. He was Mutant #0001.

He reached down to her with a spindly arm, and helped her to her feet with apparent difficulty. In the physical world, it was easy to forget Magneto's advanced age, because he burnt with such power and passion. But here, in this corner of his mind, he was an old man, stooped and frail. For a moment, Jean couldn't bring herself to hurt him. She had to remind herself what he was capable of, what he was doing. She had to gather her shattered resolve.

But it would have made no difference, anyway.

The concrete chamber was already fading around her, and she could feel the floor of the throne room beneath her back again. She was exhausted. She couldn't move, couldn't even open her eyes. For a long moment, the only image in her mind was that of Magneto's gray eyes, and she felt a tear on her cheek.

And then, there was nothing.

Holocaust's weapon arm was almost pressed into Rogue's face.

She had closed her eyes and gritted her teeth, awaiting the lethal blast.

The Beast was on his back, nestled in the remnants of a lab stool that had shattered when he had fell on it. He was winded, he didn't want to move, but he fought to override his weakness. He dragged himself to his feet, but he felt as if he were moving through treacle. He was too slow. He couldn't possibly reach his teammate in time to save her life.

"Holocaust, no!"

The interjection had come from the female scientist: the one who had stayed behind when her colleagues had taken flight. She wore round, rimless glasses, and her blonde hair was tied back into a severe bun. She had only half-risen from behind the lab bench that sheltered her, ready to drop again if the battle resumed. She was trembling, and Hank admired her for having had the compassion to intercede on Rogue's behalf despite her obvious terror.

Or had there been something more to it than that?

Holocaust rotated the top half of his bulky armor, awkwardly, and glared at the scientist. She gave him a desperate, meaningful look. And, when he returned his attention to Rogue, he lowered his weapon arm and raised his equally huge fist instead.

But the two X-Men had had the moment's respite they needed. Rogue scrambled out of the way of a punishing blow that buried Holocaust's fist in the floor. As he fought to pull it free, a stool hurled by the Beast bounced off his head, widening the crack in his protective dome.

The scientist ducked again, with a high-pitched shriek—and the next thing Hank knew, a blast of energy came his way. He leapt above it, and it destroyed a shelving unit behind him. It seemed to him, though, that the blast hadn't had half the power of the last one he had seen. Holocaust was weakening, his life essence pouring out of his breached containment suit. Rogue must have seen it too, because she dared to get nearer to her foe, taunting him. Assailed by punch after earth-shattering punch, he gave ground, arms flailing wildly, and Hank was able to reach the metal cabinet against which his teammate had earlier lain.

It was locked—but the doors were already damaged, and it didn't take much effort to wrench them off their hinges. A wave of cold air hit the Beast: the contents of the cabinet were refrigerated. The top shelf held a rack of thin vials, each containing a measure of a translucent, red-tinted liquid. The other shelves were empty—apart for the bottom one, in which another vial sat in a rack of its own, filled with a darker red and more viscous substance. He reached for it, forcing his hand to stop shaking in anticipation, ignoring the cold burn against his skin as he lifted the vial to his eyes and read its label.

He read his own name, and knew that this was the sample of his blood that Sebastian Shaw had stolen. The sample that contained the super-cell.

And his lips stretched into a broad, toothy grin as he confirmed what he had deduced: that Magneto's scientist hadn't cared about Rogue's life at all, she had simply not wanted Holocaust to fire his weapon at this cabinet because of its precious, irreplaceable contents. He looked at the vials on the top shelf again, and he knew that this was the realization of his greatest dream. The cure to the Legacy Virus. Every one of those vials could save one life.

And he had to destroy them.

It was a matter of logic. If he succeeded in getting the cure out of Genosha, then it wouldn't matter that Magneto had it too. But if he failed—and there was a good chance of that—then the master of magnetism couldn't be allowed to keep it either. Even so, the Beast felt a hollow pain in his stomach as he forced himself to yank the full rack from the cabinet and let its contents shatter on the floor.

The Legacy-busting super-cell existed only in one place now, as it had before: in Hank's blood sample, which he tucked carefully into a belt pouch. He remembered seeing a freezer cabinet in Shaw's jet: he had to get the blood into it, and get it away from here. And he couldn't let anybody or anything stop him.

Now that he had this vial in his possession at last, he couldn't face the thought of having to destroy it too.

Startled by a tremendous crash behind him, he whirled around—to find that Holocaust had been felled again. And this time, he wasn't getting up. Rogue stood over him, an expression of supreme satisfaction on her face, her fists still clenched. "How's that for déjà vu, sugar?" she gloated. "You getting your tail busted by the X-Men again!" With a cruel glint in her eyes, she added: "I bet your masters'll be none too happy about that."

"You assume correctly."

The Beast started again, his eyes darting across the lab to find Magneto in the doorway. He was standing upright but hovering a foot or so above the floor, having evidently approached in silence on the crest of a magnetic wave. Hank's heart sank into his stomach, and his hand went to his belt pouch. Rogue didn't have time to react at all. Magneto gestured toward her, and she stiffened, her eyes rolling back into their sockets and the merest gasp of pain escaping from her throat. Then, she collapsed across the armor of her fallen foe.

Magneto floated into the room and inspected the destruction around him with a hooded gaze, which lingered longest on the sundered metal cabinet and the broken glass beneath it.

He turned to Hank, and loomed over him, his face dark but his eyes aflame. And he held out a purple-gloved hand, and spoke in a stern voice that brooked no argument.

"You have something of mine, I think."

Waking from unconsciousness was not covered in the X-Men's formal training, but it was certainly something that they had to get used to.

On this occasion, Storm hadn't been out for long, and a quick touch to the thin cut on her temple told her that the injury wasn't serious. She dismissed the muzzy feeling in her head with a combination of experience and willpower, and assessed the conditions of her teammates. Wolverine, as usual, had recovered quickly and was coaxing Phoenix awake. Ororo doused Nightcrawler and Iceman with a miniature rainstorm, which shocked them to their senses and also served to replenish Bobby's vital moisture. In the meantime, Phoenix and Wolverine worked together to lift the beam that pinned Cyclops—although Ororo noted that Jean didn't employ her telekinesis.

"We have to get after him," insisted Cyclops, sounding as if every word was an effort. "The Beast and Rogue can't handle him on their own."

"Just one problem there, boss-man," said Wolverine, sniffing the air. "We got company!"

He turned to face the doorway, adopting a battle-ready stance, even as Sebastian Shaw appeared. The Black King cast a disdainful glance at the feral Canadian, then held up a placatory hand. "I am not here to fight you," he said.

"Then why *are* you here, Shaw?" asked Storm coldly.

"How did you get free?" asked Cyclops tersely.

Shaw looked at the X-Men's leader with a pained expression. "Please, Mr. Summers. To judge by the condition of your team, I would say that this is your day for underestimating your opponents."

"If you came here to gloat, Shaw—"

He shook his head grimly. "I came to find Magneto. Where is he?"

Nobody answered him, but Shaw surveyed the room through narrowed eyes, and then nodded to himself. "The laboratory, no doubt." He turned to leave.

"Hold on, Shaw!" Cyclops took two steps toward him, fingering the controls on his golden visor. Normally, Storm knew, he would have activated it with his palm studs; the overt gesture was for the Black King's benefit. "You don't expect us to just let you walk out of here and rejoin your partner, I hope?"

"It would be in your interest to do so," said Shaw smoothly. "There is no reason for us to fight any more. My intention is to end this, if you'll let me."

"You have asked for our trust before," said Storm with a hint of bitterness, "but you do little to earn it."

Shaw inclined his head as if accepting the criticism. "In this case, however," he said, his dark eyes gleaming, "I don't think you have much choice in the matter."

CHAPTER 15

THE Beast stared up into Magneto's fiery gaze, and time stretched like elastic as his clawed fingers surreptitiously teased the vial from his belt pouch. He ought to have destroyed it by now—he was gambling with billions of lives—but he couldn't bring himself to do it. Not until he was sure that there was no other choice.

"I developed this cure for the good of mutantkind," he insisted hoarsely, his tongue feeling swollen in his mouth. "I beg you, don't force me to destroy it!"

Magneto's silver eyebrows knitted together, and his lips peeled back from his teeth. His hand remained stubbornly outstretched. "I will use it to save lives. Nobody will be left wanting if they are prepared to renounce their prejudice. On that, I give you my word."

"And I accept it," said the Beast quietly. "Unfortunately, I cannot accept your desire to make a distinction between those who deserve life and those who do not."

"If you destroy that cure," said Magneto, "nobody will be saved. You'll condemn thousands of Genoshan citizens, and many more, to death."

"Perhaps so—but such an action would, I believe, end your mad scheme to extend the contagion."

"Perhaps it will not," said Magneto with a sudden flash of anger. "Perhaps I will release the reengineered virus anyway, and give humanity a taste of what we have had to endure."

"I don't believe you possess such a nihilistic streak," countered the Beast. "And I doubt the mutant Messiah is yet ready to martyr himself to his cause." He shook his head. "No, Magnus, I can't let you have my blood. I will not have the resultant death toll upon my conscience. But I appeal to you as a fellow mutant—as a fellow human being—to allow me to keep it. Let some good come of this."

"Would you give up *your* dream so easily?" Magneto's demeanor had changed again, and Hank could see something of the vulnerable, abused child within him: the child who had vowed to reform a cruel world, but who had buried his own innocence in the process. He could see the pain, the desperate plea, in the depths of his deadliest foe's eyes. "You are all that stands between me and the better future for which I yearn. I swear, I will kill you, Henry, before I allow you to extinguish that hope."

The Beast swallowed, and his voice was barely a whisper now. "Then I'm sorry, Magnus. I'm sorry for us all."

And he tightened his fist around the precious vial, and crushed it.

The ensuing silence seemed so loud to Hank that it roared in his ears. He fully expected Magneto to exact bloody revenge for his action, but it hardly mattered now. He looked down at his right hand, opening his fingers and staring numbly at the fragments of glass and the blood that he had spilt. Blood on his hands. It seemed an apt metaphor.

And suddenly, he realized that the blood was no longer dripping, or soaking into his blue fur, but rising. In defiance of gravity, it gathered into a red mass before his startled eyes, and floated away from him. It took him a confused half-second to appreciate that Magneto was drawing the blood to him by controlling its iron content. The master of magnetism wore a harsh smile of triumph.

With an anguished cry, the Beast threw himself at his foe, feet-first—a desperate, futile attack. He rebounded from a magnetic force field, and was borne to the ground by a heavy, invisible weight upon his shoulders. He struggled to rise, but found himself on his knees at Magneto's feet. "I warned you, Henry. I am too close to my goal to suffer any obstacles in my path. The cure is mine, and nobody will take it from me."

"I think you know," said a stern voice, "that that isn't true."

Hank gasped with relief, and not only because he felt the magnetic pressure upon him lessening. The voice had belonged to Cyclops—and he was accompanied by Phoenix, Storm, Night-crawler, Iceman and Wolverine. The footsteps of the six X-Men crunched against the debris left by Rogue's destructive battle with Holocaust as they entered the laboratory and lined up before their oldest enemy. They appeared battered and tired, but defiant.

"As I keep telling you," said Cyclops, "the X-Men will always stand against you."

"You're too late," snarled Magneto. "I have the cure!"

"But you can't protect it and fight us at the same time," said Phoenix. She glanced meaningfully at the blood sample, which hung suspended at Magneto's shoulder, maintaining the shape it had had in the vial even though there was no vial any more. "You're holding it together by force of mind alone. The slightest lapse in concentration, and you'll lose it."

"Then you should know one thing before you seek to engineer such an outcome," he said coolly. "By my reckoning, it is eight o'clock. In Hong Kong and Perth, therefore, it is midnight. I am aware that you deactivated the trident firework in Sydney—but by now, the second and third devices have been launched. Their infection has been spread. And as you rightly say, my dear, any offensive against me will result in the destruction of the one thing that can counter it. So, my friends, are you still as eager to begin a fight that will doom the majority of the world's population? Or are you prepared to accept my terms at long last?"

To Hank's surprise, Cyclops laughed in Magneto's face. "Another thing you need to learn, Lensherr: there's always a third option."

Sebastian Shaw was standing, a shadowy figure, in the doorway. A young couple stood behind him, and Hank thought he recognized them from pictures in the X-Men's files: members of Genosha's cabinet, although he couldn't call their names to mind. Shaw cleared his throat, and said: "The launches in Hong Kong and Perth have been aborted. And my assistant, Tessa, is contacting our other branches worldwide as we speak. Regrettably, the Hellfire Club's solstice celebrations will pass not with a bang but with a whimper."

"Shaw!" A dangerous undercurrent rumbled in Magneto's voice. "I expected this betrayal, of course—but I didn't think even you would be so blatant."

"I have not betrayed you," said Shaw. His tone was even, his expression grim. "But the situation has changed. While you were busy fighting these children, your aides couldn't reach you with vital new information."

Magneto raised an eyebrow, and the Beast found that he was holding his breath, waiting to hear what the Black King had to say.

Sebastian Shaw took a pause, as if entirely for dramatic effect, before ending the suspense. "The cure doesn't work," he said.

And, for several seconds afterward, nobody spoke.

"What treachery is this?" Magneto spat the words, but his erstwhile ally was nonplussed in the face of his anger.

The Beast had some idea what he was feeling. His own head was awhirl with thoughts. He couldn't accept that, after all he had been through, all he had put the X-Men through, it could end like this. A part of him knew, of course, that it was for the best, that Magneto couldn't proceed with his plan now. But Shaw's cold, hard assertion had robbed him of hope.

Even when he had been prepared to sacrifice the Legacy cure, he had had the comfort of believing such a cure possible, knowing that he had found it once and might do so again. Now, there was nothing. No. He *wouldn't* accept it.

Three weeks ago, the Beast's teammates had visited a possible future in which Selene had had the Legacy cure. His cure. And it had worked for her—hadn't it?

Shaw had seen that future too. Hank wanted to remind him of it, to contest his awful claim. But it was likely that Magneto knew nothing of the averted timeline in which the Black Queen had ruled New York—and if this was an elaborate bluff, a way of wresting the cure from him, then he couldn't risk blowing it. Biting his tongue, he waited and listened.

"If you won't believe Shaw," urged Cyclops, "at least listen to your own people. Jennifer? Phillip?" Shaw stepped aside, and the two cabinet members came forward.

"It's true, Magnus," said the man. "Raul Jarrett is dead."

"The virus returned," expanded the woman, "stronger than I've ever seen it. It ate through his system in a matter of minutes. There was nothing we could do."

"I have just contacted Tessa in Sydney," said Shaw. "She is having your other young guinea-pig examined—but it appears that she too is showing symptoms of a relapse."

Hank swallowed. Ruthless as the Black King might be, the X-Men would never have gone along with a plan that involved murder. And if Raul Jarrett wasn't really dead, then Magneto would find out the truth soon enough. Worse still, the story made sense—as Phoenix now pointed out. "How do you think we escaped from the Hellfire Club in Sydney, when Miranda was holding us powerless? My abilities returned to me, Magnus. We didn't realize it, but the Legacy Virus must have been affecting her mutant gene even then."

"We knew there was a remote possibility of this," sighed Shaw. "The super-cell must have become unstable when it was taken out of Doctor McCoy's bloodstream. It worked for him, but it won't work for anybody else."

"It is feasible, Your Eminence." Hank had almost forgotten about the blonde scientist, but she emerged timidly from her hiding place now. "And if it's true, it would mean that each Legacy sufferer would have to evolve his or her own unique super-cell."

"In short," said Shaw, "he would have to go through the same tortuous process as McCoy did—which is, of course, impossible since Selene destroyed the Kree equipment and records at our Pacific research facility. The work we did there cannot be duplicated."

It was a good story—perhaps too good—and Hank almost allowed himself to be convinced by it. He probably would have been, had it not been for Selene.

But then, Magneto let out a roar of pain and frustration, and swung an arm with savage force as if knocking aside some invisible opponent. The blood sample that had hung in the air beside him exploded, showering the occupants of the lab with sticky red droplets. And Hank realized that, even if Shaw and the others had been lying, even if the cure had worked after all, then it had just been lost forever. He leapt forward with an anguished cry, but stumbled to a halt in the stomach-wrenching knowledge that there was nothing he could do.

His dream had died.

"You idiot!" he raged instead. "We could have studied that cell. We could have tried to understand it, found a way to transplant it successfully or recreate the circumstances of its creation." His voice tailed off, sounding smaller and smaller in his own ears.

"It's over!" snapped Magneto. He directed a glare at Shaw. "Our business partnership is terminated." The Black King acknowledged him with a curt nod as Magneto stalked toward the door, his cloak billowing behind him.

Wolverine barred his path. "Forgetting something, aren't you?

You've put the X-Men to a whole heap of trouble, bub—and we ain't paid you back the half of it yet!"

Magneto rounded on him with naked contempt. Then, the Beast followed his probing gaze to the rest of his mutant foes in turn. They would fight him if they had to, but Hank saw—as Magneto must have seen—that they were weary, their resolve sapped by the fact that there was nothing left to fight for. Only a pound of flesh that would have done them no good at all. Nightcrawler was helping a dazed Rogue to stand, and Iceman was surreptitiously leaning against a charred bench for support. Even Cyclops looked unsteady on his feet.

Hank felt the same as he imagined they did. He wanted to go home.

"I have no interest in another futile confrontation," said Magneto, and he sounded tired too. Tired and old—but still forbidding, still rigid. "You are intruders in my country, all of you. Leave within the hour, and I will take no further action. Fail to do so, and you will be dealt with as enemies of the state. Farewell."

He turned away again and strode out of the room, and this time Wolverine let him go, albeit with his fists clenched and his lips curled into a hateful sneer.

"So, this whole mission was a flaming waste of time!"

The X-Men's Blackbird aircraft had just taken off from Sydney, giving its eight occupants their first real chance to converse since their reunion in Genosha. Nevertheless, Rogue had settled back into her comfortable seat in the back of the plane, hoping to get some sleep. She was exhausted—and, even with the Blackbird's souped-up engines, New York and Salem Center still lay several hours away. Wolverine's gruff voice had shaken her out of the beginnings of a doze, and she sighed ruefully and pried her eyes open.

"I wouldn't say that," objected Cyclops. "If we hadn't become involved—"

"Then Shaw would have called the whole thing off anyway," said Wolverine, "as soon as that Miranda woman fell ill again."

Iceman pouted. "Trust Emma Frost to send us on a wild goose chase!"

Cyclops shook his head firmly. "It would have been too late by then. The Legacy bomb in Sydney would have been detonated; perhaps the ones in Hong Kong and Perth too."

"It might not seem like we accomplished much," said Phoenix, "but by delaying Magneto's plan for as long as we did, we probably saved the whole world."

Nightcrawler grinned. "Again? This is almost becoming embarrassing!"

"Don't get too excited, elf," said Wolverine sourly. "The world won't appreciate it."

"Makes me feel a little better, anyhow," mumbled Rogue. She cast her mind back to the long, heavy silence that had fallen in the wake of Magneto's departure from his laboratory. The silence that had said that nobody had won today, because the prize itself had been lost.

Shaw had been the first to speak, assuring the X-Men as he had taken his leave of them that it *hadn't* been a pleasure. Storm had pointed out that he was leaving the wounded Holocaust behind, to which Shaw had replied that his pawn, having failed the Hellfire Club again, was of no further use to him. "Will you never learn?" Ororo had sighed, exasperated.

"Incidentally," he had said as a parting shot, "I trust you can make your own travel arrangements from now on? You aren't welcome to share mine."

Cyclops had used a low-intensity, high-duration optic beam to fuse the cracked part of Holocaust's armor, preventing him from hemorrhaging any more life-sustaining energy. His act of mercy had sparked a predictable but mercifully short dispute with Wolverine.

And, finally, Jennifer Ransome had offered to send the heroes on their way. One of her cabinet colleagues, an unsavory type by the name of Cormack Grimshaw, had the ability to convert people into binary electronic impulses. He had transmitted the X-Men to the Blackbird's comm-set via a modem: all in all, not an unpleasant way to travel, so long as you didn't think too hard about it—and Rogue had certainly appreciated the fact that it was almost instantaneous. Remembering the hired motorboat, and thinking that the Xavier Institute could do without yet another bill for damaged or lost goods, she had asked Jenny if she could also retrieve the vessel and return it to its owner in Madagascar.

"We are rather assuming," said the Beast, "that the cure was ineffective from the outset. There is an alternative possibility: one to which I have been giving much consideration."

Phoenix nodded. "I thought about that too. The cure worked for Selene, didn't it?"

"Could she have found a way to stabilize it?" mused Nightcrawler. "Something she didn't tell us about? We've never really understood how her abilities work."

"It is possible, yes," said the Beast.

"But it's also possible," conjectured Cyclops, "that the cure *did* work—and that somebody tampered with it before it could be used."

"All of which," said the Beast, "leaves a palpable question mark hanging over the identity of this hypothetical noble soul."

"Could it have been Tessa?" asked Storm.

Cyclops frowned. "I doubt it. She's always been fiercely loyal to Shaw." Ororo's eyes narrowed thoughtfully, but she didn't argue. Rogue wondered what she was thinking.

"You don't suppose . . . ?" she began. She tailed off in mid-sentence. It was a ludicrous idea. Wasn't it?

But Phoenix continued her train of thought. "Somebody who had the means, and was close enough to Magneto to have the opportunity. . . ."

"But just unhappy enough with his plans. . . ." said Nightcrawler.

"And treacherous enough," interjected Storm.

". . . to have the motive. . . ."

"Best hope you're wrong," growled Wolverine, resting his heels on the seatback in front of him. "'Cos if you're right, it means we've all been played for suckers. We've just been the pawns in another Hellfire Club game!"

"As far as I'm concerned," said Cyclops firmly, "only one thing matters. In the hands of somebody like Magneto or Selene, that cure was a threat—which we've ended. We might not have the cure ourselves, but even so . . . I think we won this one."

The Black King of Hong Kong stood in his rooftop garden and surveyed his domain.

He never felt more powerful than this: than when he stood at the heart of his self-built empire and looked out over the city that he had come to think of as his own. He had influence here. Between his immediate employees and his wider network of contacts, he could issue almost any decree and expect it to be carried out. And if there were still larger empires to be won, other Kings and Queens to be toppled, then that was good too. It gave him something to work toward: a goal that, on bright mornings like this, he was confident of achieving.

Shaw's current objective was comparatively modest, but he approached it with no less determination and flair than he applied to all his ventures. The Hellfire Club's solstice celebrations had fizzled out, but he would compensate for that with the grandest, most hedonistic New Year party that the organization had seen in generations.

He didn't need to turn and face his assistant. He outlined his instructions and knew that, without having to take notes, Tessa would absorb and act upon them. It was only after he had dismissed her that she gave voice to a question. "Sir?" she said. And Shaw half-pivoted toward her, arching an eyebrow. "Did I do the right thing?"

He didn't have to ask what she meant. He took a deep breath, pursed his lips in thought, and finally admitted: "The X-Men provided a useful distraction. I am satisfied with the outcome."

"I'm glad," smiled Tessa. She hesitated for a moment as if hoping to learn more. When Shaw remained silent, however, she didn't prompt him. She gave a brisk nod, turned and left.

For a minute or more after her departure, he stared at the door to the stairs that had closed behind her. And then, without having consciously willed it, without even having been aware of the shadow rising within him, he clenched a fist and drove it into one of the pagoda's struts. He was shaking in frustration, and he had to close his eyes and breathe through it.

She was just another pawn, he told himself. A commodity to be used and discarded. He had allowed himself to become uncommonly close to this one, almost reliant upon her—but that had been a mistake. And he had learned his lesson now. An ambitious man could not afford to be weakened by sentiment. He didn't yet know for sure that Tessa would betray him—he only suspected that she was like all the others after all—but the seed of doubt had been planted in his mind, and it was enough. When the moment came, he would be ready for her.

By now, she would know what he had done. Most of it, anyway. He had given her enough information for her computer-like mind to work out the rest.

Tessa had always known that her employer was working with Magneto under sufferance, that he intended to keep the hard-earned Legacy cure from him. Unfortunately, Selene's highly visible intervention had made that impossible. Lacking the physical power to defy his partner, Shaw had been forced to bite his lip and hand the stolen blood of the Beast over to him. But he had had no intention of living in a world ruled by that zealot; a world in which all the real power lay in the hands of one man, and that man was not Sebastian Hiram Shaw.

Fortunately, his influence extended far beyond Hong Kong; even further than Magneto had realized. Until recently, the prosperous Genoshan capital, Hammer Bay, had seemed an ideal site for a new Hellfire Club chapter. Therefore, Shaw had been pulling the strings of its captains of industry for some time; he had even imported many of them. And, at his strongly worded request, more than one such person had resisted his instincts to abandon the suddenly war-torn city for more stable markets elsewhere.

Magneto had had six scientists working in shifts to duplicate the Legacy cure. It had been a simple matter for Shaw's agents to track them down and identify the weakest of them. The master of magnetism controlled his servants through fear, but Shaw had always believed that money—in enough quantity—was a more powerful incentive. In this case, he had been proved right. The transaction had taken place under Magneto's nose.

Of course, the Black King knew the power of fear too. He had sent Holocaust to Hammer Bay, ostensibly as an additional layer of security, claiming that he would feel happier with one of his own agents guarding the Legacy cure. But the presence, and veiled threats, of the otherworldly creature had given his hapless pawn the spur he needed to get the job done.

The scientist had exposed the Beast's blood sample—and the few vials of the cure that had so far been extracted from it—to a small dose of microwave radiation. Just enough to weaken the super-cell, for it to start to break down almost imperceptibly. The results had been unpredictable—and, as it transpired, almost too slow to become evident. Perverse as it seemed, Shaw was grateful to the X-Men for deactivating the trident firework in Sydney, and for kidnapping him. They had bought him time—and they had given him an excuse to be in Magneto's command center at the critical moment.

He had destroyed the hope of mutantkind rather than let it fall into the hands of a despot.

He smiled at the thought that some people might have considered him a hero. But then, like Tessa, those people would have been unaware of the whole truth. They couldn't have known how handsomely Shaw had been rewarded for his calculated act of betrayal.

He felt in the pocket of his smoking jacket for the precious vial. He ought to have secured it in his wall safe by now, but he enjoyed being able to touch it like this. As a tangible reminder of his great achievement, it helped him to dismiss his nagging worries about Tessa and his sundered Inner Circle, to concentrate on what was important.

The vial had been smuggled out of Genosha at some expense, and much risk to the smuggler, while Shaw and the X-Men had delayed Magneto in Sydney. It contained the cure, of course—and this sole remaining sample was pure, untainted. It would work.

The only drawback was that Shaw couldn't use it yet, at least not openly. For one thing, he would attract the X-Men's attention again, although he felt he could handle them. Selene, too, if it came to it. Magneto, on the other hand, was a different proposition. If he suspected what Shaw had done, he would seek recompense—and he was not an enemy to be made lightly.

But Shaw knew how to bide his time. He was used to playing the long game. First, of course, the cure would have to be duplicated in sufficient quantity. That would take time. Then, a few additional months down the line, he could start to use the cure, surreptitiously at first—and if challenged, he would claim to have come by it some other way. Nor would he waste the intervening weeks. He had plans to make. He had a powerful tool at his disposal, and it behooved him to employ it strategically, to maximize its potential worth to him.

In the end, then, this was all that mattered: that Sebastian Shaw had set out to cure the Legacy Virus, and to keep that cure to himself. And that, despite his trials along the way, he had achieved that goal.

The Black King had won.